# The Brothers Harper

By Michael Slayter

eBook ISBN: 979-8-89795-245-8
Paperback ISBN: 979-8-89795-246-5
Hardcover ISBN: 979-8-89795-247-2
Fawcett Publications

# ACKNOWLEDGMENTS

To my wife, Jane, for her patience and guidance

To the Seasoned Readers Book Club for their
support and encouragement

Book cover design by Noah Slayter

# PROLOGUE

Family is a safehouse of unconditional love, where alliances and connections overshadow time and distance. Joy and sorrow are commonplace and met with laughter and compassion. The strength of family becomes visible when we see it nurture growth, celebrate differences, and give support without judgment. We are profoundly grounded by shared memories, from ordinary moments to what seems to be unbelievable. Family is not defined only by blood or genes, but by those who choose to stand beside you, offering warmth, understanding, and a sense of belonging that makes the world feel a little less daunting.

Author Unknown

# CHAPTER ONE

December 10, 1960 – East Berlin, East Germany

The storm was waging outside like a hurricane, but with snow blowing instead of rain. Helga Röder managed to open the door and step inside, or better, was blown inside, where the warmth greeted her like a scowling aunt waiting for the wayward girl to come home. She faced the eyes that waited for her to speak and said, "They are on their way. We must meet them Saturday before sundown to make sure they get across the border. I have decided: I am going with them this time."

Two of Helga's cousins in East Germany had been trying to cross over to West Germany for several years. They both worked for the local government and had access to critical information that would be helpful to certain parties in the western half of the country. Three times, they tried, and it seemed that each time they attempted it, an obstacle raised its ugly head and blocked their way. Anna Richter, a trusted friend, said she had information about the guard schedule on the outskirts of town, beyond the barbed wire and barricades, where dense forest and searchlights surrounded any potential portals of escape. Twice, they almost made it through, only to find themselves struggling in the wilderness, hungry and cold. They found a road both times but realized they would have many miles to walk, days, in fact, if they intended to continue in that direction. Both times, they turned back and were able to retrace their steps back into the city.

The third time was almost catastrophic. Helga had managed to steal diplomatic identification cards that would have allowed them to cross over on one of the few scheduled trains, but at the last minute, she realized the cards they held were obsolete. The East Germans would periodically change the format of the cards and issue new ones only to those who were known to be bona fide diplomats. They left the train station just as the Stasi, the East German secret police, came aboard to check all passenger credentials.

"Anna, how could I be so careless? The Stasi almost caught them. Maybe I'm not the best one to make this happen."

Anna was reassuring. "Helga, they will make it, and so will you. I have an idea."

Anna worked for the local utility company and was a persuasive woman when she knew what she wanted. The wall had not been constructed yet, and there was a slow trickle of human souls successfully finding ways to cross into the West. Anna knew of a poorly guarded section supplied with electrical power from the very company she worked for.

"Helga, I have a friend named Karl who will do almost anything I ask of him. He bought me a charm bracelet last week and said it was for friendship. I can see where he is leading me, and I won't have any part of it. But this once, I don't mind telling him a small lie. Let me see what I can arrange."

The next day, Anna saw Karl in the office. She had made sure she was dressed in a manner that balanced between elegance and mild seduction. She wore a form-fitting pink top with a matching skirt that was not revealing but could easily provoke a man's imagination.

She asked him, "Karl, where is a good place to get lunch nearby? I always bring mine, but I didn't have time this morning. I need to buy something to bring it back to my desk to eat."

Karl couldn't believe his ears. "Anna, why don't I take you to lunch? You don't need to eat here at your desk."

Anna fluttered her eyes and feigned a moment of shyness, then found her coat and agreed to go with him. During the cold walk to Karl's favorite diner, he boldly tried putting his arm around Anna's waist as they walked. She looked at him and smiled. They found a table in a corner, and Karl ordered a glass of wine for each of them.

Anna was a model of naivete. "So, Karl, tell me exactly what you do. I've heard you talking about transformers and – what do you call them – relay stations?  What are those things?"

Karl could not allow this opportunity to pass by. He went into a detailed description of power grids and high-voltage lines.  He impressed her with the fact that he could work with such equipment without interrupting any electrical service.

"I would love to see that.  I've never been in the field with men who know about these things.  It would make me a better employee, don't you think?" She ended her question with a weak smile and reached across the table to touch his fingertips.

Karl was almost speechless.  "Well, yes!  I could arrange to give you a tour.  How about tomorrow?"

"No, I'm busy tomorrow.  How about Friday? That's just three days from now."

"Ah, yes!  Definitely, yes.  I can arrange my work schedule to include an inspection of one of the relays, and I'll show it to you."

Friday came, and Karl was like a child at Christmas.  At three in the afternoon, they met at the main relay station and walked through the open gate that appeared to be rusted at the hinges and probably rarely ever closed.  Just inside the fence, Anna noticed a small, uninhabited building that contained tools, spare parts, and unclassified junk.  She continued her façade of interest in power grids, and Karl went into lengthy, detailed explanations about switches, circuit breakers, transformers, and insulators. As he was about to switch his lecture to another subject, Anna put her arms around him and showed him something else to think about. She kissed him long and hard until they heard voices coming into their field of view. She made the transition like a pro.

"Karl, what are these big boxes for?" She asked her question and waited for the intruders to keep walking. The men hesitated when they saw her, dressed for the office and not fieldwork. Karl took her cue and answered her question with a tone of authority and experience.

"These are the main transformers for the various sections of town, as you can see on this map here." He pointed to a diagram, all the while looking to see if the others had left yet. They hadn't. Anna was studying the diagram closely.

Finally, she looked at him and said softly, "I think they might suspect something if we stand here too long. Maybe we better go."

That night, Anna met with Helga and fleshed out her plan.

"You need to be at the restricted zone at the intersection I told you about. You do remember, yes? There's a café right there where so many come to take their breaks during the day. Bring your cousins there at sundown tomorrow. It will be the weekend. You can get lost in the crowd. Don't bring anything bulky like suitcases. We will be traveling light."

Helga nodded. She knew the exact spot.

The next day was Saturday. Helga casually walked to the café just before sundown, and her two cousins, Claus and Friedrich, approached from the other direction. They made eye contact but didn't join as a threesome. Both men lit a cigarette while Helga seemed to be digging in her purse. Suddenly, all the construction lights, as well as the streetlights, went dark. Anna had known that the guards in that area would be sparsely assigned that time of day, and, under the cover of the dim light, three silhouettes clamored through the unguarded gap.

In the darkness, a single gunshot rang out.

Minutes later, Helga stumbled over crumbling construction debris and felt a jolt of pain in her ankle. Claus noticed and came running back.

"Hast du weh?"

She got to her feet and limped toward him. "Yes, I hurt my ankle. Claus, I told you to start speaking English. How do you expect to work for the Americans?"

"Wieso?"

"Why? Do you think…"

He interrupted her and said, "Yes, you are right, but this is not the time for this. Here, let me help you."

As Helga, Claus, and Friedrich darted down dark alleys that would take them away from the barricades, Anna emerged from the relay station with a large crescent wrench in her left hand and a severe burn on her right hand. Sparks were flying around and among the transformers. She walked two blocks to the unlit gap in the border and crossed through herself.

As arranged by Anna, Helga and her two cousins met with their American counterparts about a quarter mile further in. She introduced herself.

"Gentlemen, my name is Helga Röder."

The two men stepped forward and shook her hand.

"I'm John Pleasance, and this is Henry Harper. We're both Staff Sergeants in U.S. Army Intelligence. So pleased to meet you."

Helga finally spoke. "Yes, thank you. We have much to tell you. And we would be pleased to help you in any way we can, but do not ask us to go back there." She pointed to the east. "Never again."

Henry gave a sharp whistle, and a car pulled alongside them. They all got in, and the car immediately headed back in the direction that they had just come from.

Helga almost screamed, "Wait! Where are you taking us?"

"Don't worry," said Henry. "Just a couple of blocks. We have one more passenger to pick up."

The car turned a sharp corner and stopped abruptly. The door opened, and Anna climbed in, holding her burned hand gingerly with the other.

"John, I need a doctor."

Helga looked at her with confusion written all over her face. Anna forced a weak smile.

"You didn't think I was going to stay there, did you? Have you ever met Karl? Have you ever seen Karl? Have you ever kissed Karl? It's enough to make anyone want to escape!"

Helga was still confused. She asked Anna, "Do you know these men?"

"No, but we have communicated by shortwave. I didn't tell you because the less you knew, the less chance of you – well, if you had been caught. I…"

Helga nodded.

Henry was listening and said, "We have nice hotel rooms for all of you, courtesy of Uncle Sam."

They arrived at a hotel near Tempelhof airport. Their driver left them at the door, and the two Americans saw their guests in full light for the first time. They all looked tired and weary with smudged, wrinkled clothes.

John seemed to notice Anna first. She was tall, thin, and had a very light complexion that matched her pale, straight, blond hair and blue eyes. She seemed to have a more confident air about her than Helga. Anna was the planner, the risk taker. The hotel doctor arrived and bandaged her hand with instructions to see him again the following day. He left her with pills for the pain, which she took immediately.

By mere chance, Henry was sitting next to Helga in the lobby. She wasn't as tall as Anna. Her hair was also blonde, but not the near albino tone as Anna's. She had a cute, thin nose and expressive, amber-colored eyes shielded by thin eyebrows. He noticed she had a peculiar way of cocking her head to one side, almost unnoticed, when she was listening. It reminded him of a puppy hearing a strange sound for the first time. He was talking to her and looked down, noticing the delicate contour of her ankles. Somehow, she didn't fit the mental picture he had of someone who had repeatedly attempted escape from a brutal environment.

Being slightly older than Henry and outranking him by only a few months, John took the lead in the discussion.

"I assume everyone here speaks English."

The two women nodded yes, and Helga's two male cousins looked at each other and shrugged. It was obvious that some translation would be necessary.

John simply said, "Okay, there's no reason to get into details tonight. Let's get you settled in your rooms. There are new fresh clothes waiting for you and a hot bath. We'll have supper brought to your rooms as soon as you let them know what you want. We'll meet in the dining room for breakfast. Does that agree with you?"

And so began a two-year relationship involving the two American soldiers and the two German Frauleins as they practiced eavesdropping on electronic communications from East Germany. Even though John and Henry were listed as Army personnel, they were assigned to the 6913th Radio Squadron Mobile, an Air Force unit in Bremerhaven. For the two women, most of their jobs involved translating what was being heard and being able to tell what was truth and what was fictitious fodder, planted to purposely mislead anyone who might be listening. Eventually, Claus and Friedrich became more fluent in English, and the Americans gave them both jobs as staff car drivers.

With Helga's magnetic personality, Henry developed more than a working relationship with her, although the official policy frowned on off-duty fraternization. But that word hardly described how Henry's feelings were evolving for this wonderful creature. One day, after about a year, those feelings were amplified when fate put her in danger of the regime she had left in Berlin.

She translated a message that came from East Berlin, wrote a summary of it, and sent it to Henry. Her code name changed every week, but this time, she was careless and signed it simply, 'Helga R.'

The next day, the Military Police came into her office area with a strong sense of urgency. The captain of her section approached her desk with two husky MPs.

"Helga, go with these men. Do what they say."

She looked around frantically for an explanation. "Why? Where are you taking me?" Her mind was exploding with images of betrayal, of memories from seeing what the East German police were capable of, and her reflexes told her it was happening right there and there was no safe place in the world for her.

Her fears were quickly dispelled when she was taken back to her private quarters and there, waiting for her, was Henry. At first, she wasn't sure of anything, but Henry set her mind at ease.

"Helga, the bad guys have traced your whereabouts to this place. The MPs intercepted some infiltrators at the main gate, and they had documents on them that told us they were looking for you. We must get you to a safer place. You're going to the

British zone for a few weeks. It's for your own good. You need to pack."

And so, she was moved. Henry managed to find a reason to travel to the British zone several times while she was there. Three months later, she came back.

A year later came the tragic day when Henry's orders arrived, directing him back to the States, and he was eventually discharged from the military. He never asked Helga to come back with him, but she clearly knew he wanted to ask her that question. On the night before he left, she laid to rest any second thoughts that he might have.

"Henry, I can read your mind. I care very much for you, but I have something here I must complete. My family has lost a great deal in this war. My country needs to heal and grow again. I need to be here to help it happen."

Henry's heart was full of mixed feelings. Maybe he had not impressed her enough to pull her away from such lofty ambitions. Maybe it just wasn't meant to be.

"Where will you go?" she asked.

"It looks like I'll go to Ft. Dix in New Jersey. That's where I'll be discharged. Then I'm thinking about going to Florida, where I grew up."

"Why Florida?"

"Oh, you should see it!  The winters are warm, and everything grows there.  Just stick it in the ground and it grows.  There are things that actually bloom in the winter.  Can you believe that?"

Her response was faint and distant.  "Sounds beautiful.  I didn't know you were such a gardener."

"I'm not.  I just know beautiful things when I see them."

She took him in her arms, kissed him, and said, "This doesn't mean we cannot stay in touch.  Let me know where you settle."  Their last night together was long and memorable.

# CHAPTER TWO

Kissimmee, Florida. It was the Spring of the year 2000. It was the year everyone called Y2K, and the masses thought all computers would go crazy. Internet scams had been running rampant, selling all manner of protective software, and there had even been predictions of the end of the world. It turned out to be just another typical year for most folks. That is unless you were the Harper brothers, and nothing was typical about these two. Aaron was ten years old, and Daniel was eight. Both attended Lake Toho Elementary School, and they rode the same bus together, morning and afternoon. It was a short ride each way, with a half-dozen stops along the way, but enough time for Daniel to stir the pot.

"Dan, stop it! Leave my backpack alone!" She was a year older than Daniel, but Cheryl Carpenter was an easy target for his teasing sense of humor.

"Aw, c'mon. What ya' got in there? Anything to eat?"

"Yes, my lunch and some chips. Now, go away!"

He made a clown face and said, "I'll bet you have some cookies in there."

He reached for the backpack again when eleven-year-old Teddy Slovak grabbed him by the collar and yanked him back so hard he fell on his back.

"She said to leave her alone," Ted said firmly.

"Mind your own business, Teddy!" Daniel was in the process of trying to stand up again.

"You want to start something?"

He reached for the front of Daniel's shirt, pulled his shirttail out, and had his other hand cocked back and ready to deliver a bloody nose punch when Aaron Harper grabbed Ted's fist from behind and gave him a solid punch in his back. Ted turned around, and Aaron put his palm in the boy's face, sending him sprawling just as the bus was pulling into the school parking lot. The driver, Mr. Peabody, watched the whole thing through his mirror but was too busy driving to intervene. A load of school children all scrambled to exit the bus, and Ted never had a chance to restore his dignity. Both brothers stepped over the fallen boy and moved with the crowd toward the door. Peabody shook his finger at both Harper boys, and they knew what that meant.

Once outside, Aaron dragged his younger brother around the corner of the building and shoved him against the brick wall.

"Danny! What's with you? You start a fight on the school bus, and you know Mr. Matthews is going to find out! You're lucky I was there to break things up this time before you got your face mashed in."

Daniel was not impressed. "I didn't start a fight! I was talking to Cheryl. And I don't need your help! I don't need anyone's help!"

"That was a dumb thing to do, and you know it. Teddy is her so-called big boyfriend, and he almost made you pay for what you did. What were you thinking? He's bigger than you, and he's older. You knew that. Geez, what am I going to tell Dad?"

Daniel pushed his brother away. "Tell Dad? That's all you talk about – tell daddy, tell daddy. Well, go ahead. I don't care! You're his favorite anyway."

Aaron rolled his eyes. "That's not true. But I know he's going to ask me about it. Now, let's get to class before the bell rings."

"I can take care of myself!"

"Can you? Does our mommy still tuck you in at night? Huh? Talk about favorites!"

They were both still throwing verbal jabs at each other as they walked around the corner toward the entrance, and Ted Slovak was waiting for them. "Just you wait," he growled under his breath. "I'll see you both on the bus this afternoon."

Time for recess came and both boys were called to the office of Timothy Matthews, Assistant Principal. Matthews was fifty years old, had taught elementary school up until this school year, and managed to snag the assistant principal's job at the last minute before the hiring deadline closed. He had a slender build and was completely bald, and most of the children loved him. At assembly time, they hung on to his every word, but when the occasion called for it, his firm look spoke volumes. He scowled at the two Harper boys.

"What am I going to do with you two?" His authoritarian voice had nails and spikes in it. "This is three times in the past three months that there has been some kind of incident on the school bus. I've spoken to your parents about this problem more than once, and I guess I'll have to call them again. Daniel, it seems you started the whole episode this morning, right?"

Before Daniel could answer, Aaron spoke up and said, "It's not his fault, Mr. Matthews. Uh, he can't help it. He's, ah – he's got pills at home that help, and I think he forgot to take them this morning. Yeah, that's what happened. I heard Mom reminding him, but I didn't see him taking anything. Really, he's okay now."

"Medication? Pills? Pills for what, Dr. Harper?" Matthews leaned back in his chair and waited for another one of Aaron's contrived fables.

Aaron looked at the ceiling and searched his imagination. "He's got antidisembarkment disorder, sir. Real bad sometimes."

"Is it contagious?"

"No, sir, but if he eats too much peanut butter, it happens."

Matthews smiled to himself. "Well, let's hope it doesn't show itself again today, okay?"

Aaron tried to sound convincing. "No sir, it won't. I promise. I'll keep an eye on him. You know, a close watch."

Timothy Matthews strained to keep from smiling outright. He had to admit that they were cute boys, and Big Brother certainly knew his protective role. They left, and Matthews picked up the phone.

The afternoon school bus run went without incident. Ted Slovak wasn't on it because his mother had picked him up early to make a dental appointment. Their father, Henry Harper, met them at the door. Evelyn, their mother, stood behind Henry with a passive look and said nothing.

"Come on in, boys. Put your things away and meet me in the garage."

Their father had never raised a hand to discipline either of them. He didn't have to. His intimidating figure, all 6'2" of him, was enough to conjure up all manner of imaginary outcomes, and the boys fell in line with his words. He employed a crew of workers that tended to his immense fields of flowers at Harper's Gardens, and he knew how to exude authority.

"You know why I have you out here. I won't have my boys behaving like that on the bus or anywhere else in public. So, here's the deal. I need the garage swept out and all the garden tools cleaned and put away. You know where they go. Then empty the trash and hose out the trash cans. I want the inside of those cans spotless. After supper, you'll finish your homework from today's classes, and there will be no TV tonight. Tomorrow morning is Saturday. I'll wake you at 7:30, and I'll have some yard chores for you to do after breakfast. Understood?"

They both nodded. As soon as he left, Aaron turned to his brother and hissed, "Look what you got me into! There goes my Saturday! I don't know why I help you with this kind of stuff." Daniel just shrugged.

An hour later, Henry came to check on their progress. Daniel was struggling with the dustpan and broom while Aaron was cleaning tools.

Henry maintained his stern approach. "Daniel, it's not that hard. Broom in one hand and the dustpan in the other. Just do it."

Aaron spoke up, "Dad, his hands aren't as big as yours. He can't handle that job."

"Then swap with him." He looked at his younger son and said, "Daniel, do you think you can do anything right?  Looks like you aren't man enough yet."

Aaron saw his brother's face turn red and twisted.

The boys exchanged jobs, and Henry left, chuckling to himself.  Aaron shook his head and said, "I'm sure as shit not going to help you the next time!"

They both looked up and saw their mother coming into the garage from the back door.  She glanced into the kitchen and, seeing that Henry was out of earshot, she said to Aaron, "Here, let me help you."  She took the broom from him and said, 'Now, hold the dustpan while I sweep."

Saturday morning arrived with a cloud of dread.  Their father was never ambivalent about consequences.  He put them to work, as promised.

The weekend came and went.  Monday morning issued forth, and Henry Harper was sitting at his desk at Harper's Gardens when the phone rang.  The caller ID showed the call as coming from the school.  He rolled his eyes and picked up the phone.

"Good morning, Harper's Gardens.  May I help you?  Yes, wha - Again?  Yeah – Okay, okay, I'll be right there.  Just give me a few minutes."

At the school parking lot, Henry pulled into the last visitors' parking place.  Timothy Matthews saw him through his office window and met him at the door.  He had a sheepish look on his face.

"Come on in, Henry.  Let's talk."

Henry noticed that neither of the boys were present. Matthews reached into his drawer, pulled out a magazine, and handed it to Henry.

"Daniel had this in his backpack. Look familiar?" The cover of *Penthouse Memories* was staring him in the face. He looked closer at the cover and saw ink lines that circled certain body parts along with the written words, 'boobies' and 'tits.' Matthews continued, "The boys aren't here right now because I know this is something you can deal with at home. I'm not one to squash a kid's curiosity, but he just can't be bringing this stuff to school." He paused for a moment and continued, "I'm not going to ask where he got this."

"Well, not from my house, that's for sure. Are you sure he brought it from home?"

"We just know that the janitor saw him looking at it with his brother and two other boys at recess. When he was questioned, he quickly stuck it back into his backpack."

"Give it to me, and I'll deal with it when they get home." He walked to the car, sat for a minute, and opened the magazine. He felt a grin come over his face, and then he laid it down on the seat beside him and started the engine.

When the boys got home, he walked into the bedroom they shared with the magazine folded in his back pocket. Dan looked up at his dad like a deer in the headlights. Aaron was busy paging through a comic book.

"You fellows have a good day at school?" They both nodded. "Anything big happens? Anything I need to know about?" Aaron began turning pages more forcefully. Dan continued his innocent stare. "Anyone give you something to look at? Something secret?"

Aaron looked at his brother with a menacing glare, then returned to his comic book. The body language was clear to Henry.

"Daniel, what happened at school today?"

"Nothing, really, Dad. Nothing happened."

"I hear you have a new taste in reading material. You may as well tell me about that." Daniel's eyes began to well up with tears, and Aaron laid his book down.

"It wasn't his fault, Dad. It was Ted Slovak. He was getting back at Dan for what happened Friday on the bus."

Henry approached both boys and said, "I'm listening. Go ahead."

Daniel chimed in before his brother could say anything else. "I can tell it. You don't have to tell it for me. Ted came to me on the bus and said I should read this magazine he had. He told me to stick it in my backpack and don't take it out until we were out of class and at recess. I had just started to look at it when Mr. Armstrong saw me with it.  Honest, Dad. That's how it happened."

"Armstrong?"

"That's the janitor," Aaron volunteered.

Henry spoke gently.  "Okay, you see, Mr. Matthews thinks you got it at home.  I had to tell him otherwise, and that would be the truth, right?"

Aaron spoke first, trying to sound as composed as he could. "That's right, and Ted Slovak was -"

"Ted Slovak is an asshole!" Daniel screamed. "He did it just to get me in trouble."

Henry smiled.  He knelt in front of his boys and wrapped his arms around them both.  His tall frame seemed to collapse and bring his eyes to their level. "Okay, calm down.  You're not in trouble.  Now listen to me.  If either of you ever have any questions about the kind of stuff you saw in that magazine, just ask me.  I don't want you learning the wrong stuff from the wrong people."

"Not even Mom?" Aaron asked.

"Don't ask your mom. Ask me.  She would be too embarrassed to explain anything like this."

Both boys appeared relieved, and Daniel wiped his eyes with his fists.  Henry was at the door, about to leave, when Daniel's next question stopped him in his tracks.

"Dad, if they're not called boobies, what are they called?"

***

Seven years later, Aaron was a senior in high school, and Dan was a sophomore. There was only an inch difference in height, and both had their dad's blonde curls and blue eyes. Aaron was part of the Drama Club, and Daniel played sophomore football. At school plays, when Aaron had a part, Henry was always the first to rise for a standing ovation, even if the performance was lousy and childish. At football games, Dan played defensive end, and the voice of their mother, Evelyn, could be heard above the crowd's cheers, especially when Dan made a tackle in the opposing team's backfield. She knew the team's playbook backwards and forwards.

Both boys had dates to the Christmas Ball at school and had their parents' permission to double date with Aaron driving, saving Henry and Evelyn the trouble of being taxi drivers for Dan and his date. It started out as a suggestion that no one can remember exactly who brought it up first and then evolved into an expectation that Aaron was beginning to regret. It would be a first for both boys for a variety of reasons. They had never been together on a double date, and Dan was new to the dating game. Aaron was old enough to drive, so the decision was considered a no-brainer. The afternoon of the big dance, the two boys were making their plans. They would be going in Aaron's car, a used

Chevy Camero that Aaron had saved up for over the last three years.  His plan was to take it to college. At that moment, he had the hood up and was polishing the chrome-plated valve covers.  Dan was chewing on a granola bar and watching his brother.

"What are those things you're polishing?  Dan leaned against the fender and pointed at Aaron's work.

"Don't lean against it!  You'll scratch the finish. I just got through waxing and buffing it."  As Dan stepped away, Aaron took out his handkerchief and wiped his brother's fingerprints off the finish.

"My God!  You act like this car is a person.  And who cares what's under the hood?  Who are you going to show it to?  Your next date?"

Aaron stopped and looked at his brother.  "That reminds me, who's your date for the Christmas Ball?"

"Amy Tucker.  I asked her yesterday, and she said 'yes.'

That's when the shouting match started, and Aaron's voice seemed to dominate.  "Amy Tucker? No!  You can't take her!"

"Why not?"

He closed the hood and glared at his brother. "You know why not!  She and I just broke up two months ago.  And you want me to be driving with my date in the front seat while you and Amy are smooching around in the back seat?  No way!  Not in my car!  I've just finished cleaning it and waxing it, and the inside is spotless.  I'll not have you canoodlin' in the backseat of my car!"

"Making out in the back seat!  What a great idea!  Thanks for suggesting that!  How do you know that's what we'll be doing?"

"Because – I know this girl!  She's had her hands on practically every guy in school.  Besides, she's a senior.  You're just a sophomore!"

"Every guy?  That includes you?  Maybe she likes football players better than stage actors."  He ended his remark with a giggle.

"Look, you don't want your reputation to be – you, you just don't want to do this!"

"How come?  What do you know that I don't?  What's she like?  Is she a good kisser?  Does she French kiss?  I can't wait, man."

"You will not go out with her!"

"Who are you?  My mother?  What do you care?  You'll graduate in a few months and be gone.  And I'll be here all by myself – and with the marvelous experience of making out with an older woman, getting me ready for anything else that comes along.  Don't you just love it?"

That evening, both boys were in the front seat as they picked up Daniel's date first.  From the back seat, Dan could see his brother constantly glancing in the rearview mirror. At one point, Amy waved her fingers at the mirror and kissed Dan when she knew Aaron was watching. Aaron's date ended up sitting close to him, blocking out his view in the mirror. All he could hear from the back seat were giggles.

Once they arrived at the school, Aaron pulled his brother aside and told him in definite terms what time they would depart to go home. "Don't make me come looking for you." The brothers parted ways for the remainder of the evening.

But Aaron knew how to manage a younger brother. On the way home, he decided unilaterally that Amy should be dropped off at her home first. Then, before Dan could realize what his brother was doing, they were parked in front of their own house.

Aaron turned to his brother, the sole passenger in the back seat, and said, "This is where you get out. Tell Dad I'll be back after midnight. Have a nice evening."

Aaron and his date drove off for their own private time, leaving Dan standing on the front walk. He swore he'd get even, but the ensuing months went by too fast. Aaron graduated, went to college, and from there, the two brothers followed different paths with only brief reunions and holidays until providence brought them closer again years later.

# CHAPTER THREE

Osceola Presbyterian Church, Kissimmee, Florida –
On December 10, 2024, Reverend Aaron Harper was
just finishing his sermon. The congregation was
giving him undivided attention.

"And the Word became flesh and lived among us.
This verse from John's Gospel is said to be the
complete gospel in one…." In his coat pocket, his
cell phone let out a comical jingle that brought smiles
and giggles from the congregation.

"That better be God calling," said an elderly man
in the front row. More chuckles.

Aaron looked at the caller ID after realizing he
had forgotten to turn off the ringer. He contemplated
only a second and put it back into his shirt pocket.

"As I was saying…" This time, the ringer was
off, but the vibration against his chest was impossible
to ignore. "Excuse me, folks." He put the phone to
his ear and said quietly, "Not now." He hung up and
laid the phone on the pulpit next to his notes.

Several minutes went by, the service was
finished, and Pastor Aaron had finally given the
benediction, while a light rain had begun falling
outside. Most of the congregation stood in line to
exit the building, umbrellas in hand, but a few
lingered in the narthex of the one-hundred-fifty-year-

old church to chat and exchange the typical snips of rich gossip that always permeated the social atmosphere before and after each Sunday service. Most of the members were seniors, well over 65, and a few young families with children. The demographics were like that of other Presbyterian churches. Live oak trees older than the building itself guarded both sides of the entrance, complete with the ever-present Spanish moss and azalea beds that surrounded each tree in every direction. One block to the east was the city hall, and the local police station was at an equal distance in the opposite direction.

Aaron shook hands with those in the process of leaving. He tried to appear attentive to Clara Bench, an eighty-five-year-old woman who consistently told him the same news every Sunday. She walked stooped with a cane, taking steps less than a few inches per stride. Her face had a leathery, sun-drenched complexion divided infinitely by wrinkles that branched and coalesced like a roadmap. Her daughter lived in New York and worked on Wall Street. She had promised to come to Kissimmee for Christmas, as she promised every year, but invariably failed to do so. As always, Clara broke down in tears, as she does every Sunday, with a line of people stacking up behind her, waiting. Aaron had her script almost memorized. Just as he thought she was finished, his cell phone vibrated again in his coat pocket. Instinctively, he reached for it but changed his mind.

"Aren't you going to answer that?" Clara said as she wiped her eyes.

Aaron fished the phone from his pocket, looked at the caller ID, and said, "It's my brother, Daniel. I'll call him back later."

"Oh, yes – Dr. Harper, your brother. Must be important, calling on a Sunday. Go ahead; call him back. I've got nowhere to go right now. I can wait."

Aaron reached for the outstretched hand of the man behind Clara, and she understood, as she does every Sunday, that the pastor has other parishioners to greet. Two minutes later, the phone buzzed again, then stopped.

"Could you pardon me for a second?" He turned and hit the speed dial button for his brother's number, and Daniel answered after two rings. He sounded a little irritated, but that was nothing new.

"Hey, I tried to call you a couple of minutes ago. You didn't answer."

"I know. We were in the middle of worship service, and I – "

"Alright, look, Aaron, I don't have time to be calling you about stuff that's none of my business."

Aaron stepped away and plugged the opposite ear with his finger. "Excuse me? Dan, what are you talking about?" His voice was becoming obvious to the exiting crowd of churchgoers.

"What am I talking about? It's Dad! I'm trying to take care of business here, and he's called me three times in the last thirty minutes. He called my phone number, thinking each time that it was yours. He wanted to talk to you, not me! So, would you please deal with it?"

Aaron covered the microphone and apologized to the parishioners who were waiting to be both acknowledged and to bless him with the usual sermon critique and their own private commentary of the scripture. He then stepped around the corner and down the steps to the sidewalk, realizing the rain had stopped. Two of the church elders followed him at a safe distance onto the sidewalk but still within earshot. Consistently, these two gentlemen felt it was their duty to eavesdrop on the pastor.

"Dan, I will deal with it. I just can't do so at this very moment. But wait, why would he call your number in the first place? He's got both numbers. Like I said, I'll -"

The line went dead. He turned and smiled at the faces staring at him, realizing he hadn't tempered his voice on the phone.

"I'm sorry, just a little family friction."

John Pleasance was a longtime friend of the family and one who Aaron could depend on for advice and guidance, but one who never tried to steal the glory of things accomplished. He was the senior elder for the church, semi-retired, and a part-time bank manager during the week. John was a rather plump little man in his early 80s with white, wavy hair combed straight back and an aquiline nose. Aaron's father always said John looked like the hood ornament on an old Mercury. He always spoke with an understanding demeanor. "Yes, we know about your family friction, as you call it. That was your brother, Dr. Harper, on the phone, right? Was this about your father? How is he? What is his name? Oh yes, Henry. Henry Harper. He used to attend church here, didn't he?" He ended with a chuckle. John had known Henry for years, and the dry humor was not lost on Aaron.

"Uh, yeah, Dad's fine. He just gets a little confused sometimes."

"I think it's more than that," John said, shaking his head. "I heard about his disappearance last week from the facility. The police found him walking through a residential neighborhood, right? The Henry Harper I once knew would never get lost anywhere. Doesn't that worry you?"

Aaron tried to defuse the conversation. "Don't believe everything you hear, John. He just got turned around a little. Actually, it's not a facility; it's an assisted living community. He's been there only a little while, a few short years, and he goes for walks all the time. He knows his way around. Dad's fine. But it seems I do need to call him. Would you excuse me?"

Aaron Harper, thirty-four, was the solo pastor of Osceola Presbyterian Church in Kissimmee, Florida, and had been in that position for eight years. He graduated from Austin Presbyterian Theological Seminary in Texas nine years ago. Jane, his wife of nearly nine years, was a bona fide Texan from San Antonio, a dutiful pastor's wife, totally dedicated to her husband's calling, and a flawless example of motherhood to their two sons, Joshua, who was six, and Adam, a four-year-old. Both boys had red hair, like their mother.

Aaron's brother, Daniel, was two years younger and had a bachelor's degree in biology and a doctor's degree in veterinary medicine, both from the University of Florida. Daniel always had a loving affinity for horses and now owns a thriving equine practice in Ocala, Florida, where the density of thoroughbred farms in Marion County approached that of the State of Kentucky. With thoroughbreds came family money. In that county, one never saw barns or fences in need of painting, and the stables were designed to house champions. But with such opulence came expectations. Daniel was a type-A person who gave others, with few exceptions, little opportunity to disagree with him. He purchased the clinic and the goodwill of the business from an older veterinarian, Dr. Roger MacArthur, who was looking to ease into retirement by working part-time for whoever bought the clinic. Daniel was single and lived only to work. He spent his office hours working both at the clinic and from the back of his truck. He was open for business seven days a week. Twelve-hour workdays were nothing new to him because of his popularity. New veterinary graduates sought him out for guidance and consultation, but he was sparse with giving away free time or advice to anyone. He dreaded the day that Roger would decide to retire completely, but he hadn't taken the time to find a replacement.

No two brothers could ever have been so different in so many of their mannerisms and their personalities. Both, however, were about six feet tall, broad-shouldered like their father, blonde, blue-eyed, and with an infectious smile. That's where their similarities ended.

Aaron stood on the sidewalk outside the church and dialed his father's number. Henry Harper answered the call on the second ring.

"Hello? Aaron? I've been trying to call you for weeks! Have you been out of town?"

"No, Dad. I've been right here all the time. I called you last Wednesday, and I came to see you, remember?"  He waited and gave his father a moment to process.  "We talked about the upcoming Superbowl and how much my two boys are growing. You said you got a card from Mayor Pollock, remember?"

"Yes, I did – it's right here.  How did you know about that?"

"You told me, Dad.  You told me all about how you and the mayor were friends in high school and played football together."

His father's phone was silent.

"Dad?  You still there?"

"Oh, I'm sorry.  What were you saying?"

"That's okay.  Look, I've got some people standing outside the church waiting to talk to me. How about I come by to see you this afternoon?"

"Yes, well, you go ahead and talk to your friends. I'm sure I'll see you at some point."

"Dad, I just said -" He was interrupted by the dial tone.

Henry Harper was eighty-two years old.  Before retirement, he had been the sole owner of Harper's Gardens, a large wholesale nursery that supplied most of the flower shops in Osceola County.  He had purchased the business when it was just a small flower shop and then developed it into a huge enterprise as he bought various plots of land, one by one until he had over one hundred acres of flowers of all sorts. People out for a casual Sunday drive would slowly idle past the main gate and try to gaze at the waves of color flowing in the breeze. Henry's main crop was marigolds, of which he had thirty-five acres started from seed. Landscaping companies knew they could always find hibiscus, bougainvillea, and plumbago at Harper's to showcase new construction sites. Disney was his biggest client, especially in April when Epcot opened its flower show to the public. When he retired, he sold the business and the property and simply stuck the money in a savings account, despite the advice many gave him about putting it into a trust so it would transfer over seamlessly when the time came.

He and his wife, Evelyn, had been married 20 years when they concluded, with great disappointment, that they would never be blessed with children. Several doctors told them there was no medical reason for Evelyn to be barren. Just a case of bad timing, they said. They were encouraged to keep trying, but the doctors' words of wisdom did not dispel the negative effect on the relationship and on Evelyn's state of mind. She gradually entered a world of depression and despair at the expense of the intimate physical and psychological connection between Henry and her. But not entirely. Despite her depression, there were moments of clarity in which Evelyn recognized Henry's occasional need for intimacy, even to the point of exchanging mutual, but minimal, enjoyment.  Eventually, Aaron came into the world and then, Daniel, two years later.

Aaron, at age twenty-five, was almost through seminary when his mother had a massive stroke and died when she was seventy-two years old.  Henry never completely finished grieving.

For the last three years, Henry lived at Meadows House, an assisted living organization at the invisible border between Kissimmee and Orlando.  It consisted of several buildings, all of which were five stories high, each with a gracious first-floor lobby filled with overstuffed chairs, sofas, artwork, and soothing background music.  The lobby furniture was arranged in clusters as though separated by invisible walls to create isolated pockets of warmth and privacy.  Picture windows with bright, floral curtains added an element of grace and cheer to the texture of the room.  Each floor had a nurses' station, but one wouldn't know it because each one looked more like a coffee station, and no hospital atmosphere or anything institutional broke the warm, inviting ambiance.

Henry had a single-bedroom apartment with a small kitchen, living room, breakfast nook, and French doors that led to a small room, which could be an office or parlor or just a catch-all.  The bathroom had all the details required by those on the cusp of needing personal help but not having yet lost the dignity of total independence.

It took about thirty minutes for Aaron to complete all the expected post-worship service conversations and lock up the building. He often wondered how pastors in larger churches managed to get away in time for lunch on Sundays. Of course, they usually had a full staff that took care of things like checking all the restrooms, checking the answering machine, and adjusting the thermostats.

His car was parked in the lot behind the church. It was a 2010 Mazda Miata with a faded red paint job and a cracked vinyl convertible top. It wasn't a muscle car like the Camero he had in college, the one that sucked up the fuel at an alarming rate and stopped at every gas station. The Mazda engine ran like a clock and got good gas mileage, but the exterior appearance needed help. And that was Aaron's escape from the stress of pastoring a church. Since he bought it used five years ago, he had spent hours trying to restore it to its original sparkle. It was a thankless task of rubbing and polishing. He embellished the interior with new replacement seats and a hand-tooled cover for the dash. The gear shift knob had an outline of a Christian fish. His vanity plate read, '1 PresKiss.' Twice, he came close to having the body repainted professionally, but that was expensive and took all the joy out of doing things himself. But the heart of the car was under the hood, the 2-liter engine, a six-speed manual shift, and the rack and pinion steering. When no one was looking, he enjoyed winding it up, shifting gears, and drifting around corners. He admitted to himself that he never outgrew his love for fast cars.

Meadows House was a ten-minute drive from the church through some back roads off the beaten path. It took Aaron between orange groves on either side of the road, and this time of year, the fruit was nearing harvest time. But the road, with no turns or curves for several miles, spoke to his foot on the gas pedal. He had the top down, and he loved the musical sound of the engine when it hit third gear. Up ahead, another car was approaching with flashing headlights, so he slowed down. As he suspected, a Florida State Trooper was parked behind a cluster of trees, watching and waiting. Aaron waved to the cop as he drove by, 5 mph below the limit.

At Henry's apartment, Aaron knocked on the door and waited a full minute before cracking the door open and glancing inside. At 1:00 O'clock in the afternoon, Henry was still in his pajamas and robe, asleep in his old, thread-worn recliner with his arms and legs draped open in an undignified manner. He had not heard his son's arrival. Aaron noticed his dad's hair was uncombed, and he had not shaved in several days. His robe lay untied, and the food stains on the pajama front suggested several meals had gone by without him changing clothes.  Dirty dishes filled the sink, and a small saucepan was on the stove lined with congealed oatmeal.  The bedroom was no better.  The sheets were pulled away from the edges of the mattress, and a faint yellow pattern covered a dinnerplate area of the bedspread.  There was a discernible odor of ammonia in the room, and clothes littered the floor.  On his dresser was a pile of used tissue paper, assorted change from his pockets, cuff links, ties, a pair of socks, and a stack of framed photographs.

Aaron paused long enough to look at some of the pictures.  The small half-bath door was open, and the toilet had not been flushed.  Aaron pushed the handle down and immediately regretted having done it.  The water level in the bowl rose to the rim but didn't overflow.  *Try getting a plumber, even in a place like this, on a Sunday.*

He walked to the phone and called the front desk.  "Yes, this is Aaron Harper.  I signed in a couple of minutes ago.  Yes, thanks for remembering.  I'm visiting my dad in apartment 30, and I cannot believe the mess I found here.  Has anyone checked on him in the last few days?  Just a minute – hang on a second…"

Henry's voice croaked like an old frog.

"What? Who's there? Who are you? What are you doing in my house?"

"Dad, it's me – Aaron. Me, your firstborn, remember?"

Henry blinked his eyes and rubbed the top of his head. "Aaron, yeah, Aaron. What's, what's the problem? Why are you here?"

"You called me, Dad. Hang on. Let me finish talking to the front desk."

Aaron described his findings to the weekend receptionist and told her the priority should be to unstop the toilet. He then made it clear that he wanted to talk to whomever wore the manager's hat that day. He was given a promise that the manager would be there shortly. Satisfied for the moment, he turned to his father.

"Dad, when's the last time you showered?"

Henry stared at the floor and shrugged his shoulders. "This morning?"

"No, Dad. You probably haven't cleaned yourself up for several days. We need to take care of that."

"So, if you know how many days it's been, why'd you ask? What are you doing here, anyway? You never come to see me. Your brother, Aaron, does all the time."

"Dad, I'm Aaron. Are you talking about Daniel? Has he been here? He said you called him twice today."

"I didn't call anyone today. Hell, I don't even know where my phone is. I just – I can't remember where – I guess it's - I don't know. Your mother would know if she were still here." Aaron saw tears welling up in the old man's eyes.

"Don't worry. We'll find it. Say! How about I go down the hallway and bring back a cup of coffee for both of us? You can put some clothes on while I'm getting it. Have you had lunch?"

Aaron started for the entrance when he heard a knock at the door. Before he could reach it, his dad shouted, "Who's there? What the hell do you want?"

Aaron opened the door, and a stately Hispanic woman in her mid-50s stood in the hallway with two maintenance men. Her name tag read 'Dorothy.'

"Did you call the front desk, sir? What's the problem?"

"Come take a look for yourself." Aaron arched his eyebrows as he spoke. Dorothy grasped his silent message and politely stepped inside.

"Oh, my," she said quietly. "Looks like we need a little help with domestic tasks. When's the last time he had laundry done?"

"I have no idea. If I may say so, my brother and I depend on you folks to keep track of things like that.

But laundry is not the worst of it.  Go look at his toilet, the one off the bedroom, and see for yourself."

Aaron waited in the kitchen while she disappeared in the next room.  Within seconds, her voice came screeching forth through the door, "Alfonso, get in here!"

Both maintenance men looked at each other and quickly followed the sound of her voice.  Aaron could hear a 3-way conversation in Spanish, and Dorothy appeared, making bold strides with her arms folded.

"Mr. Harper, I am so sorry this has happened. From the looks of it, he's used that bathroom for several days without flushing it.  And this kitchen, it's a disgrace.  We need to talk.  Your father obviously needs the next level of care, and we should have seen this long before it happened."

"In all fairness, I was here five days ago, and it wasn't like this.  Something eventful must have happened to him since then."

"When is his next medical appointment?"

"I'll check on that.  Right now, I need to get him out of here for a couple of hours while these men work.  Do you have a clean-up crew who can make a dent in this mess?"

"Mr. Harper, I regret to say that such services are not part of the level of care he's paying for.  We have cleaning crews, but -"

"I'll pay for it."

"Well, first we have to -"

"I said I'll pay for it. But, if the truth be known, it wouldn't be this bad if someone had checked on him. I know that's part of what we're paying for."

"I can understand that you're upset. Yes, tomorrow we'll have someone here."

"No, today! I'm taking him to my house right now, and I'll be back before supper. I'll have him cleaned up and dressed for the dining room."

"Yes -"

"Which reminds me, I thought he ate in the dining room. Why are there dirty dishes with pots and pans in the sink if he's supposed to be eating with the other residents? I would think someone would have noticed his absence."

Dorothy clasped her hands together and took a step closer to him. Her eyes took on a steely look, and she said slowly, "Mr. Harper, I just work on the weekends. It seems you have several questions that should be directed to the full-time manager. He will be here tomorrow. In the meantime, I will do my best to restore some order to this situation. All I can ask for is your patience." She continued to glare at Aaron and waited for him to acknowledge what she had just said.

Aaron nodded and smiled. "We'll be back in time for supper." He went into the bedroom and started rummaging around for underwear and clothes. Helping his dad dress was a new experience. It reminded him of dressing his two children not too long ago. In fact, everything about his father reminded him of a child's mind in a man's body.

Once they got into the car, he called his wife, Jane. She answered after several rings.

"Aaron, where are you? I thought you said you wouldn't be long."

"I know, but Dad's apartment was a disaster. They're supposed to be cleaning it up. Ah - listen, do we have ingredients for a sandwich of some type? He hasn't eaten all day."

"Your dad? Are you bringing him here?"

"You'll understand when you see him. He looks worse than the apartment. I'm bringing a change of clothes for him and his shaving kit."

"That bad? I think I'll take the kids to the mall. How long is he staying?"

"I don't know. I'll wait a couple of hours and call to see if they're done cleaning here. Oh yeah, the toilet was stopped up as well."

"Oh my God! Okay, come on. Maybe the kids will keep him entertained after you clean him up. You say he hasn't eaten today?"

"Probably not."

"We were going to have last night's leftovers. I'll see if there's enough."

"Well, I was thinking of something like an afternoon snack until I get him back here for supper."

Jane listened patiently. "Okay, give me a few minutes before you leave."

"We're already in the car. Thirty minutes? I can drive slow." He paused. "Hey, I love you."

He drove his dad on a long, circuitous route to the house, first past the big marina on Lake Tohopekaliga, with a fleet of private boats sat bobbing in the water. Then they stopped at the fishing pier and just gazed off in the distance.

"Dad, is there anything you want to see while we're out? Jane's fixing us something to eat. Are you hungry?"

His father looked at him with a blank stare. His eyes seemed to be looking at something a million miles away, or maybe his mind was fantasizing about something unimaginable. Finally, he blinked and focused on his son.

"Jane? You said something about Jane?" His gaze turned back to the lake with the sunlight coming out of the west, reflecting on the small whitecaps. There were several bass boats anchored among the reeds and bullrushes. "Looks like the breeze is picking up out there. That's always good for fishing. The bass bite best with a little chop on the water."

"Dad? You remember that? That's wonderful. Remember when you used to take Daniel and me

fishing?  We went right over there off that far point."
He pointed to a cluster of water lilies along the far
bank.  "There's a deep drop off, and you knew that's
where they'd be.  I always enjoy remembering those
fishing trips."

"No!  The drop-off is over there!  Next to those
cypress trees.  I know – I was there last week.  And
the National Guard came and said I had to leave.
Those sonsabitches think they own the lake!"  He
started to open the car door, but Aaron stopped him.

"Okay, Dad.  I think we better get going.  Jane's
probably waiting for us."

Jane Harper was less than two years younger than
Aaron.  She was a flaming redhead with a knock-out
figure and a definite Texas twang in her voice.  They
had met during Aaron's last year at Austin
Presbyterian while she finished her degree in English
at the University of Texas.  Their first conversation
was almost their last one when he questioned the
historical importance of the Alamo in Texas history.
Their dialog progressed from Texas history to the
passion she had for family values, and that convinced
Aaron that she was worth pursuing to see where it
led.  And pursue he did.  They married shortly after
his graduation.  She accepted the unpredictable life
of a new minister, picking up substitute teaching jobs
here and there, not knowing where they would be
working or living from month to month.  For a short

while, he filled the position of associate pastor in Bryan, Texas, until he heard about the opening in Kissimmee. There was a need for schoolteachers in Kissimmee, so Jane had no trouble finding a rewarding job. Aaron's father was of sound mind and body when they moved to Florida. Harper's Gardens was flourishing then, overflowing with orders. But that was then.

Aaron's car pulled into the driveway, and both boys, Joshua and Adam, stood at the front door and waited for the car to stop. As soon as they saw Aaron get out of the car, they raced to greet him, each wrapping their arms around a leg. Henry made his exit from the little sports car slowly, carefully, refusing any help, keeping one hand on the side of the car as though the ground beneath him might begin to shake. Both children spotted him and retreated behind their dad, peering around him to gaze at what appeared to be a boogieman, uncombed, unshaven, disheveled, with slippers on his feet.

Henry spoke first. "Who - who are these kids?"

"Dad, these are my kids – Joshua and Adam. You remember them, don't you?" Henry looked at his son with pleading in his eyes and a silent question on his lips. That's when Jane spoke up from the front steps. There was never a time that Aaron regretted choosing her as his lifetime mate. She stood there wearing a pale green striped slipover blouse and jeans, both of which offered more than a hint of her figure.  Her red hair fluttered gently in the breeze.

"Henry, you old outlaw!  I got a big hug for you!  C'mere!"

"Jane!  Oh my, Jane!  Aw, hell, you look great!  Hang on, I'm moving as fast as I can."

Aaron watched the scene play out as it had many times.  Henry had memory problems with names and faces, but not with Jane.  For some reason, the time he first met his new daughter-in-law, Jane's appearance and personality had made a permanent impression on him years ago.  Ignoring his grungy appearance and obvious lack of hygiene, she met him halfway on the sidewalk, engulfed him in a huge bearhug, and kissed the side of his face, whiskers and all.  *They don't make women like her anymore,* Aaron thought.

It took five minutes to get Henry, his belongings, Jane, and the kids inside the front door.  Henry acted like he had never seen their house, although he had been there a multitude of times.

"Dad, let's get you into the bathroom where you can shower.  I brought your razor, but I think you need a barber, as well.  We'll attend to that tomorrow."

Aaron handled the small duffel bag of clothes and guided his father toward the bathroom down the hall.  Once inside, he helped Henry strip down and held his father's hand while he stepped into the tub and turned on the water. The last thing Aaron did was adjust the flow, draw the curtain, and sit on the nearby toilet seat to wait.

He could hear Henry quietly cough and sputter as the water hit the shower curtain. He heard the soap drop, and his dad cursed, but the process didn't stop.

"Hey, Dad, be sure to get all the cracks and crevices cleaned out." That was the phrase Henry used to use on both Aaron and his brother when they were small boys.

From behind the curtain, his father's voice sounded low and muffled. "I know how to take a damn shower, son."

To Aaron, he almost sounded normal. If only he could turn the clock back. Yeah, and do what? Pray harder? Ask God for a different outcome?

He heard the water turn off. Henry slowly drew the curtain back and stood there, dripping. He slicked his hair back with his hands and reached for a towel. Aaron started to dry him off, but Henry gently took the towel from him. "I got this. Thanks anyway."

Aaron thought, *What a difference a simple shower makes.*

Dressed and combed as much as possible, Henry slowly made his way into the dining room, where Jane waited with an afternoon snack of bacon, lettuce, tomato sandwich, and a glass of iced tea. Henry sat and quickly devoured every crumb, then sat silently and stared at the tablecloth for several seconds. Aaron and Jane sat across from him, watching. Slowly, his eyes began to moisten until tears flowed freely. He said nothing; he just sat there, his eyelids fluttering and his lips trembling.

Aaron spoke softly. "Dad, what's the matter?"

Henry cleared his throat and croaked, "Your mother used to make sandwiches like this one. She knew I enjoyed them. Thanks, Jane, for remembering."

Joshua and Adam came into the room and stood next to their grandfather, Joshua, holding a stuffed toy shaped in the image of a small horse. One eye was missing, and the stuffing was exposed through a small tear in the fabric.

Henry was suddenly the perfect grandfather. "Joshua! What's this? Who do you have with you?"

"His name is Buddy," Joshua said softly.

"What's that? I didn't hear you."

"His name is Buddy," the child said a bit louder. "He lost his eye. And the dog chewed on him."

"Does that make you sad?"

Joshua nodded. The corners of his mouth began to turn down.

Henry pulled him closer and said, "Well, you know what? It's almost Christmas time. That's a time to be happy. Hey, let's sing something! Do you know Jingle Bells? I'll bet you do! Let's sing it!"

In a flash, he had both boys smiling with his clown-face antics and hand gestures. Aaron patiently waited for the moment to pass, knowing that his father would soon be back into his world of clouded judgement and lost memories.

Jane rose from her chair, walked around the table, stood behind Henry, and put her arms around him. He reached backwards, gave her a gentle pat on her shoulder, and stood up. "I need to get back to my apartment. Can you call a cab for me?"

Aaron looked a bit surprised at first, then remembered that streak of independence his father always had. "Dad, I'm going to take you back. I want to see if they've fixed your toilet." It sounded like a good enough answer.

Back at Henry's apartment, the toilet seemed to be in a functional status and the bed looked fresh with clean sheets and tight corners. The kitchen was still a mess, and dirty laundry lined the floor like a carpet. Aaron started by filling the dishwasher to capacity, closing it, and pushing all the right buttons. Nothing happened. None of the panel lights came on, and no water flowed. Nothing.

"Well, shit!" he muttered. "Dad! How do I make this thing work?"

Henry shuffled into the kitchen, opened the dishwasher door, rattled the top tray, then slammed the door shut. "Now try it. Not that button, this one. Simple mechanics, preacher!" To Aaron's relief, the machine roared to life, and his father's wide range of moods and levels of comprehension continued to amaze him.

An hour later, all the pots and pans that couldn't fit into the dishwasher were clean and on the drying rack, and Aaron had the countertop clean. He quickly gathered up all the dirty clothes, filled out an inventory slip, stuffed it all into a laundry bag, and dropped it outside the door in the hallway.

"I'll ask the front desk to have someone come in here tomorrow to vacuum and mop. This whole apartment needs sanitizing."

"I'll take care of it tomorrow, son. I'm sorry you had to see it like this. But thanks anyway. You need to go home to your family now. I've got this."

Aaron hugged his dad and promised to see him bright and early the next morning.

Monday was Aaron's usual day off. People often think preachers only work on Sundays, but much time and effort go into preparation for a worship service as well as all the other tasks that go along with a house of worship. The church secretary, Sally Butterfield, was experienced in acting as a Monday buffer, keeping the calendar clear on his day off. She knew every member of the church, their kids' names, who they were having secrets with, and who drank too much. The church was in bad need of an associate pastor, but the budget could not support such a luxury right now. Beyond Monday, there was always an appointment book that controlled his life, filled with meetings, conference calls, counseling sessions, and visits to the homebound.

Aaron pulled into the parking lot of Meadows House at 9 AM and went straight to the front desk. The receptionist was a new face, a young woman named Andrea, according to her name tag. The first things he noticed were her false eyelashes and heavy mascara. The second thing was her lowcut, yellow, flowered blouse that strained at the buttons and looked like it had been intended for a smaller woman.

"Hi, I'm Pastor Adam Harper. Do you think I could have a moment with someone on the management staff?"

Andrea stood with a big smile and straightened her short, tight skirt that barely covered all privileged parts. "Let me go see, Pastor. They had a quick meeting this morning, and I think they're finished."

Aaron scratched his chin and made an effort to keep his thoughts on the straight and narrow. Andrea returned in less than a minute with a jiggle in more than just her step.

"The manager says he can see you in about an hour. I'm so sorry. He's tied up right now."

"That's okay. I have some things to do first, so that works fine."

She responded with a smile and a flutter of eyelids.

Aaron walked to the facility barber shop and arranged to bring his dad there in the next few minutes. As he exited the elevator, he was hoping that Henry was up and dressed, and he heard music playing from the direction of his dad's apartment. It got louder as he approached, and he found Henry, up and fully dressed, prancing around the room with a vacuum cleaner while a recording of *Jailhouse Rock* blared from his stereo.

Aaron had to yell to be heard. "Dad! Dad! What are you doing?"

"What? Speak up, son. I can't hear you!"

Aaron closed the door and turned down the music. He looked at his dad and couldn't help but smile. Moments like this were becoming less and less frequent, and he decided to savor the joy of seeing his dad happy, even if it was temporary.

"Where'd you get the vacuum?"

"Some kid who didn't speak English came in here and started running the damn thing, and I told him to give it to me and go do something else. I don't know if he understood me, but he left. That's okay,

I'm done here.  I'll just leave it out in the hallway.
What brings you here?"

"I made you an appointment at the barbershop
downstairs.  Is that okay?"

Henry pulled a clump of hair down to his nose
and said, "You think I need it?  Ha!  Sure, let's go.  I
think I can work it into my busy schedule."

Aaron followed his dad into the bedroom in
search of socks and shoes.  He noticed the stack of
framed pictures were now neatly arranged in a simple
pattern on the dresser top.  He picked up one to look
at it, and his father quickly took it from his hands and
said, "Mind your own business."

The barbershop had three chairs, two of which
were occupied.  The third was assigned to a young
man named Albert, according to his name on the
mirror behind the chair.  He seemed to be a man of
few words as Henry climbed aboard and leaned his
head back.

"How you want it?"

Aaron stood by the chair and motioned with his
hands.  "He needs most of this taken off and leave
him just enough to -"

"I can speak for myself," came Henry's reply.

"Excuse me?"

"Are you the one sitting in the chair?  I know
what I want.  First thing, I want my regular barber,
not this kid."

Aaron mouthed the words, 'I'm sorry,' and Albert stepped back and took a cigarette from his shirt pocket. He headed for the entrance, mumbling something about working in a place like this.

The chair next to them had just vacated, and Henry quickly occupied it. "That's better," he said roughly. "Now, let's get this done."

With Henry seated, the older barber said, "Sir, my name is George. Do you remember me? How would you like your hair cut? You need a shave as well?"

Aaron picked up a magazine while Henry and George engaged in a continuous dialog that filled the room, centered on nothing and yet on everything. He lost count of the number of times the barber stopped, walked to the front of the chair, and talked like there was nothing else in the world to do, nothing pressing, just two men connected in natural mutual bonding. Aaron had not seen his father this animated and vocal in several months. Listening, it reminded Aaron that Henry was a man of details and had always approached his sons this way, explaining ordinary things in a manner that revealed how everything fascinated him. He wanted his sons to have the same joy in living. It was a relaxing tonic to just sit there and listen to Henry being Henry.

When George was finished, the two men shook hands, Aaron paid him, and they started toward the elevator. From the corner of his eye, Aaron saw the young barber coming back through the front door.

"Hope you're happy, you old fart," the young man muttered.

Henry looked at Aaron and asked, "What did he say?" He turned around and yelled, "Hey, you, come back here! Hey, I'm talking to you!"

"Let it go, Dad. He's got things on his mind, probably."

Henry was pointing at the man and looking at Aaron with a piercing glare. "You preachers! What he needs is a good tongue-lashing and a new job. He ought not to be working here. You hear what I'm saying?"

"Yes, I hear you. But maybe setting him straight is not our job. Let's get back upstairs, and you can make me a cup of coffee."

A bundle of clean laundry waited outside Henry's apartment door. Aaron carried it inside and put it on the bed, then joined his dad in the kitchen. An hour later, they put their coffee cups in the sink, and Aaron said goodbye. The day was starting out on a good note.

Aaron's 10 O'clock appointment was with Jonathan Appleton, assistant manager for Henry's building. Try as he could, Aaron could not get the notion of 'Johnny Appleseed' out of his thoughts. Mr. Appleton was in his mid-50s, slightly plump, with a receding hairline and small mustache, and wearing a white shirt and tie with grey slacks that did not cover his ankles. Even at mid-morning, his tie was loosened as though stress had taken an early-morning toll on him. Aaron noticed the collar tabs were unbuttoned.

"Hi! I'm Jonathan. Have a seat."

"Aaron Harper. Thanks for seeing me on short notice."

"What can I do for you?"

"My dad is one of your residents, and I'd like to talk -"

"What's his name?"

"Henry. Henry Harper. He's in apartment 30. He's -"

"Hang on, let me pull up his file in the computer. Yeah, here it is. Been with us a couple of years, I see."

"Maybe a little longer than that. Have you met him? I mean, do you know him?"

The man never took his eyes off the screen. "No, not first-hand. I just started here last week. Oh, I see you had some plumbing problems yesterday."

"Yes, there's that, but I also wanted to talk to you about his care."

"Is there a problem?"

"I'm not sure. What I found yesterday surprised me. I -"

"Would you like a cup of coffee?"

"No, thanks." Johnny Appleseed seemed to be distracted as he sat behind his desk, so Aaron just waited for him to fill his own cup.

The man took a long slurp of coffee and seemed ready to settle back and listen. "Hmm, that's good. You know, coffee is the dark matter that ties the universe together." He waited for a response from Aaron and got none. "Okay, I'm sorry. Go ahead. You were saying?"

Aaron shifted in his chair and said, "Yeah, ah, I came to his apartment yesterday and found a disaster. The toilet was clogged. There was trash everywhere, dirty clothes strewn about, urine stains on the bedding, just a disaster."

Appleton raised his eyebrows but said nothing. He now seemed very focused on what Aaron was saying.

"Honestly, I thought we were paying you folks to look in on your residents to make sure everything was at least hygienic and in some semblance of order. My brother and I can't be here all the time, and I just thought someone should know what I found yesterday."

Appleton was propped up on one elbow, moving only his eyes from Aaron to the computer screen and back again at Aaron.

"So, what you found didn't match up with what you were expecting, right?"

Aaron cleared his throat, anticipating a confrontation. "Yes, something like that."

He was still leaning on his desk, his cheek resting on the palm of his hand, and he said casually, "Were you aware that your dad changed his contract with us?"

"Changed? What, what do you mean? Changed how?"

Appleton turned his screen so Aaron could see it. "According to this, he canceled his housekeeping requirement two weeks ago and turned in his meal ticket. It says here he wants to do his own grocery shopping and will cook for himself."

Aaron was momentarily speechless. Searching for words, he now realized how much variation there was in his father's cognitive abilities.

"You know, yesterday he was a blank page. I couldn't get a coherent sentence out of him until I took him to my house and then -"

"What happened there?"

"Well, he saw my wife and immediately recognized her. He connected with the grandkids after a while, and he seemed okay when I brought him back."

"How is he this morning?"

Aaron could only shrug and said, "He seems fine. He has such mood swings and memory lapses. He almost had a scene with one of the barbers, but that's another story. This whole thing is really beginning to trouble me."

Appleton was looking at the screen again. "It says here that he has early Alzheimer's Disease. Maybe it's not so early anymore. This diagnostic entry was made by his doctor over a year ago."

"Has it been a year?

"Yes, it sure has, and then some. I think we need to upgrade his care agreement. I see you also have power of attorney. And who's Daniel?"

"That's my brother. He lives in Ocala."

"His wife?"

"My brother is not married."

"No. I meant your dad. I'm asking about your mother, I presume."

Aaron felt a little embarrassed. "Oh, yeah. Mom died about ten years ago. He has no other family. Just Dan and me."

"I see. So, let's write up another care agreement for you to sign, and we'll take it from there. I assume you have control of his checkbook."

"Yes, we established that some time ago."

"Good. We don't want him buying a bunch of stuff online. There're all kinds of scams out there."

Aaron agreed and thanked Mr. Appleton. He had his hand on the doorknob to leave when Appleton said, "His next medical appointment is this Friday. You knew that, right?"

"Next Friday? Wha – no, I didn't know that. I'll see if – what time next Friday?"

"Ten O'clock. Not next Friday, this Friday. Four days from now."

# CHAPTER FOUR

Ocala, Florida.

Dr. Daniel Harper waited by his truck while two employees of Hemphill Farms brought in the next mare for him to examine. In three more weeks, it would be a new year, and the foaling season would be in full swing. In horse racing society, all thoroughbreds were considered as born on January 1st. Anything before that put them in the wrong year group. Anything much later made a big difference in training as they approached the racing age of three years old. The intensive training of a young racehorse cannot proceed at full pace until the bone growth plates in the legs have calcified and closed. Taking x-rays of the growth plates was one of Dan's essential tasks for his clients. For horses at such a young age, a delay of 5-6 months made a big difference when running against others born closer to that magic New Year's date. Consequently, January and February ushered in almost nonstop work for farm staff and their veterinarians. As soon as that was over, the breeding season started all over again. Most owners tried to breed their mares on the first ovarian cycle after giving birth. Hemphill Farms had 50 brood mares and five studs, and there was no time to waste.

Silas Hemphill was eighty-five years old and still lived in the house his grandfather had built. It was not the first house on the farm. His grandfather, Josiah Hemphill, had been a cattleman in South Florida almost a hundred years ago, building herds from the wild cattle they rounded up out of the swamps and gater holes around Lake Okeechobee. It was a tough life, and men had to settle their own differences without the help of law enforcement or attorneys. Cattle thieves were the biggest obstacles to success, and the Hemphill boys were good at eliminating the problem. Then, one day, someone took Josiah to a racetrack, and he saw his future in action. It was not in betting on the horses but in raising and selling them. He had heard about a small group of farms in Marion County that seemed to have a good sense of that business, so he sold his cattle ranch and found a job working for one of the farms. The pay was paltry, but he never told anyone of his hidden wealth from the sale of his South Florida cattle ranch. Word traveled slow in those days, and he felt safe with his secret.

Finally, a horse farm became available in an estate sale, and he outbid all the other would-be buyers. The farm had no name, so Hemphill Farms it was. There was a small ramshackle house on the place and the resemblance to a swamp cabin didn't fit his dreams, so he created a new house site and built the one Silas lived in now. It was constructed in the typical Florida Cracker house style, being low-slung in front with a tall, peaked roof and large, wraparound porch and railing. The term 'cracker' came from the use of whips and dogs to round up scrub cattle from the wild. The 'crackers' were tough men, not because they learned to be that way but because anyone else without the aptitude for that lifestyle simply didn't attempt to do what they did. Josiah passed his methods and values on to his children and grandchildren, including Silas. In the front yard, large pothos vines with pyramidal leaves the size of dinnerplates grew from the ground around some of the live oaks and reached the uppermost limits of the branches. Josiah made sure the house was big and impressive because he wanted to build his legacy around his wealth and dominance in whatever enterprise he attempted. So, Silas came from old money that started two generations back when his grandfather moved to Marion County. Horse folks in Kentucky said it was the wrong climate for thoroughbreds, and Josiah was determined to show the world that no one questions or challenges the Hemphill family. Stubbornness and arrogance became a family trait, and now, Silas displayed the family banner proudly. Two years before, Silas's wife of sixty years died, leaving him with only one child, a grown woman whom Daniel had never met.

Dr. Harper had one hand on the mare's hindquarters and the other holding an ultrasound wand when his cell phone rang. He let it ring until it stopped. Another beep told him a voicemail message had been left. It would have to wait. He finished his task and said, "Okay, who's next?" He waited a few seconds for a response from one of the farm hands. "Hey! Let's go! We're wasting time. I've got other calls down the road waiting on me."

The next mare came prancing into the treatment area with two men trying to control her while Daniel put on a clean plastic sleeve. This one would require a type of examination that he referred to as 'Going up the old dirt road.' He had just drizzled lubricant on his sleeved arm when the phone rang again. He looked at it with his free hand.

"You're a popular man today," someone said.

"It's my brother. He can wait."

As he was finishing, someone told him that was the last mare for him to examine that day. Feeling satisfied, he walked toward his truck and was about to return Aaron's call when Silas Hemphill drove up to the barn in his BMW.

"Dr. Harper, you need to look at Pistachio. He's got something wrong with his left eye. I just came from the stud barn.  I saw it myself.  I'll meet you over there."

"Mr. Hemphill, can it wait until this afternoon?  I've got another appointment a few miles from here, and I need to get going."

Silas's face turned red.  "Hey, who do you think is paying your retainer?  I don't give a continental damn how many other clients you have. When I tell you to do something, I want to see it done right then!  Don't argue with me!  I'll meet you at the stud barn." With that, he got back into his car and sped away.

Dan looked around at the others who were standing there, taking it all in.  From the back of the crowd, someone said, "You better go, doc. He means it."

"Yeah, I know," he muttered.  Why did he let anyone talk him into signing a retainer agreement? He was on call twenty-four hours a day for this one client, and all his other clients simply had to wait their turn.  What was he thinking?

In less than two minutes, he arrived at the stud barn, and three handlers were standing around Pistachio, a beautiful, twelve-year-old, solid black stallion that had sired a dozen foals the last year, all of which had champion potential.  Daniel could see the problem as he stepped out of the truck.  Pistachio was squinting his left eye, and Daniel could see a large splotch of redness even as he approached.

"What happened? Looks like an injury to me."

Silas spoke with venom in his voice. "We hired this new guy last week. Told all of us he knew how to handle a horse like this one. The first thing he did was whack him across the face with a riding whip and catch his eye with the tip. I fired his ass on the spot!"

Dan approached the horse cautiously. Pistachio had a reputation for striking with his front feet. Slowly, he reached for the horse's neck and then let his hand travel to the top of the head. Gently, he clutched a handful of the horse's ear and gave it a slight squeeze. Distracted, Pistachio stood still while Dan looked at the injury.

"He's got a small hematoma on the sclera, the white part. It'll resolve on its own. Might take a couple of weeks, maybe longer. I'll give you some medication to drop in the eye just to prevent it from becoming infected."

"Doc, he's supposed to race in two days. The track vet is going to scratch him if he sees that eye. Can't you put a needle in there and suck the blood out?"

"Mr. Hemphill, first of all, I'd have to knock him down with an anesthetic in order to do what you're suggesting, and he might still be a little woozy come race time. He might even have a trace of it in his urine sample after the race. You see, the blood is infiltrated in the tissue like a sponge. It's not just a pool of blood and, furthermore, the exertion of a race might make it worse. I'm afraid your idea is out of the question."

"Young man, who do you think you're talking to? I want him at that racetrack tomorrow! I'm in the firing mood today, and I just might fire you! And I'll see to it that you don't touch another horse in this whole damn county!"

"That's not the way I do business, Mr. Hemphill. I have respect for the owners of these fine animals, but I respect the animals as well. You do not want to force this issue!"

As the two men stood almost nose to nose, Dan caught sight of a figure stepping out of the shadow of the barn door. Coming closer, he noticed an hourglass silhouette with all the right curves and long, dark, auburn hair. She wore jeans that fit snugly and a flowered blouse that was unbuttoned enough to show a remarkable cleavage. She spoke softly.

"Daddy, what happened to Pistachio? Did I hear something about his eye?"

Silas Hemphill's demeanor suddenly collapsed at the sound of the woman's voice. He struggled to find the words.

"Uh - yeah, he had a little accident with his eye, honey. He'll be okay."

She casually walked up to the horse, rubbed the side of his face, and spoke as though no one else was around. "Hey, pretty boy. What happened to you? It's okay. Here, I got something for you." She reached into her pocket and pulled out a carrot. The horse waited patiently for her to extend it to him, then gently took it from her hand. She turned and looked at Daniel.

"Hi, I'm Melissa Gibson. I'm this guy's daughter." She smiled as she spoke and pointed to Silas. "We've never met, have we?"

Daniel stepped closer and shook her hand. He could clearly focus on the faint hint of wrinkles around her eyes and a dash of makeup that partly covered any signs of age. In the blouse pocket, he could see a pack of cigarettes. He noticed a hoof knife in her hip pocket.

"No, we haven't met. I'm Daniel Harper. Looks like you and this animal have met before."

"I raised him. Daddy let me have him years ago when he was first born. There's a story behind it, but I won't bore you." She looked at her father and said, "Did I hear something about a race?"

Silas was still sounding apologetic. "Well, that was the plan until this happened." He pointed to the horse's eye, and Pistachio tossed his head and stamped his feet. "We were going to race him the day after tomorrow down in Tampa." He suddenly spoke as one, choosing his words carefully, and glared at Dan. "But I guess that is out of the question now, right?" He turned and stepped toward his car, then stopped and looked back at Dan. "Didn't you say you had business elsewhere?"

As the BMW sped away in a cloud of dust, Aaron took a deep breath and realized that Melissa was still standing in front of him with a question on her face.

"What was that all about?" she asked.

"Ah, your dad has his own ideas about medical treatment. This horse won't race for a couple of weeks at least." He stopped and changed the subject. "I haven't seen you around here before. Are you just here for a visit?"

"Well, no – well, yes. I grew up here. I'm going through a sticky divorce in New York, and I had to come down here just to get away from the lawyer drama. Once it is settled, I plan to move back here to be closer to my dad. He's by himself, and I need a climate change, weatherwise and otherwise."

Daniel noticed the hazel color of her eyes with flecks of gold. She wore just a touch of lip gloss. Then he realized he was staring.

Looking at his watch, he said absently, "Shit, I have to go. My day is a busy one."

Melissa smiled broadly and said, "Well then, shit, you better go, brother!"

He took a step towards his truck, then remembered something. "Melissa, let me get the eyedrops for your horse. Hang on a second." He fumbled around in one of the truck compartments until he found what he was looking for. Handing it to her, he gave her quick instructions, said goodbye again, and got into his truck. Torn between staying a few more precious minutes or heading down the road, he started the engine and waved.

With a small grin, he watched her in the rearview mirror and said to himself, "Holy crap!" His day had just gotten better.

Then he remembered his brother. His phone was connected to the sound system of his truck. The wonders of Bluetooth.

Aaron answered quickly. "Hey, Danny! How's it going?" He knew his brother didn't care for the name 'Danny.' He said it was for children only.

Dan responded flatly, "It's going. What do you want?"

"Uh, yeah. It's Dad. I found a real mess yesterday, but we got that straightened out. Now he has a medical appointment on Friday at ten. I was wondering if, you know…"

"Are you kiddin' me? Really? You know what time of the year it is? You know I barely have time to take a crap this time of year. It's like this every year. So, before you say anything else, think about what I just said."

Aaron was accustomed to his brother's bluntness, but it still got on his nerves. The response was expected, and he kept his cool.

"Okay, I can call and get it changed to Monday."

"Right, that's your day off. Wish I had a day off once in a while."

"Danny, we all make our own bed to lie in."

"If it's that damn easy, why did you call me?"

"I just thought you'd like to know. And also, you should know I've had to change Dad's care plan. We can't have any more scenes like the one I saw yesterday."

"Was it that bad? I mean, we put him there so other folks could take care of him. Just tell them to do their job."

"Dan, I'm not making this up. Dad took it upon himself to change his treatment contract. He can't be trusted with those kinds of decisions. We need to keep a closer eye on how he's being cared for, and I could use a little of your help doing that." All he could hear was his brother breathing. "Hey, you there?"

"Yeah, I'm here!" He was almost yelling on the phone. "Dammit, why does this have to happen in December? Look, let me get through the next couple of months, and I'll step up to the plate with you."

"That's what you said last year. It never happened, as I recall."

"Yeah, I know. Last year, two of the farms had an abortion storm in their breeding mares, and I didn't have time to piss, much less take care of Dad. They lost over half of the pregnancies that year."

Aaron noticed his brother's tone of voice almost sounded apologetic.

"All I can do, Aaron, is promise to try. Hey, look, I gotta' go. Call me later and let me know how Dad's medical appointment turns out."

Aaron could hear Daniel's truck radio change stations, and he knew the call was over.

At the end of the day, Dr. Harper came to a stop in front of his office, which was attached to a small equine clinic. After he purchased the business, he added a state-of-the-art surgery room that doubled as a recovery room. It was lined by a layer of tartan rubber to keep 1000 lb animals from injuring themselves as they struggled to come out of anesthesia. In the back, there were several small outdoor pens under a metal roof intended for patients who required daily attention. The purchase of the clinic included a small ranch-style house next door, and he called that home when he wasn't working. After he finished veterinary school at the University of Florida, he took a two-year preceptorship in equine medicine and surgery at Texas A&M. Dr.

MacArthur, the previous owner and now part-time associate, was helpful when he was on duty, but that was about half-time, maybe a third. So, Dan soldiered on almost like a solo practitioner, taking one day at a time.

Working for him was Simon Drister, an older man who knew horses like a mother knows her children. Like the house, Simon also came with the purchase of the clinic. He could handle horses by himself, and Dan trusted him to give treatment to those patients he kept at his clinic while outside calls took up the rest of the day. Under Simon's watchful eye, three other trained veterinary technicians had been recently hired to help in surgery and kept the clinic in running order. When there was nothing requiring him to stay at the clinic, he rode with Dan as he made his rounds in the truck. Dan had tried to talk to Simon about family and other social connections, but he was a man of private issues and usually clammed up when Dan broached the subject.

It almost seemed providential that both brothers had secretaries who were grey-haired, in their sixties, and treated their employers like doting grandmothers. Dan's front office employee was Tricia Fulgate, a 65-year-old woman who knew how to talk on the phone, make appointments, and was a skilled bookkeeper. A widow with three grown children and a pack of grandchildren, she found purpose in working for Dan because all her family had moved to other parts of the country, leaving her with an empty house and no agenda. She had worked for the previous owner and knew the clientele better than Dan did. She was well paid, but she would have worked for far less just for the chance to connect with people on a daily basis. Doctor Dan, as she called him, had just walked in the door, smelling like sweat, barnyard, and saddle soap. She knew to let him have at least a few seconds to gather his thoughts before giving him a list of phone calls to return.

"And the last one is from Hemphill Farms. Weren't you there today? Anyway, this woman, who I have never heard of, said she was from Hemphill Farms, and she had a question for you. Her phone number was not the usual one for that place, and I looked it up, and it's a New York area code. Imagine that!"

"Okay, I'll take care of it. How was the scheduling today? Do I have any time to breathe tomorrow?"

"Yes, I blocked off eleven to one so you could stop and have lunch somewhere. I scheduled your last morning appointment with Dreyfus Stables, and it's right down the road from that Italian place you like. What's the name if it?"

"Tuscany Plaza. Yes, I like that. Thanks for thinking about me. Shouldn't you be getting home right about now?"

"Home to what? No, I'm in no hurry. Sit down; I'll place these calls for you."

Tricia proceeded to place call after call, and as he spoke to each client, she worked the profit and loss sheets for the clinic. Daniel did notice, however, that she absorbed every word he spoke on the phone. When he was down to the last call, she started to dial, but he stopped her.

"Tricia, I'm not so sure about this one. Better, let me call it myself. Really, you should go home. It's almost 7 O'clock."

Tricia cocked her head to one side. "So, is she one more in the stream of women I see going in and out of your little love nest next door?"

Dan showed a slight grin and started to speak, but Tricia interrupted him. "Dr. Dan, you're too old to be acting this way."

"What way?"

"Like an overgrown, horny teenager!"

"Ha! That's me, I guess. I love you most of all, Tricia. Now go home."

Reluctantly, she gathered up her purse and a tot bag that held who knows what and headed for the front door. Daniel watched her drive off as the phone was ringing at Hemphill Farms.

"Hello?"

"Hi. This is Dr. Harper. I have a message asking me to call this number."

"Yes, Dr. Harper. This is Melissa. We met today. You looked at Pistachio's eye, remember?"

Daniel felt his pulse quicken ever so slightly. "Yes, we did meet. Good to hear your voice again. What can I do for you?"

"Well, it's what I can do for you. First, I wanted to apologize for my father's behavior today. He's getting up in years, and he thinks he owns the world and everyone in it."

"Not a problem. My dad's getting older as well. I know what you mean."

"Does he live in Ocala?"

"No, he's down in Kissimmee at an assisted living place."

"Really? What's the name of it?"

"It's ah, it's – umm, sorry, I seem to have a mental block right now. The name escapes me." As he stalled for time, he began flipping through Tricia's card file to find the name of his dad's residence.

"Well, anyway," Melissa continued, "I was wondering what you might be doing for dinner tonight. Dad's off at some committee meeting, and since you're on your own tonight - "

Dan couldn't believe what he was hearing, but he knew how to play along. "What makes you think I'm alone tonight?"

"Well, I just assumed that you know, take a chance and – oh my!  I'm so sorry; I did not mean to intrude.   I just thought, well, maybe I wasn't thinking."

"Meadows House!  That's where my dad is.  It just came to me."

"What?  I was talking about something else."

"I know.  Something else.  Um, do you know where Dreyfus Stables is located?"

"Yes, but why do you ask?"

"Then you probably know of a place called Tuscany Plaza.  Sound familiar?"

"I've seen it.  Never been in it."

"I can pick you up in fifteen minutes.  I need to clean up first."

"No, you take your time," she stammered.  "I'll meet you there."

Dan could not remember the last time he had been approached like this by someone of the opposite gender, especially one he just met hours before.  His social radar was beeping, but he decided to ignore it. It was usually his initiative that got things going, and he was proud of his own track record.  His clients knew he was a swinging bachelor, and the few who knew more details about his private life didn't seem to care. He was good at what he did professionally, and that was all that mattered to them. The parking lot at Tuscany Plaza was moderately full and well-lit. There was a slight chill in the air, even for Florida. The entrance was bedecked with Christmas wreaths, red berries, and a large golden bow on each of the double doors. Inside, the vestibule was lined by white, gossamer material held up by evergreen branches with twinkling lights. There was a definite aroma of pine and cinnamon. Several benches stood against the walls, intended for those waiting for a table, but only one person sat there, patiently waiting for someone else. Dan felt like he was in a freeze-frame picture, allowing him to drink in every detail of what he was seeing. She wore a lightweight, emerald green coat with a high collar that framed her face. A cozy, cream-colored scarf fell loosely around her neck. The ends casually drifted to one side. High on one shoulder perched a delicate gold brooch, catching the light as she moved. The unbuttoned coat draped open and showed the warmth of her stunning figure. Finally, he saw she was wearing dark-wash jeans and knee-high boots made of rich brown soft leather. Her face held sparse makeup, tastefully applied, giving a soft glow to her face. Her auburn hair was loosely styled and draped over her shoulders in natural cascades. Dan stood still as a statue, mesmerized by the sight and totally captured when she turned her head and smiled at him. He felt underdressed.

"I – I hope you haven't been waiting long. I came as quick as I could." He couldn't help but wonder how she managed to be dressed so elegantly in the short period of time after their phone conversation.

Her voice matched her appearance. "Not to worry," she said softly. She tucked her hand in the crook of his elbow and said, "Let's find our table. I told them to save it for us. Tell me, do you prefer Daniel or Dan?"

"My mother called me Daniel, and sometimes my brother does, but no one else."

Dan felt like a teenager on his first date. The restaurant's interior was definitely Italian, with statues of nude figures in the corners and renaissance artwork on the walls. Mandolin music played softly from somewhere in the background. The waiter brought them menus and glasses of ice water. Dan looked at the offerings and was totally lost. He had been here before but only for lunches. Pizza and sub sandwiches had been his usual diet. The evening menu was completely different. Then he spied something he could relate to - shrimp and angel hair pasta. He closed his menu and looked at Melissa.

"I gotta' tell you this: you look fabulous tonight. I feel like I just crawled out of some barn." He wasn't sure, but he thought he saw a hint of blush on her face. Then, her sense of humor kicked in.

"Oh, these are just my street clothes. You should see when I really dress up!"

Dan's face broke into a broad grin.

She smiled and asked, "So, what are you going to have?"

Dan tried to act and sound well-versed in such things and said with a voice of mock experience, "I think I'll have the shrimp and angel hair pasta. One of my favorites."

"And what kind of sauce?"

He paused for a moment and continued, "Oh, you know – just the usual. How about you?"

She gazed again at the menu, pursed her lips, and said slowly, "I'm still looking."

"This menu is a bit different from their lunches. I've never been here at night. Have you? I mean, at night, you know. Totally different. Actually, I haven't been here in a while. My secretary suggested it to me a couple of years ago, and - " He noticed she wasn't listening but still looking at the menu.

"Okay, I've got it," she said calmly before looking up. "Where's our waiter?"

Dan nodded in the direction of the kitchen, and their waiter quickly came to their table. He was dressed in black pants, a white shirt, and a red vest.

There was a hint of a Mediterranean accent in his voice.

"Are we ready to order?" He looked at Melissa. "For the lady?"

She put her menu down, looked at him, and said, "I'll have fried calamari and caprese salad, then linguine di mare, the one with all those wonderful seafood bits. Can you tell me what's in it?"

The waiter folded his arms and spoke with authority, "Madam, it has lobster, clams, mussels, and shrimp. The sauce is very spicy. You will love it." He turned to Dan and asked, "And for you, sir?"

"Ah, shrimp and angel hair?"

"That's it?"

"Ah well, we'll probably have a dessert later. But yeah, for now, that's it."

The waiter smiled and left. Dan shifted in his chair and looked around as though to see who might have witnessed his simplicity in dining.

"You don't eat out much, do you?" she asked.

Dan took a long sip of his water. "I guess you got me on that one. Say, how did you know I was single?" He leaned forward and said softly, "And I think that twinkle in your eye is hiding some mischief in you." She leaned back in her chair and raised her eyebrows with a grin. "So, tell me about yourself," he asked.

Melissa thought for a moment, then said blankly, "Not much to tell. I was born in Ocala, raised on a horse farm in Florida, and married a man from New York who I met at the race track. Now, I'm about two steps away from being on my own again. That's about it. And - oh, most of the workers on our place told me I needed to meet you. That's how I knew."

He smiled and decided to switch gears. "Your dad. He's had the farm a while, right?"

"All his life. He was an only child, and his father left the whole outfit to him. I remember my grandfather from when I was a child. You think my dad is hard? Grandpa Hemphill was an ordained bastard. Back in his day, the horse business was a tough way to make a living. He had at least a half-dozen handguns in the house in various rooms. All of them loaded. He said he never knew when he might need one. I had a cousin visiting once. He found one of them and shot out the bedroom window. My grandmother never told Grandpa or my parents. She just had someone come fix the window and told us to stay out of their bedroom from then on."

Their conversation was interrupted by the waiter bringing their order to the table.

"Are there still guns in the house?"

"Yep. One day, I asked my dad to teach me how to shoot, and he came up with four different kinds. I can shoot a .45 better than most men."

Bit by bit, they both opened up to each other. Dan's sense of humor seemed to fit hers with no strings attached.  They had finished their main course, and Dan tried to get back to a previous subject.

"And you started out telling me you had a dull life!" Dan said with a chuckle.

"And what about you?" she asked.

"Me?  No, you're not finished.  What's the New York connection?"

Melissa picked up her napkin and said, "Not something I like to talk about."

"Why not?"

"Let's just say the divorce was based on infidelity, okay?"

"He was seeing someone else?"

"Several.  He kept going on business trips, telling me he had real estate investments everywhere.  I knew he had lots of money, so I believed him.  Turns out, he was a slum lord.  Had apartment buildings all over the State of New York.  Most of them he rented out.  A few, he used for his own purposes."

"How long were you married?"

She stared at the ceiling.  "Five years.  Do you think we could order dessert?"

Dan read the body language and said, "Hey, I'm sorry.  I was being nosey, and I shouldn't have asked such personal questions." He reached across the table and touched her hand.

She gave his hand a quick squeeze and said, "Limoncello."

"Huh?"

"That's what I want for dessert, Limoncello."

Dan took a deep breath, looked at the waiter, and said, "Yeah, me too. What she's having."

She slowly released his hand and whispered, "And now it's your turn. Tell me all your secrets, and I mean it this time, pal."

The waiter had taken their order and left. She gazed at him with a look of expectation, waiting for him to speak. Before he could say anything, a voice interrupted them.

"Eh, Doctor Dan, you come for dinner now! Wonderful!"

It was the voice of the owner, Nicolo Panarelli. He was a first-generation Italian with a wife, seven grown children, and too many grandchildren to count.

Dan spoke first. "Nicolo, my friend, how are you? So good to see you!"

"So, you take time off your busy work to have dinner with us? I see you here so many times, but always for lunch, never dinner. And you bring this pretty face with you. So glad to meet you, ma'am. My name….ah, Nicolo. And you?"

"Melissa. Melissa Gibson. My father owns Hemphill Farms. I'm from New York."

"Ah, you see? They come from everywhere, and they find this place. Even people like you, Doctor Dan, no?"

"Nicolo, it's always a pleasure to come here."

The owner clapped his hands together, wished them the best, and disappeared into the kitchen.

Melissa insisted on continuing. "Now, where were we?"

Dan swirled the ice in his glass. "Okay, I was born in Kissimmee. My dad was the owner of Harper's Gardens just south of town. He supplied floral shops all around the central part of the state. His biggest client was Disney. Dad had about a hundred acres and employed about 50 workers, some immigrant, some not. My mother died from a stroke ten years ago. Dad's retired now. Good thing he got out of the business when he did."

"On the phone, you said he's in an assisted living place."

"Yeah. My dad's gone 'round the bend, I'm afraid. My brother's spending more and more time with him. I feel guilty that I can't get down there more often."

"You have a brother?"

"Oh, yeah. Older brother. He's two years older than me."

"Is he a vet like you?"

Dan grinned. "No, you won't believe it. He's a preacher. A Presbyterian preacher."

"You grinned when you said that. Are the two of you close?"

"Ah, that depends on what you mean by close. My dad always seemed to show a preference for Aaron. I'm sorry, his name is Aaron. I was always the kid in the family. Aaron was the prize sibling. He graduated from Presbyterian College of South Carolina on a full scholarship and went on to seminary out in Texas. Then there's me, little ole' Dan. I got a degree in biology with a minor in botany from the University of Florida and went on to vet school there. I was at the top of my class both times, and you would think he'd be proud of me, at least because of my side interest in plants. But that didn't happen. He moaned and groaned about his precious Aaron living in Texas, and finally, he found a church in Kissimmee. You would have thought my dad had died and gone to heaven when he heard Aaron was moving back to Florida. Not only that, but he was bringing his Texas wife with him, cowboy boots and all. Yeah, Dad loves his oldest son. I fit in wherever there's a gap in the agenda."

Melissa was listening intently. When Dan stopped for a moment, he noticed she was looking at him oddly. He glanced down and then back at her.

"Too much information?"

She took a sip from her water glass and asked, "How old is your father?"

Dan thought for a second and said, "He's eighty-two. He has a birthday coming up in a few months. Why?"

"And how old are you?"

"Me? I'm thirty-two."

"And your brother is thirty-four."

"Yeah."

"That means he was forty-eight when Aaron was born. What age was your mother?"

"She was a year younger than my dad. Why?"

"That's almost late in life to be having children."

"To hear them tell it, they wanted children more than anything else. Mom once told me that by the time they had been married almost twenty years, she had practically given up on the idea. My dad took me aside and told me about Mom's bouts of depression. She wouldn't stay in the room when he talked about it. He said back then, he was about ready to give up on her as well, and, all of a sudden, bingo! Here's Aaron, folks! Maybe that's why he's so partial to his oldest, but that still doesn't make it fair."

"When's the last time you talked about this, I mean, to anyone?"

"You mean like a shrink or a counselor?"

"To anyone.  Girlfriend?  Close buddy?  Anyone."

"Well, for one thing, I don't have a girlfriend or a close buddy because I'm too damn busy running a semi-solo practice."

"That's not healthy, Dan.  You're going to burn out if you're not careful."

"That's what my preacher brother says, too.  He took a minor in family counseling while he was in seminary, but that doesn't make him a frickin' expert.  Besides, wouldn't that be a little weird?  Him talking to me?  Like, maybe he's the problem?"

"At least he's concerned about you.  How well do you know his wife?"

"Jane?  She's a doll.  Pure and simple.  Heart of gold.  And they have two great kids, little ones, two boys.  Just like their daddy and their uncle."

"What are their names?"

Dan looked at Melissa, rubbed his eyes, and looked at her with a sly smirk.  "What is this?  Are you trying to make me feel guilty?  I'm sorry, I don't remember their names.  Wait, I have it in my wallet, just a minute."

Dan pulled out his wallet just as their dessert arrived in elegant glasses.  He looked at it, then turned to the waiter with a look of uncertainty.

"Doctor Dan, is all okay?"

"Is this what we ordered?"

Melissa chuckled under her breath. "What were you expecting?"

"I thought it was some kind of pudding!"

"No, you don't eat out much, do you?"

The waiter politely told them the dessert was on the house, courtesy of Nicolo. Melissa had taken three sips of hers when he held a scrap of faded paper in his hand and pronounced proudly, "Joshua and Adam! That's who they are."

"How old are they?"

"Ah, four and six – I think."

"I won't ask you who is the oldest."

"Please don't. I've embarrassed myself enough tonight!" He finished with a boisterous laugh. Melissa smiled.

They finished their dessert, and Dan paid the tab, even after she offered to split the check. Melissa excused herself and headed for the ladies' room. While he waited, drumming his fingers on the table, he noticed her cell phone next to her napkin. It made a pinging sound, and he instinctively picked it up, then felt conspicuous and guilty doing so. But he couldn't help but notice that the ping was a reminder of an overdue event. It said, 'Call Trevor about dinner.' He quickly laid it down, then turned it so it was exactly as she left it. He looked around to see if anyone had noticed his sneaking a peek.

Melissa returned to the table, and Dan stood to help her with her coat. They thanked Nicolo for a wonderful evening and stepped out into the parking lot. There was a faint chirp of crickets in the air, not a common thing this time of year, but it gave a slice of substance to the night air.

"My car is over there," she said while pointing to a brand-new Lexus a short distance away.

"Well then, let me walk you to your car."

"It's just right there, I'm okay."

"Then it's not that far for me to walk with you. I know I said it before, but you look great tonight."

For the first time that evening, he saw an unmistakable blush come over her face. He reached down and took both of her hands in his. "Maybe again sometime?"

"And I'm sure you'll find time, right?"

He shrugged his shoulders and laughed. There was a moment when he thought something else was about to happen. But she reached into her coat pocket and brought out a cigarette and a small butane lighter. She handed the lighter to Dan, and, like a true Southern gentleman, he lit her cigarette and handed the lighter back to her. She took a long draw and blew smoke out in a large cloud. He leaned forward, hoping for a taste of her lipstick, but she held up her car keys between their noses, and he got the message clear and simple.

She was about to turn toward her car, and Dan let his impulsive nature get the best of him. He blurted out, "Who is Trevor?" He immediately regretted his own words. The air in the parking lot was suddenly very still. No creature sounds came from the nearby woods.

Melissa's face slowly became distorted and angular. Her eyes were mere slits.

"Trevor? Who's Trevor? You know how to ruin an evening, don't you? Of all names, why are you asking about someone named Trevor?"

"I'm sorry. Your cell phone was right there, and it had a message about Trevor. It wasn't like I dug into your purse or something. It was just there in plain sight." Trying to salvage what he could from the conversation, he said, "Okay, just forget I mentioned it. Again, I'm sorry."

"Forget it? Just like that?" She tossed her cigarette down, stepped on it, and continued to stare at the gravel beneath her feet. She finally looked up, and her face had softened. "Okay, you were being honest with me, so now it's my turn." She cleared her throat and continued. "Trevor is someone I had been seeing, and he had made a date with me for tonight. I had second thoughts about it at the last minute, cancelled the date, and so, there I sat, all dressed up and with nowhere to go. End of story."

Unshaken, Dan saw his opening. "Not quite. The end of the story is when you called me. I wondered how you got dressed so quickly. But that's alright. I don't mind being second on your dance card. That is if there's the hope for moving up on the list and having another night like this."

"Thanks for a lovely evening, Dr. Harper," she said dryly, then turned quickly and got into her car.

As she drove away, he had mixed feelings about the evening, but there was something about her, something he couldn't quite grasp. "So, what was the problem with Trevor?" he mumbled to himself. "That might be good to know in the future."

# CHAPTER FIVE

The following Monday arrived without fanfare. Aaron had managed to change his father's medical appointment and snagged an early time window. A cancellation had given him an opening at 8:30 that morning. The doctor's office in Kissimmee overlooked the lakefront and the marina and sat among a cluster of single-story brick buildings with dwarf palmetto trees separating the walkways. Next door was Pirate's Cove restaurant.

A medical assistant called them into an exam room, and Dr. Roche followed about five minutes later. He was casually dressed, wearing a loose-fitting shirt with the tail hanging loose. It was accented with muted silhouettes of palm trees. There were no white coats to be seen on anyone. The only clue as to his profession was the stethoscope around his neck.

"Henry, good to see you. You, too, Pastor Harper. How's the fishing, Henry?"

"Oh, you know, two or three times a week. Depends on the weather." It was the same question on each visit with Dr. Roche and Henry always gave the same answer. Only this time, Henry gave much more detail about how many he had caught, how big they were, and how each one of them fought. He ended his story by telling how his wife cooked them.

Dr. Roche had been the family doctor for many years and had followed Henry's journey through all the red flags of dementia and beyond. Aaron never ceased to be amazed at the doctor's finesse in questioning Henry while he went through the motions of a physical examination.

"So, how do you cook your catch? You fry them in some kind of batter?"

"Yes, well, Evelyn does. She uses peanut oil. Says it cooks hotter and seals in all the flavor."

Aaron could see the doctor's subtle glance in his direction. Henry's wife had been dead for over ten years, just as Henry's mental condition began to show itself. Nevertheless, Dr. Roche continued his dialog without missing a beat.

"Henry, your heart sounds like it's working a little too hard. I've got something that will help. I'll call it in for the druggist to fill, and we'll see how you do with it."

Henry nodded and looked at Aaron.

"Don't worry, Dad. I'll pick it up." Seeing that Dr. Roche was finished, he said, "Dad, why don't you hit the men's room before we head back? I'll meet you in the lobby."

As soon as Henry was out of earshot, Dr. Roche said, "Pastor, there's nothing wrong with your dad's heart. He's becoming more delusional since the last time I saw him. This new medication will just take the edge off. There's really nothing we can do to reverse the progression, but I'm not telling you anything new, am I? You need to make the staff at Meadows House aware of his progression and this new prescription."

Aaron nodded his head and thanked the doctor. He walked into the lobby and waited for Henry. After a few seconds, his dad walked out, and Aaron's eyes were immediately drawn to the front of Henry's trousers. The belt was only loosely buckled, the zipper was down, and a large wet spot covered most of the front.

"Dad, let's go back into the men's room and fix this." He pointed to Henry's problem, and his father's face turned red. Thirty seconds later, they emerged with the zipper in its proper place and Henry's shirt tail dangling outside the waistline of his pants, covering the evidence. It was not the first time Aaron had used this tactic to disguise Henry's lack of focus when relieving himself.

After he deposited Henry in his apartment with instructions to change his pants, he was in the process of making another appointment with the staff to discuss the next level of care. As he waited, Jonathan Appleton came through the front door and recognized Aaron. His appearance caught Aaron off-guard, and he almost called him Mr. Appleseed.

"Good morning, Pastor," Appleton said in a strong voice. How's everything?"

"I just got back from my dad's medical appointment. He's upstairs getting comfortable."

"And how did that go?"

"Oh, just catch and release, like always." Appleton smiled at the metaphor, and Aaron continued. "But I need to update the staff about the new medication and what the doctor said."

"You want to do it now? I've got a minute or two to spare."

Aaron tried hard to be brief, but Appleton had more questions than Aaron had expected. He finally left feeling that his dad was in good hands. Now, to call his brother, update him and he could get on with his day off.

After three tries with no response on his brother's cell phone number, he decided to call Dan's office. Tricia answered quickly.

"Harper Equine Clinic, can you hold, please?"

Tricia Fulgate always had such a pleasant tone on the phone. She was truly a blessing for his brother. After a minute, she came back on the line.

"Thank you for holding. How can I help you?"

"Tricia, this is Aaron Harper. Good to hear your voice. How are you doing?"

"Oh, Pastor, I'm glad it's you. Your brother is in a real tight spot. He had a bunch of appointments today, and he had to cancel all of them because of the fire."

"Fire? What fire?"

"Oh, you haven't heard? The barn fire at Hemphill Farms. The main barn caught fire early this morning. Several horses were burned, and Dan is in a real pickle because he's run out of I.V. fluid; the emergency shipment he ordered came here to the clinic instead of going to the farm, and now he's trying to be two places at once and so - "

"Tricia, hang on. You're saying he needs supplies that are at the clinic, and he can't get away to come get them? Where's his helper?"

"Simon? He's out of town. Dr. Dan gave him the day off weeks ago."

"Tricia, get all the supplies he needs and stack them by the front door. I'll have someone there shortly to pick them up."

"Can you do that? Who will you call?"

"Tricia, I'll explain it later, okay?"

Aaron knew the Chief of Police in Ocala, Willis Tisdale. He had been on the Kissimmee police force for many years before he took the job in Ocala. Aaron continued to maintain an open line of dialog with him over the years. A quick call and Tisdale promised someone would immediately come to the clinic and act as transport for what Dan needed.  In the meantime, Aaron called his wife.

"Jane, can you do without me for a couple of hours?"

"Why?  What's up?"

"Dan's got his hands full with a barn fire.  His helper is out of town, and he's in a tight spot."

"How can you help him?"

"I don't know, but I have a feeling he needs to see a friendly face."

The drive to Ocala was 75 miles, and Aaron's Miata made it in less than an hour.  When he arrived at Hemphill Farms, he could see Dan's clinic truck parked outside of what was left of the barn.  The front of the building was reduced to ashes and black char.  The rear of the building was still standing.  The fire department had already left.  Hemphill's farmhands were busy like a nest of ants.  He could hear Dan's voice as he approached.

"No, goddamn it!  I said the bottle of lactated ringers, not straight saline.  Try listening to me!  Go back to my truck and get it. Hurry up!"

A young man of Hispanic appearance emerged and walked quickly to Dan's truck, shaking his head. Aaron approached him and asked, "Can I help?"

"No entiendo…"

"That's okay, I heard what he said.  Here, this is what he wants."  Aaron immediately saw the bottles of lactated ringers and handed two of them to the young man, who practically ran back to the barn. He heard Dan's voice again.

"What took you so long? I didn't ask for two!"

Aaron stood at the door and watched his brother work the scene. He was truly a professional and very much in charge. Three horses were standing with grooms holding I.V. bottles while Dan tended to bandaging legs on of several others. He happened to look up and see his brother standing there but didn't stop what he was doing.

"You come to watch the show?"

"No, I thought you could use some help."

"Yeah, well, maybe. You speak English?"

Dan had a way of maintaining his sense of humor in the worst of conditions. Noise coming from a nearby stall snatched his attention away from Aaron, and he quickly trotted over to the problem and replaced a needle that had pulled out of a horse's jugular vein.

When he emerged, Aaron asked, "So how bad is it? How many horses were hurt?"

"Three were burned badly. I've already put two of them down. Pitiful sight. Most of the injuries were caused by panic. I've been suturing and bandaging for the last two hours. The insurance company is going to shit when they see this claim."

"Okay, I'm here if you need me."

Dan returned to the leg he had been bandaging and spoke without looking up, "Right, nice of you to come. Thanks. We're just about done here. I've been here since 5 AM. What time is it?"

"Almost noon. You must be tired."

"Yes, and I have one more tough job."

"What's that?"

A screeching female voice could be heard from the back of the barn. "No, you sonofabitch! Not like that! You're scaring him! Dan, hurry up and get back here!"

Dan exhaled loudly and said, "That's the job, speaking now."

Aaron spoke almost in a whisper. "Whose voice is that?"

"Not now, brother."

Dan had finished his last suture and was wrapping an elastic bandage around a fetlock when the source of the voice came around the corner. She looked like she had just battled two alligators and came out on the losing end.

"Dan, who is this?" she blustered.

"Melissa, this is my brother, Aaron. He's just here to help wherever he can."

She paid no attention to Aaron. "Well, hurry up, Pistachio won't let me put these damn eye drops in. He's still freaked out by the fire."

Dan put one more turn to the wrap he was applying, and both men walked down the line of stalls to the last one where the black stallion stood, pawing the ground and shaking his head.

"Have you looked at him yet?" she asked.

"Melissa, I had to triage the injuries when I got here…"

"I asked if you had looked at him!"

"I didn't look close at your horse, but at a glance, he didn't seem to be in any life-threatening danger. There were others more critical."

In the presence of the two men, she gradually seemed to gain control of her emotions. She wiped her eyes and blew her nose. "I'm going outside for a smoke. Take a look at him and come tell me if he's okay."

As she left, Aaron looked at his brother and simply raised his eyebrows.

Dan kept talking while they stepped into Pistachio's stall. "I know, she's a piece of work. Her name is Melissa Gibson. She's the daughter of Silas Hemphill, who owns this place. On a good day, though, I kinda' like her."

"I don't remember you mentioning her. Does she live here?"

"I just met her a couple of days ago. She's down from New York to spend time with her dad. Actually, she's going through a divorce and wants some peace and quiet. None of us were bargaining for this." He waved his hand at the barn.

"Sounds like you know quite a bit about her. You just met her?"

Dan scratched his head, looked at his brother, and said, "Well, we did have dinner together." Pistachio was tossing his head and making Dan's efforts less than easy.

Aaron folded his arms, and a slow smile came on his face. Dan stopped and looked at him.

"I know that look. Just let me live my own life, okay?" He paused while looking at the horse's eye. "Oh, shit!"

Melissa was coming back in through the doorway. "What? What's wrong?"

Sometimes, explaining a worrisome finding to an owner is harder than treating it. This was one of those times.

"Melissa, Pistachio must have hit his head or something like that during the fire. Must have hit it awfully hard. There's some swelling of the tissue around the eye."

"So? Swelling? That's it?"

"No, there's more. This eye has some nasty problems."

"Yeah?" The look on her face was going from curiosity to stark terror. "Tell me!"

"He has a luxated lens. That means the lens has popped out of the capsule that holds it in place. It's pushed forward and is pressing on the inside of the cornea."

"Meaning what?"

"He's going to lose sight in that eye. I'm sorry."

"No! You fix it!" Her voice sounded nearly hysterical. "Aren't you the hotshot horse surgeon I heard about, or are you some kind of phony?"

"My surgery training did not include ophthalmic cases, but this one is a no-brainer. Take him to the vet school in Gainesville if you want. They have folks there who will give you multiple second opinions. But don't wait too long because this condition will set up inflammation that will prevent any kind of surgery they might elect to do. I'd call them today."

"Call, hell! I'm loading him up right now, and you're going to call!" With that, she turned and walked toward the house. Halfway there, she turned and screamed, "Emil, hook up the goddamn trailer!"

Aaron stood transfixed after listening to their conversation. He reached into his shirt pocket and fished out a ballpoint pen and a scrap of paper. "She must be a joy to have dinner with. What was her name again?"

"Melissa Gilbert. I must admit, I didn't know this side of her. Oh, well. It was good while it lasted.

Now I have to call someone in Gainesville. Know any good horse eye doctors?"

"I'm afraid not. That's your territory. By the way, I see you got all your supplies delivered."

"Yes, Tricia had the Ocala police bring it to me. Great imagination, that Tricia!"

Aaron started to say something but didn't. Silas Hemphill came around the corner of the barn, talking to a police officer who was holding a cell phone in front of him. Aaron caught part of the conversation.

Silas was emphatic. "Yes, I see you have a picture of a car with the license plate showing. So what? Where did you get that?"

"One of your employees was apparently up and around at a late hour and saw this car leaving around 3:30 this morning."

"Yes, that would be Carlos. He does a security check for me every night. Just walks around with a flashlight. Enough to scare off anyone who might – wait a minute, who called in the fire alarm?"

"Carlos did. And he caught this picture with his phone before the blaze started. Apparently, he was using the flashlight on his phone to do his late-night check on things. We ran this plate number, and it belongs to someone named George Stillman. Do you know him?"

"Stillman? I fired his ass three days ago! He was nothing but trouble around here. You don't suppose he would have - "

"Could be. We'll pick him up and find out why he was here at such an odd hour. Sorry, but we have to isolate your barn as a potential crime scene. Can you move your horses to another barn?"

On the way home, Aaron called his contact person at the Kissimmee Police Department. Officer Stan Kemper came to the phone.

"Pastor Aaron, how's life treating you? It's good to hear from you."

"I take it like it comes, Stan. No other way to do it. I just keep the faith."

"Yeah, and I'm sure Jane and the kids keep you on the straight and narrow. Okay, I know you didn't call to practice a sermon on the phone. What's up?"

"Stan, you know how sometimes I ask you to do a background check on potential church employees?"

"Yeah, go on."

"If you can't do this, just say so. I need a check on someone for my own purposes."

"Not for the church?"

"No, for me."

"Hmm. It's not exactly kosher. Kosher, is that a Presbyterian word? Never mind. Okay, on the sly, I'll have to charge it to the church and -"

"And I'll pay for it myself."

"Okay, what's the name?"

"Melissa Gibson from New York. Her father owns Hemphill Farms in Ocala. Big horse farm. All thoroughbreds."

"You have any other identifying information? Social security number? Age?"

"I don't have her number, but she looks to be in her mid-forties. I heard she's going through a divorce up in New York if that helps."

"This is starting to sound a bit juicy. May I ask what prompted your curiosity?"

"Maybe later. It may be a dry run."

"Give me a couple of weeks."

"You're a good man."

"And you're a sneaky one. For a preacher, that is."

The call to Gainesville was successful. The vet school promised to see Pistachio as soon as Melissa got there. Dan just hoped she would be more hospitable and polite in the presence of high-powered faculty folks. By late afternoon, he was finishing up his outside calls. Some had cancelled and found another veterinarian because tomorrow was already filling up, according to Tricia. He was within a mile of the clinic when his phone rang. The caller ID indicated a New York area code.

"Hello, this is Dr. Harper."

"Dan, it's me. I'm here at the school. The vet on call took one look at Pistachio and said the same thing you did. He gathered a bunch of students around him so they could see it, too. He called it irreversible damage. They've got to take the lens out. One vet said they should take the whole eye, but the head guy, I forget his name, he said he could save the eye for cosmetic reasons only. His racing days are over. I can't let a one-eyed horse even near the starting gate. It would be too dangerous."

"Melissa, I'm sorry to hear that. When will they do the surgery?"

"They said tomorrow. I'm going to drive home now. It's not that far, a little over 30 miles."

"Okay, drive careful."

"Dan?"

"Yeah?"

"I'm sorry I blew up like I did. Too much on my mind."

"That's okay. Will I see you sometime soon?"

"How about tonight? When I'm not tending to horses, I'm a pretty good cook."

"Your place or mine?"

"There're too many people at my dad's house. I need some quiet time."

"I'll stop and pick up some steaks."

"And a bottle of Merlot." She giggled as she said it.

Dinner that night was a success. Melissa was the captain of the gas grill. The steaks were done to perfection, and she coordinated that with sweet potatoes, green beans, and salad. They killed the bottle of wine. After dinner, conversation led to the couch, and all was right with the world. They both fell asleep and woke up around midnight. Dan spoke first.

"Hey," he whispered. "You awake?"

She rubbed her eyes and raised her head from his shoulder. "Barely. You?"

"This is the best midnight wake-up I've had in a long time." He leaned down and kissed her.

"Let's not spoil the moment. You want to continue in the next room?" Dan was thinking he must have died and gone to heaven.

The next morning came early. Dan raised up from his pillow and looked around the room. There was no sign of Melissa. A sudden but faint clatter of dishes told him she was in the kitchen. He grabbed a bathrobe and found her with a skillet in her hand and a smile on her face.

"Breakfast?" she asked. "How many eggs?"

Dan walked to her and leaned forward. She took a step back. "Brave man, trying to kiss a woman with a hot skillet in her hands."

"So put it down and give me a moment."

Melissa complied and kissed him like they were completing what they had started but not finished the night before.  The faint smell of smoke interrupted them.  Dan turned off the burner in question.

She whispered in his ear, "Geez!  Look what you made me do!"

"You been up long?"

"Not long.  I called my dad, and he said the cops have George Stillman in custody.  He's singing like a canary.  They'll put him away for a while."

Dan wrapped his arms around her one more time. She kissed him again and pointed to the stove.

**"Okay, okay, let's eat.  Then we need to call about your horse.**

**I've got a busy day ahead of me."**

# CHAPTER SIX

The following Sunday, Aaron was halfway through his sermon, and he saw two figures enter through the back of the sanctuary. The sunlight was coming through the doorway behind them, and he could only see their silhouettes, but he could make out the fuzzy outline of a man and a woman. The old hardwood floor squeaked as they came in and sat in a back pew. When the usher closed the door, his vision adjusted, and he was surprised to see Dan and Melissa just settling into their seats. He glanced down at his notes and continued.

"Referring to our New Testament reading today, the Rabbinic standard in those days, taken from the book of Amos, was that forgiveness should be given 3 times. But Peter thought he was being generous by doubling that amount and adding one more for good measure, making the number seven. But Jesus' answer was 7 times 70, which meant forgiveness was limitless.

But before we can ask God to forgive us our debts, we must feel the need for forgiveness. We must have a sense of sin. We sometimes have the wrong concept of sin. We picture a sinner as someone who is a thief, a murderer, an adulterer. The New Testament uses different words for sin, most of which tell us we have missed the mark and not lived up to God's expectations. Our first mistake is not having faith. Like the *faith* of a child who takes your hand in the night, a child with hope. Hope is the shimmering light on the horizon that keeps faith plugging forward."

The end of Aaron's sermon came quickly, and after the benediction, he walked to the narthex to greet folks as they left. Dan and Melissa stepped back and waited until the crowd had cleared.

"I hadn't heard you preach in a while, brother. You still have that sanctimonious charm."

"Dan, it's so good to see you down in these parts. Melissa, so good to have you join us in our worship." He turned to his brother and asked, "What are your plans today?"

"This good woman convinced me I was working too hard, and we decided to take Sunday off. That's what the bible says, isn't it?"

Melissa spoke up and said, "I guess that rule doesn't apply to preachers, does it?"

"I take my day off on Mondays whenever I can." He was struck by the stark difference in demeanor that he saw in her. She was not the same person he had seen at the barn.

"So, what are your plans today?" Aaron asked, looking for more details.

Dan started to answer, "Well, I...". He was interrupted by Melissa.

“We would like to take you and your family out for lunch if you have the time.”

Aaron’s curiosity was aroused by this unusual offer, but he maintained a smooth transition into his response. “Let me call Jane and see what she has in store for us, and we can go from there. Excuse me for a second.”

Aaron stepped aside and dialed his home phone. Jane had attended an earlier service that morning and had gone home to prepare for the rest of the day. Aaron’s call was unexpected.

“Hey, my dear, you’ll never guess who came to church today. Dan and a new friend of his. Her name is Melissa. Yeah, that’s the one. They want to take us out for lunch. The whole family. Kids and all. What do you think?”

When he hung up, he was smiling. To his brother, he said, “Pick the place, and we’ll meet you there.”

The windows of Pirate’s Cove looked out over the lake and the Kissimmee marina. Dan and Melissa were waiting at the entrance when Jane arrived with Joshua and Adam, and at about the same time, Aaron found a parking spot. Dan made the introductions and had the children’s names on the tip of his tongue. Jane remarked on the Christmas decorations inside the dining room and immediately connected with Melissa, who surprised everyone by telling the group that she had previously been an interior design artist. To Jane's credit, she knew how to keep a conversation going.

"That's an exciting profession. I am always in awe of people who can look at a room and see it in a different context. How do you do it?"

Melissa was glad to respond. "It takes practice, but eventually, we start to see repeat possibilities with designs we used on other jobs. It's like building a vocabulary. If you know how to use certain effects, you can see places where to apply them. We've got a barn to rebuild, and my dad wants me to come up with some interior ideas."

"For a barn?" Aaron was amazed at the idea.

Melissa was patient with her answer. "Have you seen the barns around the Disney area? You would think royalty lived there. But the scoop shovel in the corner is a dead giveaway that it's really a barn. The horses don't care one way or another."

"Did you have many clients in New York?" Jane asked.

"Only a handful at a time. I tried not to load my schedule up to the point of not doing a good job."

"What was the name of your agency?"

"Sunshine and Lollipops," she replied. "We specialized in making rooms look open and airy with skylights and bright colors. It's the Florida look, we call it, and it's not restricted to just this state. It was my attempt to remember my childhood."

"Where did you go to school for that?" Aaron asked.

"I went to the New York School of Interior Design. That's about the time I met Jack."

Dan was in the process of imbibing a bite of filet mignon, and Melissa's remark stopped him with his mouth open. He paused only for a moment and said nothing. Aaron noticed his brother's body language.

Jane continued her attempt to appear interested. "So, tell me about Jack."

"He's my ex. Well, almost. It was like I told Dan a few days ago; it's getting nasty, so I came to visit my dad to get some relief from the constant nagging."

Dan had put his fork down. "Nagging?" he said.

"Well, he thinks I'm foolish for leaving him, and he calls every day wanting to know where I am."

"You haven't told him where you are?" Aaron asked.

"You don't know this guy. If he knew where I was, he'd be on a private jet and taking over the town of Ocala by storm in just a few hours. The guy is so possessive."

Dan was listening intently and glanced at his brother, who had a subtle frown on his face. He returned the look and silently mouthed, "What?"

Neither of the women saw the cryptic exchange of looks between the two brothers.

Dan deftly changed the subject and said, "Anyone for looking at the dessert menu?"

The two children cheered loudly, and all the adults laughed. At the peak of the moment, Aaron saw Officer Stan Kemper from the police department leaning against the bar across the room. They made eye contact, and Stan motioned a hand gesture with his thumb and little finger held up to the side of his face. Aaron read his lips, saying, "Call me."

They finished their meal, and both women excused themselves to the ladies' room, leaving the two brothers and the children at the table.

Aaron spoke as soon as they had privacy between them. "Did you know about Jack?"

"She mentioned her ex-husband, but I didn't know his name.

"From what she said, it sounds like he's trouble for her and anyone else mixed up with her."

"Is that a hint? Is big brother still looking after me, huh?"

"No, just a statement of fact. I know you can take care of yourself."

"Do you? You believe that?"

"Dan, don't get your britches all twisted. I was just saying - "

Dan rolled his eyes and said, "I got your message. I'll be careful, Mom."

Aaron was about to continue when the children started wandering away from the table. He gathered them up just as Jane and Melissa were coming back from the ladies' room.

Dan was the first to speak. His voice had a tone of abruptness. "Melissa, you ready to go?"

She spoke slowly and looked warily at Dan. "Well, I guess so. Jane, it was so nice to meet you. Aaron, good to see you again." She stooped down and gave each of the boys a quick hug. Before she could say anymore, Dan had her by the arm and was headed to the door.

Jane had a child on each hand and asked as soon as they were outside, "What's with you and your brother? You have words with him?"

"No, it's fine. Just a point of discussion we had."

"I've seen that look before. You and your brother are so alike. You wear your feelings out there for the whole world to see. I guess you'll tell me when you're ready."

Aaron just nodded. Because of the last-minute plans, they were at the restaurant in separate cars. Jane gave him a quick kiss and turned toward her car with the boys. "I'll see you at the house," she said.

In the parking lot, Aaron sat behind the wheel and reached into his pocket for his cell phone. Stan

Kemper had given Aaron his private number, and he answered quickly.

"Hey, preacher. Glad you called. It's about this woman you wanted me to check on."

"Yeah? That was quick."

"Yes, I know. Missing persons department in New York acts quickly."

"Missing persons?"

"Yeah, some guy named Jack Gibson filed a report. Any relation to this woman you're interested in?"

"If it's who I think it is, he's her ex-husband, or will be soon enough."

"Okay, so here's what I did. I was just out for a stroll, walking to my office this morning, and as I walked past the church, I saw your brother going in with this woman. She turned around, and I got a picture with my cell phone. I sent it to NYPD, and they did a facial recognition. That's who they're looking for. She's the one you were having lunch with today."

"Okay, so you found her. Now what? She's here of her own free will. Do you have to tell them where she is?"

"I don't know what to do. This guy, Jack, could be trouble. He's been brought up on charges of racketeering, fraud, extortion, you name it. And each time, he gets the charges dropped. Probably got multiple judges in his pocket. I got a feeling if I tell the guys in blue up there, they're gonna tell him she's in Florida. It won't take long for him to figure out where she is."

"And you already sent them a picture."

"Yeah, there's that part, too. The sign in front of the church was in the picture. Now they know where she is." Stan took a long, deep breath. "I might have screwed up when I did that."

Aaron paused before continuing. "Well, if she's trying to avoid this Jack fellow, maybe we should tell her that he might turn up here."

"Yeah, and there's one other thing. And this is off the record. She been in and out of a psychiatric ward twice in the last three months. The NYPD has been called to their residence numerous times for domestic disturbances. Also, Jack is her third husband. The first one committed suicide, and the second one had a heart attack. The second one was much older than her and had more money than God himself. I didn't find out much about the first one."

Aaron was staggered at this piece of information. He thanked Stan for his help. *What has Dan gotten himself into?* Aaron thought. *I've got to tell him.*

He waited until he got home to call Dan. Jane was busy around the house and didn't notice his look of distress. He could feel the perspiration forming on his forehead as he heard Dan's cell phone ring. His brother answered quickly.

"Hey, Aaron – Look, I'm sorry I blew up at you. I know you were just voicing your private thoughts. I appreciate it. Melissa and I are okay. We're just friends, nothing big." He paused and then said, "Aaron, are you there?"

"Yeah, I'm just trying to collect my thoughts about all this."

"What's there to collect? Jack's up there, and she's down here. Sounds like the best deal."

"Yeah, but there's more to it. I know you're going to be mad at me, but I did something that looks like none of my business, so just stay calm and hear me out. Is she with you now?"

"Yeah, why?"

"When you get a moment alone, call me."

Five minutes later, his phone rang. Aaron was halfway through explaining what had transpired with the background check when Dan could restrain himself no longer.

"You nosy sonofabitch! What do you mean background check? Who authorized you to do that, huh? Is this what preachers do in their spare time?"

"Dan, listen to me. I know you're pissed, and you should be, but I have something to tell you."

"Yeah, I bet you do! What could you tell me that I don't already know? She's older than me, she's been married before, and she's getting a divorce. Right?"

"Yes, this is her first divorce. She didn't need anything like that for the other two."

"Huh?"

"Dan, you need to sit down. I have a lot to tell you."

When Aaron finished, there was silence on the other end. "Dan? Dan? You there?" He could hear his brother breathing hard. "Dan, I'm so sorry for jumping into your life like this. If I had it to do over, I probably would have stopped, except now, with what I know, I'm so glad I did."

Dan was still steaming but finally answered, "Okay, so now you've told me. But that doesn't change the fact that I really like her. I did notice her taking some medication on the way home. I'll find some way to ask her about it. It doesn't matter if she's older than me. I'm not looking for the mother of my future children. Hell, I don't know if I even want kids. I'm just tired of living by myself." He took a deep breath and let it out with a sigh. "Just this past year, the evenings seem so – empty. I go home to an empty house. I've got no one. I come home, and there's no one else there. I remember what it was like growing up. Mom and Dad were always there for each other. I stayed so focused throughout school and my postdoc training - I never took the time to really put some balance in my life."

"When will you see her again?"

"Probably tomorrow, I guess. I hope."

Aaron felt his heart breaking as he listened. He suddenly realized just how vulnerable his brother was right then. He had this big hole in his life that had been ignored, and now this woman was pointing it out and filling it at the same time. Was she just playing with him? Dan had never talked to him like this, even when they were younger. There was always such competition between them, efforts to win the affection of their father, to prove they each were more deserving than the other. They knew their mother did not show preference; she just loved them both for what they were.

Aaron had always been a mother hen type, always caring about other people, worrying about hurting their feelings, all the things that make for a good future minister. Dan, on the other hand, played defensive end in high school and took pride in blind-siding the opposing quarterback at least twice in each game. He felt it a loss if he didn't send some poor ball-carrier off the field, limping.

In the classroom, both boys had excelled. Both were given academic scholarships, which helped the financial outlay promised from their parents. They were told that as long as their grades were decent, they needn't worry about working while going to college. Aaron was a perfectionist from the start, and it drove him to excel in all his classes, both undergrad and seminary. Dan, from the start, knew what he wanted out of life. Vet school had been his ambition since fifth grade, and he knew of the competition for the limited number of slots each year. It would have been even harder if he had applied somewhere out of state, like Auburn or Virginia Tech. But, with his grades and other credentials, his application to vet school rose to the top like fine cream. He was accepted quickly, and he graduated with honors.

But academics could do nothing for the situation they were in now. They were two brothers, and they were beginning to feel a connection, a real connection, one of the few times in their lives, and for unfortunate reasons.

# CHAPTER SEVEN

As always, Monday was the day for Aaron to visit his father.  He noticed two police cars at the front entrance but thought nothing of it.  He had barely gotten through the door when Andrea, the receptionist he had met on the previous visit, came running to him, babbling something about "your dad' and 'restraints' and pushing him toward the elevator.

"What, what's this?  What are you talking about?"

"Your father!  They tried to clean his apartment, and he clobbered one of the janitors!  They have the police up there now!  Go!"

Aaron didn't bother waiting for the elevator but took the stairs in record time.  He was out of breath when he reached his dad's door, and he could hear Henry's voice sounding like a megaphone.

"Why are you doing this? Who are these people? Get out of my house!"

An unfamiliar man's voice responded as Aaron crossed the threshold.  "Just sit still, Mr. Harper.  We need you to calm down."

Aaron was shocked at what he saw.  The room was in total disarray, with overturned furniture and curtains in the middle of the floor.  Henry was in the living room, seated in a kitchen chair with both hands restrained in the back by handcuffs. Henry was still in his pajamas and barefoot. Two policemen stood next to him, trying to catch their breath. One was rubbing the corner of his mouth with the back of his hand.

"Dad, what happened?"

One of the officers approached Aaron and would not let him closer. "Sir, you need to stay right where you are. This is for your own safety."

"He's my father! He has Alzheimer's Disease! Why is he in cuffs?"

Henry looked at his son with desperation in his eyes. "They broke into my house! They unlocked the front door and broke into my house!"

Just as Aaron was about to offer more explanation, Jonathan Appleton came through the door in a huff. "Good morning, officers. Why are you here? Why is this man in restraints? He's a patient, for God's sake!"

Both policemen tried to talk at once. Finally, the one with two stripes on his sleeve said, "We got a call from your front desk that an assault was taking place in apartment 30 of this building. That's all the detail we had before we got here. The dispatcher said the caller sounded frantic. We tried to reason with this man when we got here, and he tried to assault Officer Tibbets, so we did what we're trained to do."

Henry was still struggling to get out of the chair, and both policemen had their hands on his shoulders. Aaron walked up to his dad and knelt in front of him.

He tried to convey a tone of calmness and empathy. "Dad, who broke into your house? Where did he go?"

Henry was obviously confused. His eyes were wet, and saliva made small droplets of foam at the corners of his mouth. He just shook his head.

Appleton took charge of the situation. "Officers, this is not a criminal scenario; the man is a demented patient, and we need to transfer him to another unit. Kindly take those cuffs off." He turned to Aaron and continued, "Pastor, I'm sorry this happened. Apparently, Andrea heard of the confrontation and let her imagination paint the wrong picture before she called 911. She should have called one of our attendants. I'm so sorry this was blown out of proportion."

At this point, everyone in the room was feeling reasonably calm, including the police. They took the handcuffs off Henry's wrists and had Jonathan sign something, taking responsibility off their hands. Aaron happened to look toward the door and saw a very frightened face belonging to a middle-aged janitor who was holding a bag of ice over one eye.

Aaron asked him, "Were you in here trying to do your job? Did he hit you?"

The man nodded.

Jonathan interrupted. "Pastor, we will handle it from here. It would be best if you do not get into conversation with those involved. Can you stay with your dad for a while? Do you have the time?"

"Of course. I'll see what I can do to straighten this place up in the meantime. What happens now?"

"Stay here. I'll be back to talk to you. Won't take long." Jonathan put his hand on the shoulder of the wounded janitor and led him back into the hallway. The two policemen were the last to leave and shut the door behind them.

Aaron turned to his father and said, "Dad, what you did was not very nice. You could have hurt that poor man. He was just coming here to vacuum and mop."

"Aaron! He didn't even knock! He just broke in! He shouldn't have done that. He shouldn't have done that...". Henry sat back down in the kitchen chair and began to weep loudly.

Aaron pulled out his phone and dialed Dan's office number. Tricia answered and listened to the full account of the morning, hearing Henry in the background, promising she would pass it on to Dan.

An hour later, he was back home, hauling in a small box of what appeared to be paper junk from Henry's apartment, and Dan called back.

"Hey, man!  What's happening?  I heard Dad's in some kind of trouble."

"Yes, well, the biggest part of it is over.  He had some kind of hallucination and thought the janitor was a thief breaking into his house.  He really pounded the poor guy.  The cleaning lady he was with went screaming down the hallway, and the front desk called 911.  The manager had not arrived for the day and got there just after I did."

"How's Dad?"

"He's confused.  He was acting like a blubbering idiot when I got there.  I don't know if it was his general state of mind or the handcuffs the police put on him."

"Holy shit!  They had to cuff him?"

"Yeah, and we really need to come to a decision about moving him into a higher level of care.  I don't know about you, but I'm not ready to put him in some ward where all the patients are walking around like zombies, you know, drugged like that movie – what was it?"

"Something … nest, yeah, cuckoo's nest.  I remember now something flew over the cuckoo's nest.  I never saw it, but I heard of it.  Anyway, I agree with you.  We got to do something."

Aaron heard another voice in the background. "Where are you?  The background sounds different."

"I'm just coming out of the surgery room. I've got Melissa with me. I'm teaching her to be an equine scrub nurse."

Aaron felt himself grimace when he heard her name. "Yeah, well, that's nice. When can we get together and talk about Dad?"

"We don't need to. You seem to have it under control."

"Danny, this is our dad we're talking about. It'll be a major change. Don't you want to be part of the decision process?"

"Nope. Not today. I was up most of the night with a colic case, and I'm halfway through a busy day already. I'm running on an empty tank. So, don't try to take me on any guilt trip."

Aaron couldn't think of anything rational to say except just 'goodbye' and 'say hi to Melissa for me.' When he hung up, there was a sense of gloom hanging over his little home office. He had a sermon to prepare and phone calls to make, but his mind was wrapped around the life and legacy of Henry Harper and the apparent wedge between himself and his brother, a wedge that had been there for years and now was more visible than ever and getting bigger. Had he done irreparable damage with his police inquiry? Was he out of line with what he did?

In a cardboard box he had brought from Henry's apartment, there lay a stack of cards and old photos of Henry and Evelyn from the time they married until she died. The earliest were taken at Harper's Gardens when the family first bought the business. Later, they would let the two boys run and play in the open fields before planting. A woman named Alison was among the first employees they had. He saw pictures of her standing with the family and several others in front of the shop during their grand opening. She was Henry's assistant manager and was a lifesaver so many times when the Harpers were up against business issues and didn't have the experience to know what was possible. They sponsored a Little League baseball team and there were pictures galore of both boys in their uniforms. Dan was the more athletic of the two, even though he was the youngest.

There was also a scrapbook from years gone by that had more current mementos, like the invitation to his own graduation from seminary. Dan's graduation picture from vet school was on the facing page. And then there was a photo of Henry when he was elected president of the Rotary Club. Evelyn, both boys and Alison were standing beside him.

The last thing he found in the box was his dad's diary. Here were countless notes and comments about trivial things like the weather, an invitation to Epcot, and baseball scores. About halfway through there were notations about both boys being born and how happy it made Evelyn and him to finally have children in the house. As he leafed through it, an empty red envelope fell out, and Aaron picked it up. It was a Christmas card envelope addressed to the nursery office and postmarked twenty years ago from a post office in Tampa. The hand-written return address was simply 'A.K., Tampa.' He thought the post office required an official return address of some kind. Maybe not. He stuck it back into the diary between the pages. There were other cards from various cousins and relatives.

Looking through all the reminders of the full life that Henry lived, he realized that someone now had to make all of Henry's decisions. And it didn't look like Dan was going to be a major player in that process. He closed the book and put the box away. The whole day, from the beginning, seemed like a dream, but he couldn't decide if it was a bad dream or a wake-up call. Finally, he buried his face in his hands and whispered, "Lord, just tell me what to do. I can't do this alone. Guide and direct me. Forgive me when I fail to listen to you."

Just as he raised his head, he saw that Jane was standing in the doorway. He considered her the most unselfish person he had ever known. She was his anchor in a storm and a sail when the winds were in his favor. She walked behind his chair and wrapped her arms around his shoulders, kissed his neck and gave him a long squeeze. She turned her head to see his face and saw tears on his cheeks. She needn't ask what his thoughts were. She had heard enough of the phone conversation that she could piece together what was going through her husband's head. She knew he held a lot inside, a defense trait that ministers seemed to develop out of necessity. But it was usually about someone else's family, someone else's wayward child, someone else's shipwrecked marriage. This was about his family, his dad, his brother.

Jane turned Aaron's desk chair to face her and looked at him squarely like she would one of the children. For a full minute, she just looked at him, then pulled another chair into position and sat with him, knees to knees.

Aaron finally spoke. "I know, I've got a lot inside. You're thinking I need to get it out and talk about it."

Jane said nothing, but her eyes said, 'Tell me more.'

"Everything's a jumble, Jane. I'm trying to focus on what my dad needs and not neglect my congregation. Henry Harper is one person, and the congregation is so many more than that. I feel so conflicted."

"If I said something like that, what would you tell me, Pastor?"

Aaron looked at her and saw the most beautiful person in his life. He felt so blessed, so safe, and so embraced in love.

"I guess I would tell you to take it one step at a time."

"Umm, yeah..."

"Starting where?"

"You tell me. What's the most important thing in your jumble of thoughts? Dig it out and start there. I can't tell you what it is, but you can figure it out. Don't try to connect the dots, not yet."

A month went by, and for Aaron and his family, Christmas had been the usual mixture of changing priorities, sending out cards, planning Advent church services and giving time to the children, both at home and at the church. New Year's celebration was quiet at the Harper House. Henry was in an intermediate-level memory care unit. It was not the cuckoo's nest as Dan had described in his own crass way. Aaron had visited other nursing homes and seen hallways filled with human figures in all manner of slow mental disintegration, some in wheelchairs, some on hallway benches with blank expressions, aimlessly watching a constant parade of people walking by with no sign of recognition or sense of purpose. He didn't see that at Meadows House, although he knew such people were in this place, somewhere. The staff seemed competent and empathetic, and Henry had not had another fit of rage, but his cognition was noticeably falling into an abyss. The staff brought his medications to him rather than depending on him to remember. He was allowed to walk the corridors at his leisure, and the outside grounds were made available only when sufficient staff were around to keep watch and make sure all patients stayed on the premises. He remembered, however, the names of the shrubs and flowers that graced the gardens of the outside area. Often, Henry would forget where his room was when he came back inside. Twice, he forgot to put his pants on before going out, much to the entertainment of the female residents. Hearing such things as this gave Aaron a growing wave of embarrassment. Henry always looked forward to the arrival of Peter, the pet rabbit which the staff members would bring out for the patients to pet and coo over. Peter's soft fur and docile disposition made him a prime therapy object, although therapy was hardly the word for it. It was more like giving glimpses of late-life pleasure that penetrated the walls that Alzheimer's had built, telling the disease that defeat was not total and that appreciation of love and beauty still existed somewhere in the depths of the human mind, even if it could not show itself to the world outside.

Aaron continued to visit his father every Monday. He finally convinced Dan to make the time to meet him at Meadow's House, and Melissa came along for the ride.  If that was what it took for Dan to engage in any way, Melissa was welcome to be part of it.

It was a little after noon, and all the residents were outside.  January in Kissimmee was still short-sleeve weather for most days.  Dan came with Melissa in his clinic truck simply because it was the most convenient vehicle at the time they had planned to leave.  Dan didn't want to waste time swapping cars and creating a motor pool quagmire.  They met Aaron in the lobby.

"Danny boy!  Good to see you!"  Aaron was in good spirits that day, and he knew that his brother had a silent disdain for the handle of 'Danny Boy.'  Even preachers have a sense of humorand Aaron knew what buttons to push on his brother.

"Yeah, Mom!  Good to see you, too." *Touche'*…

Aaron exchanged greetings with Melissa but kept his distance.

He gestured toward the interior and said, "Let's go through the lobby here and out the back way.  I left him out there on the patio.  He's having a pretty good day today."

As they exited the main lobby, they saw patients and staff sitting at picnic tables or ambling about in some random fashion.  A few were in wheelchairs.  Henry sat in an Adirondack chair with a hibiscus bloom in his hand.  He was studying it like it had a secret message somewhere inside its depths.  He looked up at the sound of Aaron's voice.

"Hey, Dad!  Look who I brought!"

Henry stared at Dan with a blank look for about ten seconds, then exclaimed, "Daniel!  There you are!  How's school?"

Dan shot a nervous glance at Aaron and Melissa. "School's fine, Dad.  I'll be graduating soon."

Henry's face looked back and forth to either side in a slow figure-8 pattern.  It was as though his line of vision was chasing an imaginary flying speck, fluttering in front of him, then rocking back and forth as if keeping time with inaudible music coming from somewhere.

"That's good," he said with a slight sway. "Your mother wanted me to find out when you'd be coming home for spring break."

Dan looked again at Aaron, with a loss of words. Aaron spoke up, "Dad, this is Dan's friend, Melissa. She's from New York."

"Who?"

"Melissa, Dan's friend."

"From where?"

Melissa stepped forward and leaned toward Henry.  "Hi, Mr. Harper.  My name's Melissa. I'm from New York and I'm down here visiting my dad.

He owns Hemphill Farms in Ocala. They raise horses there, thoroughbreds for - "

She stopped and realized that Henry was not paying attention. She looked at Aaron, and he said quietly, "Melissa, that's too much information in one dose. Just keep it simple."

Melissa raised up and took a step back. All eyes were on Henry. No one could guess where his thoughts were.

Aaron chimed in and said, "Dad, would you like some ice cream? I saw some in the lobby."

Henry nodded.

It took only a minute for Aaron to disappear and return with a cup of plain vanilla ice cream and a plastic spoon. He looked at Dan and said, "You want to give it to him?"

A look of uncertainty, then confusion, came over Dan's face. "You mean, like, feed it to him?"

Aaron nodded and handed the cup and spoon to his brother. Henry immediately directed his attention to the cup Dan was holding, never taking his eyes off the open container.

Dan started to scoop out some of the cold desert, but Aaron stopped him. "Small bites, bro. Teeny bites. And tell him to swallow."

Dan had already extended the spoon to his father, and Henry leaned forward and gulped the treat. Then he sat there, holding it in his mouth.

"Swallow it, Dad," Aaron said.  He swallowed. Dan looked at him curiously.

"Alzheimer patients forget to swallow.  I thought it was a crazy thing when I first heard about it, but it's true.  If you don't tell them to swallow, they'll forget and inhale it.  Try another one."

Dan scooped out a small bite and gave it to his dad.  He waited a second and told him to swallow. Henry responded.  Bite after bite, and they both got the rhythm of it.  Dan glanced at Melissa, and she stepped toward him.

"Mind if I try?" she asked.

Dan handed the cup to her, and her sense of engagement with Henry was flawless.  Five minutes later, only half of the small cup was gone.

"I guess it takes a while," Dan said.  He continued to marvel at the primal creature his dad had become. He suddenly felt like an outsider, someone who was just visiting as a courtesy.

Aaron came to Melissa's rescue.  "Here, let me finish this off.  He never takes the whole thing.  As she backed away slowly, he noticed a look of bewilderment and concern on her face.

"How long has he been like this?" she asked.

"Like what?  Every time I come, there's something new.  It's progressing at a fast pace now."

Melissa looked at Dan, and he saw tears welling up in her eyes.  She gently chewed on her lip and wiped her eyes. "Is this what they call the long goodbye?"

Dan put his arm around her and said, "Yeah, that's what it is. I wish you could have met him before this started."

Aaron turned, looked beyond the others and said, "Look, here comes Peter. Dad will love this. He always enjoys it."

Dan and Melissa turned to see what Aaron was talking about. An attendant was approaching carrying a very large, grey rabbit who quietly sat in the man's grip with no attempt to squirm or escape. Melissa took a step toward it and rubbed the soft fur on the animal's back.

"Wow! Feels like a chinchilla. So soft and deep!"

Henry stood up and reached out to pet Peter. His hand motion was gentle and repetitive, just his fingertips moving up and down the animal's spine. As he petted, his whole body seemed to rock in time with each stroke of his fingers. Dan, Aaron, and Melissa stood and watched with amazement. Henry was captivated by the entire process. As they watched, his motions began to increase in vigor and timing. His breathing was more intense, and the attendant noticed it.

"Henry, that's enough for today. Henry, let go; don't pinch his skin. You don't want to hurt Peter. He'll come see you tomorrow."

The man gently removed Henry's hand and backed away. Henry had a look of grief on his face, and he waved goodbye to Peter. He then turned to Melissa and looked squarely at her.

"I'm Henry Harper. Who are you?"

Aaron decided Henry had had enough socializing for one day. He motioned to one of the male staff members and told him they were leaving. The staff always appreciated visiting family members because they could devote more time to other patients who had no visitors. As they re-entered the lobby, Dan stopped and looked back through the glass French doors onto the patio where Henry still sat by himself.

"Shit! I knew this would be hard, but I didn't know it would be like this." Aaron could see his brother's lips quiver ever so slightly, and it brought tears to his own eyes.

Aaron tried to be reassuring. "He's confused all the time, Dan, but he's in no physical discomfort. I'm glad to see he remembered you."

Dan shot a glance at his brother and said, "Yeah, I gotta' get by here more often. I haven't seen him in a while, and so - "

"Yeah, I know," Aaron said quietly. "If he could put his thoughts together, I know he'd understand."

"That is so much sanctimonious bullshit."

"Call it what you want. It's the truth."

They strolled to the parking lot and started to walk in opposite directions when Melissa immediately recoiled and stepped behind Dan. He glanced down at her and saw a look of sheer terror on her face. Aaron noticed something out of order and came back to where they were standing.

"What's wrong?"

Dan repeated his brother's question, "Melissa, you okay?"

She discreetly pointed to a group of four men leaning against a dark blue Toyota with tinted windows at the opposite end of the parking lot. One of the men looked up, tossed his cigarette, and began walking toward them with the other three close behind.

"Oh, my God!" Melissa hissed.

The four men came within speaking distance, and the one in the lead stepped forward and spoke.

"Where you been, Mel? I've been looking all up and down the East Coast for you. You could at least tell me where you were going."

Melissa gathered her wits and said, "Aaron, Dan, meet Jack Gibson."

## CHAPTER EIGHT

There was a prolonged moment of menacing silence in the parking lot. Jack stepped forward and stopped within ten feet of Melissa. He had black hair combed back in sweeping waves with a touch of grey at each temple. His face had faint evidence of teenage acne, and a pencil line moustache graced his upper lip. His eyes were brown and shielded by heavy, dark eyebrows. He cocked his head to one side and made a strange clicking sound with his teeth.

"Melissa, I asked where the hell you been?"

At the sound of his voice, Aaron could envision a scene from *The Godfather*. The three men standing behind him had their hands in their coat pockets and eyes half-shut with a smirk on their faces.

After several seconds, Melissa answered, "Where I go and what I do is no longer any of your business, Jack. You need to leave now."

"Yeah, but I don't like it when I can't keep an eye on you. I'm funny that way, you know?"

"Go home, Jack. Leave me alone. You're not wanted here."

The man's eyes became piercing daggers, and his words spewed out like napalm, "No one tells Jack Gibson what to do or where to go. Especially not the bitch he's married to!"

Dan had heard enough. He stepped toward Jack and spoke in a low, direct tone. "Okay, you've had your fun. I recognize a playground bully when I see one. Now get in your car and go back where you came from."

Jack snapped his head in Dan's direction, and the other men stepped closer. One of them opened his mouth to say something when Aaron came forward and was pointing at something behind them. They turned to see a Kissimmee police cruiser that had just pulled into the parking lot. It stopped a few yards away, and Aaron walked to the driver's window and spoke to the officer.

"How's it going today, Officer?"

"Kinda' slow today, Pastor," the young patrolman said. "Everybody seems to be staying on the roads and between the ditches. It's the kind of day I like. Less paperwork."

Aaron leaned in the window and said something the others could not clearly hear. It was enough to make Jack and his goons step back and try to look innocent. Aaron lingered at the police car window a bit longer and looked over in the direction of the others. The young officer turned to look in the same direction. Within seconds, Jack and his three hoods walked back to their car and started the engine.

Melissa stood holding her cell phone with Dan beside her. Jack's driver finally put the car in gear and pulled out of the parking lot as the patrolman waved goodbye to Aaron and followed the Toyota. Melissa was dialing a number as they left. She spoke briefly to someone on the other end, then turned to Dan.

"Dan, take me home," she said firmly. Silently, they got into Dan's clinic truck and pulled away. Aaron went back inside to make sure his father was in good hands and then decided he didn't want their day together to end like this, so he decided to follow his brother and Melissa back to Ocala to finish their conversation.

An hour later, both vehicles approached Hemphill Farms, about a mile apart from each other. A dark-colored Toyota was parked under the trees fifty yards off the road, hidden behind an old barn, but with a clear view of the road traffic. When Dan's truck went by, the car pulled onto the road and trailed them at a distant pace. They didn't notice Aaron approaching behind them. He recognized their car and hoped they didn't recognize his. As he thought, he remembered they had not seen him getting into the Miata back at Meadows House. Nevertheless, he kept his distance.

Dan parked in front of Silas Hemphill's house, and they saw Melissa's father sitting in a rocking chair on the front porch. He took a long draw on the cigar he held in his mouth and released a large cloud of smoke.  Within thirty seconds, the dark Toyota appeared and stopped at the foot of the driveway. Jack and the other men exited the car and began casually walking toward the house.  Dan and Melissa were coming up the walk and weren't aware of anyone behind them until Jack spoke, and then they turned around.

Jack's voice sounded like a bull bellowing. "Okay, we've played your little game long enough, Melissa.  Come get in the car so we can head back to New York, and nobody will get hurt!"

Melissa spoke with a trembling tone but with a firm resolve.  "Are you crazy?  Jack, I wouldn't go back with you for a million dollars!  Nothing but pain and misery surrounds you.  Why would I want that?"

"You miss me, don't you?  C'mon, admit it!  You miss all the good stuff.  You never had it so good!"

"Yes, I'm sure all your sugar plum fairies have their nighties all loosened up and waiting in bed for you.  How many are there now on your calendar? Last count I saw twelve.  Tell me, why do they keep coming back?"

"You ought to know, baby.  You were getting it on a regular basis for a while there.  I'm telling you, no woman backs away from me.  Now get in the car." Jack walked closer and pulled a snub-nose .38 from his belt, which he aimed point-blank at Dan's head. No one heard Aaron's car approaching.

Jack continued, "You got to the count of three to do what I say, or I swear, I'll -"

The roar of Silas's shotgun sent birds flying and twigs from the ancient oaks floating down like snowflakes. He had obviously fired a warning shot with his Winchester 12-gauge. It was now pointed straight at Jack.

"Hey, Jackass, get your damn New York twinky ass back in your car and don't look back!" Silas showed no hesitation as he pumped another shell into the chamber. "This next round is the real thing, not birdshot. It's about time you learned not to mess with an old Florida Cracker like this one."

Jack yelled back at Silas, "You trying to scare me? You gonna' wipe out half the crowd with that old cannon? You don't got shit!" Then he looked at Melissa and spoke in a hissing half-whisper, "You think I won't do it? You think I haven't done it before? You're all out of options, Mel. If I can't have you, no one will. I'll take them out, one by one, starting with this one."

Like a ghost, Aaron quietly approached from the driveway and slowly worked his way toward the crowd to stand between Jack and Dan. He looked into Jack's eyes, slowly reached up to the outstretched arm, pulled it down slowly so the gun was aimed at the ground, and spoke calmly. "Mr. Gibson, you're not going to shoot anyone. Not today, not here." Aaron looked at him unafraid, unmovable, nonthreatening, but determined.

Jack was incredulous. His eyes blazed, and his pupils dilated. "Who is this? Oh yeah, I saw you in the parking lot, talking to that young cop. So where is he? Where's your muscle?" Jack's arm came back up as he thumb-cocked the pistol and now jammed it against Aaron's head. "Maybe I'll just take care of you first!" Drops of spittle sprayed as he spoke. Aaron just closed his eyes.

Silas's voice rang like a trumpet. "Hey, asshole! You think I'm just one old, stupid geriatric case. You better look around you before you make any more dumbass decisions."

Jack looked at Silas and grinned. Gold crowns in his mouth sparkled.

Silas then bellowed like a bullhorn, "Anybody hungry?" The metallic clicking sound of multiple guns being cocked gained the attention of everyone.

From the corners of the barn, behind two oak trees, and around the edge of the porch, seven barn workers appeared, each one looking down the sights of their guns. One man appeared from behind a giant pothos vine that encased the entire trunk of a tall oak. Another stepped from behind an azalea bush and walked closer with his deer rifle aimed straight at Jack's face and said, "Si, Señor Hemphill. What's for lunch? Yankee burgers? I like mine well done!"

The three goons had a look of panic on their faces. Seven loyal guns began walking closer from all directions, looking precisely where the barrels were pointed, and all could hear more metallic clicking sounds as the safety releases on each one were snapped off. The eyes of Jack's three men darted from one face to another until all three decided to back off and carefully step back to the car, leaving Jack by himself. Jack glanced around and saw that retreat was his best option now. Carefully, he released the hammer on his pistol and took a step back. Aaron exhaled and opened his eyes. Jack leaned toward him and whispered, "You got balls, man. No one has ever stepped in front of me like that. I'll deal with you later."

Aaron replied softly, "God bless you. Safe travels."

As the four men from New York drove away, Dan walked over to his brother and smacked him on his shoulder. "You crazy idiot! I didn't know you loved me that much." He then wrapped his arms around his older brother and squeezed.

With his head buried in his brother's shoulder, Aaron said in a muffled tone, "Yeah - well, just don't tell Jane what I did."

Both men stood with arms around each other and foreheads touching. Melissa walked toward them and joined them in a three-way group hug. Silas watched from the porch, shook his head and went back inside.  The three of them separated, looked around, and all of Silas's amigos had quietly vanished.

Melissa broke the silence.  "My God, you couldn't write this stuff.  That was totally unreal!"

"Do you think they'll be back?"  Dan asked.

"If I know my daddy, he'll have someone watching the main road all night."

Aaron's phone rang.  He talked briefly and hung up.  "Problem solved," he barked.  I told that young patrolman in the parking lot to call Stan Kemper and let him know our New York suspect was in town.  I told him Stan would know what I meant by that.  Then I got a phone picture of the license plate and sent it along to Stan.  He just called and said there's an outstanding New York warrant out there for Jack Gibson.  They're looking for him now."

Melissa had a look of total relief on her face.  She jumped over to Aaron and gave him a huge, wet kiss.  "We won't tell Jane about that part either," she said.  Then she stopped and looked closely at him.  "Wait a minute, you knew about Jack?  How did you know?"

Aaron felt himself being slowly cornered.  "No, you had mentioned him previously, remember?  Then you clearly pointed him out in the parking lot.

It was easy to put the pieces together."  Silently, he hoped she would accept the explanation.

Before Aaron could offer any more explanation, Silas had appeared on the porch again with a tall drink in his hand.  "If y'all are through with all that huggin' stuff, you want to come inside?"

Silas had the housekeeper bring out cups of hot coffee and glasses of iced tea for the group.  They sat in a spacious living room lined by dark, hardwood paneling and decorated with pictures of horses as though they were Silas's golden calves.  Tiffany lamps were in every corner.  It was a picture of history and elegance.  The room centered around a huge fireplace that was lit only when the winter chill made it a reasonable choice.  A mounted elk head hung above the hearth as a memory of a Colorado hunting trip many years before.  Large potted plants stood in all corners.  Aaron noticed the name 'Harper's Gardens' on one of the pots.  Small world.

"Are you sure those fellows are gone?" he asked.

Aaron spoke up and said, "Yessir, they're gone. That last call I got was from a friend on the Kissimmee Police department.  Those guys are in more trouble than I care to describe."

Melissa asked, "What friend?  You mentioned someone by the name of Stan.  Stan, who?"

"Stan Kemper," Aaron replied.  "Just a friend I met through the church."

"What does he do?" Melissa asked. "Anything special?"

Dan interrupted, "He's just a cop, Melissa. Nothing special." He stopped and looked at Silas. "Mr. Hemphill, you have a way of being in the right place at the right time. Thanks so much."

"Nothin' to it," Silas growled. My daughter had called and told me Mr Jackass was in the area and that he might be coming by. He was here once before, a couple of years ago. I ran him off then, too."

"Daddy, you never told me about that."

"Yeah, don't you remember? You were out of pocket as usual, and he came looking for you. Some guys never learn."

Aaron finally spoke up. "Folks, I need to get back to my own neck of the woods. I still have a list of things to do, and it seems I'm running behind. Thanks for the coffee."

Everyone stood, and Aaron shook hands all around. He gave his brother a healthy pat on the shoulder and the two men paused to just look at each other. Dan mouthed, 'Thank you.'

The Florida turnpike beckoned as he stepped on the gas pedal, and the Miata responded, keeping an eye out for Florida State Troopers. Within five minutes, he saw flashing red and blue lights about a mile behind him. *Cut me some slack today, will you,*

*Lord?* But fortunately, the lights were not in the lane he was driving in. Seconds later, the dark Toyota came streaking by him, and the trooper's car was not far behind. Up ahead, two more State cars waited on an access road and joined the chase. Ten more miles and Aaron saw a cluster of police vehicles on the shoulder surrounding the Toyota while Jack and his three companions were being handcuffed. Traffic had slowed down to gawk, and Aaron had no choice but to follow the flow of the onlookers.

"Have a nice trip home, fellows," he said to himself.

Joshua and Adam ran to meet him when he came through the front door. Jane was in the kitchen and peered around the corner. "Hey, you're home. How'd it go with your dad? You must have spent some extra time there. You've been gone longer than I expected."

"Yeah, it took a while."

"Did you get milk like I asked you to?"

Aaron stopped in his tracks. He had forgotten the milk. In fact, he didn't remember her mentioning it, but he kept that to himself. "I knew there was something I was supposed to do. Sorry."

Jane was wiping her hands. "That's okay. Maybe you can go get it after supper. I'm cooking lamb chops tonight. What else should I fix to go with it?"

He wasn't listening.  Aaron stood in the kitchen doorway, staring at the floor, lost in his own thoughts.

"Aaron, did you hear me?"

"Oh, sorry.  What did you say?"

Jane looked closely at her husband.  Her brows furrowed, and she said, "Sit here at the table and tell me about your day.  I'm almost done for the moment."

He returned her look and said, "It was an extraordinary day.  Why don't you turn off the stove for a few minutes?  I need to talk to you.  But first, I need a drink."  In the back of the pantry was a well-hidden bottle of Johnny Walker Blue, something someone had given to him as a gift two years before. It had yet to be opened.

Jane watched him closely.  Her Texas drawl seemed to be more pronounced when she was probing for information.  "Okay, Reverend, spit it out."

A half-hour later, he finished telling his wife about his day, starting with the visit with his dad and ending with the sight of Florida Troopers making a bust along the Turnpike.  She sat, almost catatonic, listening to what sounded like a TV soap opera.

"Wow!  Pour me one of those, too.  And don't answer the phone for the rest of the day."

"What if my brother calls?"

"He'll leave a message.  So, back up a moment. You knew that this Jack fellow had a criminal record?  How's that?"

"Stan told me."

"Do I have to drag it out of you?  Who's Stan?"

"He's a policeman, and he does background checks for me when we hire people for the church."

"Yeah, what else?"

"That's it.  He's the communications person for the department, and he knows lots of stuff."  The scotch was beginning to give him a mellow tone.

"He knows lots of stuff, okay.  Stuff about people from New York?  Why would he know that?"

"It came with Melissa's report.  It came with – oh shit.  It came, well, he just knows."  His words were slurring, and he reached for the bottle.

"Aaron Harper, what did you do?  No, don't pour another drink.  Tell me the whole stinkin' story."

When he finished, she sat, dumbfounded, looking at him.  Finally, she said, "I'm surprised your brother even speaks to you.  He's a grown man, and you don't need to go around checking on his personal life."  She paused and said, "Three husbands, huh? One suicide, one heart attack, and now one in jail. What did he say when you told him all this?"

"He was upset at first.  Then he was shocked at what I told him, but it doesn't seem to bother him now."

"Has he talked to her about it?"

"I don't know.  I haven't brought it up lately. Haven't really had the chance."  He smiled weakly as he spoke.

"Well, he is your brother, but I would think he can handle it himself.  Just let it go, Aaron."

She got up out of her chair and knelt on the floor beside him.  Cradling his face in her hands, she said, "You were a real hero today, baby.  You've got more courage than most men.  Just don't let it get out of hand.  You've still got me and the boys to think about.  But I do admire you, Reverend Harper. You're the man I love."  She gently kissed him, and he wrapped his arms around her.  She pulled away a few inches, looked at him and said, "What are you doing after dinner?"

The next morning, Aaron called Dan's office, and Tricia answered.

"Harper Equine Clinic, may I help you?"

"Tricia, this is Aaron Harper.  How are you?"

"Just dandy, Aaron.  I heard about your day yesterday. Quite the thriller.  You want to talk to Dr. Dan?"

"No, I was wondering if Melissa was there?"

"Oh – her.  Yeah, she's here.  Just a minute."  Her flat tone carried a message that was unmistakable.

Within a few seconds, Melissa came to the phone. "Well, if it isn't John Wayne himself!  How are you, pilgrim?"

Aaron couldn't help but smile. "Melissa, I called to tell you what I saw on the way home yesterday. Jack was stopped on the side of the road with Florida Troopers swarming around him and his three traveling companions.  They were all in handcuffs."

"No shit?  Oh, excuse me, Pastor.  Ah, no kidding?"

"No, don't put up any false fronts with me. There's a side of me that most people don't see anyway."

"So, that's what you called to tell me, huh?"

"Yeah.  That's alright, isn't it?"

"Yes, but I'm one step ahead of you.  Jack already called me to ask for bail money."

"He did?  What kind of fool does he think you are?"

"That's what I asked him.  I told him to go back to New York and face the music.  By the way, my divorce from him is effective tomorrow."

"It just occurred to me – why was he driving back toward Kissimmee?  That's going south.  You know what?  He had no intention of leaving, did he?"

"That's my Jack!"

"Let's hope that's the end of it.  How's Dan today?"

"Your brother? Dan is Dan. Work, work, work. Oh wait, he's right here. You want to talk to him? Hang on."

That was not Aaron's reason for calling, but he stayed on the phone anyway.

Dan's voice was a familiar tune. "Hey, bro! What's up?"

"Just calling to tell Melissa that I saw Jack getting busted on the Turnpike yesterday. Seems she already knew about it."

"Yeah, that idiot called her begging for help. What a ridiculous crop failure he is."

"How long did you stay at Hemphill's?"

"Just long enough to see Silas get smashed on Wild Turkey. That man can put it away. Drinks like a fish."

"Um, well, I had a little of the same for medicinal reasons last night as I described my day to Jane. She's my mother confessor, you know."

"You? You had a drink? Never knew you crossed that line."

"It happens, dude." Aaron paused, trying to measure his words and finally said, "Dan, have you asked Melissa about her previous husbands?"

There was silence on the other end. "Dan? You there?"

Dan finally answered, "Yeah, I'm here. I had to wait to answer you. You know – you know what pisses me off more than anything?  It's not that you stick your nose into my life. It's the fact that when you do, it turns out that you're usually right.  That's what really gripes my ass about you, man."

"You have such an angelic way of putting it."

"Yeah, I know. I've got to get to the bottom of that part with her.  I've been avoiding it – and I'll tell you why I'm holding back."

"Yeah?"

"How am I going to tell her the reason I know about it?  She's going to hate you for it!"

"You're holding back because of me?  She just called me John Wayne!  How can she be mad at John Wayne?  C'mon, what's the real reason?"

"I'm a frickin' coward, that's why, and she's going to hate me for asking!"

"Let me give you some advice, and you can quote this to her if you want.  Ephesians 4:15 mentions speaking the truth in love. If she loves you, make her tell you the truth.  You can tell her how you found out, and I'll defend my own side of it.  Can you do that?"

"I'm not gonna' quote a damn bible verse to her."

"I said that mostly for your benefit, not hers."

Dan inhaled deeply and let it out.  "I love you, man.  I'll stay in touch."

He hung up and glanced at Tricia, who had been listening to his end of the conversation.  Her eyes were fixed on him and unblinking.  He started to walk away but stopped and returned her stare.

"What?"

"Nothing.  It's just – nothing, never mind."

"Tricia, you've never held back when you had something to say.  What is it?"

She swiveled her chair around to face him and said, "Even a fool could tell what you and your brother were talking about.  When are you going to stop fooling yourself?"

"How do you know what we're talking about?"

"I raised three kids.  Sometimes, you act like you never left adolescence, Dr. Dan."

"It seems I am surrounded by women with strong personalities and even stronger clairvoyance.  Do you want me to sit down?"

Tricia got out of her chair and looked down the hall.  "Where is Melissa at this moment?"

Dan could feel the hair on his neck start to bristle. "I think she walked out to the barn.  Why?"

Tricia suddenly spoke in such low tones that dan could barely hear her.  "That's who I want to talk to you about."

"Melissa?  What do you know about her?"

She made a face of frustration and said, "Dan, I grew up around these parts.  Never left even after I was married, had kids, and saw them all leave.  I'm still here. I know Silas Hemphill and his family. Did you know Melissa had had an older brother who died at the age of ten?"

Dan was astonished at hearing this. "She never mentioned it. How do you know this?"

"My husband worked for the Post Office. He heard everything and brought it home to me. People would come to check their mailboxes and have private conversations, not knowing that he was on the other side of the panel, hearing every word they said."

Dan stood transfixed at what she was saying. "I had no idea," he said.

Tricia looked at him cautiously and continued. "Dan, you are all I have that resembles family, so I am going to tell you the rest of it." She stopped to let it sink in. "She's been married before."

"Yeah, I know. Jack Gibson."

"Yes, but before that. Oscar Buchanan. And before that was Stephen Miller."

Dan slowly nodded and said, "I knew there had been two others, but I didn't know their names."

"You knew?"

"Yeah, and I have a feeling you know more than I do."

Tricia got out of her chair and peered around the corner. Satisfied they were still alone, she continued, "Stephen was a nutcase. Nobody could figure out why she married him. A year after they got together, he started buying stuff online. Just stuff like televisions, barbecue grills, a snowblower - ”

“Snowblower? In Florida?”

“Yes! And the list goes on and on. Melissa finally convinced him to see someone, and the gist of it all was that they finally found out he had a brain tumor in the frontal lobe, and it was the cause of all his crazy behavior. He had a discussion with his doctor, went home, and shot himself.”

Dan stood motionless with his mouth open.

Tricia shrugged her shoulders and asked, “She never told you about any of this?”

“No, never. I guess she just wanted to move on.”

“I don’t know. Who knows. Maybe the past is too hard to relive.”

“So, that was what happened to Stephen. What about the other guy – Oscar?”

“Yeah, an older gentleman. Sat on the boards of several banks. Had more money than God. Drank like a fish and was a chain smoker. Two years after they married, she found him dead in his recliner. Just finished a big meal, sat down for a nap and never woke up.”

Dan rubbed his face and remarked, “I guess that’s the way we all want to go.” He stood and looked at his secretary. “Anything else you want to tell me?”

“Rumor has it afterwards she was being treated by a psychiatrist. Does that bother you?”

"I guess not."

Tricia shook her head and said, "Okay, I have a question. When are you going to get serious about this?"

"Serious, how?"

"I've seen her car parked at your house at all odd hours of the day and night."

"You're checking on me at night? You're worse than my brother!"

She went to the front door and looked out onto the highway. She looked to the left and said, "My house is that way." She turned and pointed in the opposite direction. "And the market I use is the other way. I drive right by here all the time, at all hours. That's how I know, smarty pants!"

Dan tucked his fingertips in his back pockets, looked at the ceiling and took a deep breath. "How do I get into these situations?"

"You don't, not since I've known you. That's my point. This isn't like you. Aren't you curious as to what keeps her coming back?"

He smiled. "I guess she's a sucker for charm and charisma."

"Dr. Dan, I mean it. You can't lead this woman on under false pretenses. Are you just living for today, or do you find yourself thinking ahead – maybe?"

"False pretenses, hmm. I wonder who's leading who? Ask me if I really care."

Tricia threw her hands up and said loudly, "You're impossible. When are you going to grow up?"

# CHAPTER NINE

The mail service made delivery to Hemphill Farms around mid-afternoon. Dan saw the truck pulling away as he arrived at about 2 PM. He had thought it prudent to take a look at Pistachio's eye, and it gave him a good excuse to drop by. Maybe Melissa would be in a talkative mood. Tricia's admonition was still burning his ears. He parked at the barn and walked toward the house. There seemed to be no activity in or around the barn. He noticed the mail carrier had left the door open on the mailbox, so he stopped there, collected the daily delivery and started walking up the front sidewalk. Out of habit, he looked through the stack of envelopes until one caught his attention. He stared at it for a moment, then looked around to see if anyone else was watching. Seeing none, he continued up the front steps and knocked on the door. Silas Hemphill opened and greeted him.

"Dr. Harper, did I call you? I don't think I did."

"No sir, I wanted to stop by and look at Pistachio. Just a courtesy call."

"Well, in that case, come in, come in. I was just about to pour myself a drink. Can I interest you in one?"

Dan laid the mail on the coffee table. Just as he was thanking Silas and declining the offer, he saw

Melissa coming down the stairs. He never ceased to marvel how someone her age could look ten years younger. She was wearing jeans and a western-style pale pink blouse with button-down pockets and small delicate floral designs on the sleeves. It was snug without being tight, and her figure was nothing to be ashamed of. She was barefooted and carrying a pair of boots and socks. There was a sparkle in her eyes.

"Hey, doc! Wasn't expecting you here. Daddy, pour the man a drink."

"I tried to," Silas replied, "But he's too pure to drink this early in the day, I guess!" The old man ended his comment with a strong belly laugh that progressed to a horrible crescendo of coughing and gagging. He walked to a nearby trashcan and spit out a large wad of mucus and saliva. He turned to look at Dan, and his face was beet-red.

"Mr. Hemphill, you okay? Something I can do for you?" Dan looked at Melissa and back at the old man.

Silas just shook his head and tried to clear his throat.

"Daddy's been promising to go to the doctor for a while. I don't know how bad it has to be for him to do something."

Dan thought for a minute and said, "Hang on a minute, I'll be right back." He walked out to his truck and was back inside seconds later, carrying his stethoscope.

Silas looked at him in disbelief. "What's that for? Are you kidding?"

"Mr. Hemphill, just let me take a quick listen. Can you unbutton your shirt?"

Silas saw his daughter walking toward him and nodding. He saw he was outnumbered, and the shirt came off. He sat there on a kitchen stool, his chest covered in grey hair and sagging pectorals. Dan moved the stethoscope to several different spots on his chest and back, then stepped back and looked at him with a sense of alarm.

"Mr. Hemphill, are you running a fever? Have you taken your temp lately?"

"What?"

Melissa asked, "Daddy, do you have your hearing aids in?"

He read her lips and answered, "No, but you can talk a little louder, can't you!"

Dan repeated his question.

Silas replied bluntly, "I'm not in the habit of taking my damn temperature on a daily basis! There's no need to!" He ended with another salvo of coughing.

Dan continued. "Melissa, do you have a thermometer?" She nodded. "Can you go get it?" He turned to Silas and said firmly, "Mr. Hemphill, you have pneumonia.  It's worse on the right side, but it's in both lung fields."

"I don't have any such thing!  You're not a people doctor, so don't pretend to be something you're not!"

"Look, pneumonia sounds are the same whether it's a horse, cow, dog or a person.  You need to be on antibiotics, and I don't have the kind you probably need.  Besides, it would be illegal for me to try to treat you."

"Yeah, like I said, you're not a people doctor, you're - "

Melissa had returned and said, "Daddy, be quiet and put this thing under your tongue.  Come on, do it."

Dan continued to marvel at how Melissa could control her father like the touch of spurs to a steed.

While they waited, Melissa picked up the house phone and called their family doctor.  Dan checked the thermometer while she was still holding onto the phone.  He held it up for her to see.

"Your temp is 102 degrees, Daddy."  She turned her attention to the phone.  "Today?  Great, we'll be there."  She hung up and said, "The doctor will see you in two hours.  I told him Dr. Harper had checked you out, and he said he knew Dr. Harper.  He said if Dan says you have pneumonia, you better believe him.  Your appointment is at 4:30 today.  No arguments.  Now go get your hearing aids."

Silas frowned, then turned and walked up the stairs Melissa had just come down.  She turned to Dan and said, "Thanks so much.  I've been nagging him for two days to take care of this."  She stopped and pondered for a second.  "So, what prompted you to come by today?"

Dan stepped toward her and said, "I just couldn't go another day without seeing you."  He kissed her gently.  "Oh, and I picked up your mail on the way in."  He retrieved the stack of mail on the coffee table and handed it to her.

She sifted through what he had handed her and paused briefly at each one.  One seemed to catch her eye, and Dan saw her glance up at him and then look down again.

"Anything interesting?"

"No, nothing to be concerned about.  Why?"

"Just wondering.  I forgot you went to high school here in Ocala.  I guess I never really thought about it."

"That's a strange question.  Why do you ask?"

"I couldn't help but see an envelope from the school alumnus group.  They must have sent it to the wrong person.  It's addressed to Melissa Miller Hemphill.  Is that your middle name?  Miller?"

Melissa stared at him and then turned her back to him. He walked to where she was standing and put his hands on her shoulders. She shrugged them off and reached in her pocket for a handkerchief. When she turned around, her eyes were red and pleading. He started to reach for her again, and she backed away.

"Melissa, what's wrong? I must have hit a sensitive nerve. I'm sorry, but tell me what's wrong?"

"There's so much I haven't told you," she blubbered. "I've tried to work up the courage, and there never seemed to be the right time."

"Right time? We've had all the time in the world. What are you talking about?"

"No, I'm not talking about opportunity. I'm talking about the most appropriate time. It just hasn't happened yet."

Dan stood transfixed at the situation. This is not how he had planned the epiphany. But, at least the ice was broken. Given the right time and place, things would come out. Not today.

"I don't know what to say. I thought we knew each other fairly well. Hell, we've shared a bed off and on for the past two months. Looking for the right time? What more could you want? They call it pillow talk!"

"So much like a man!  Get her in bed and screw around a little, and it all comes out in the wash because she's so charmed and captured by his magic personality.  The poor damsel looking for her hero, and along he comes - "

"Driving a Chevy pickup truck and wearing boots.  Yeah, I hear you.  Melissa, I don't know how to approach this aspect of our relationship.  You could have told me about Stephen, and then we, well, we could…".  Melissa was glaring at him like he was the devil himself.

"Stephen?  How did you know his name was Stephen?  What have you been doing, you bastard?  Checking up on me?"

Dan looked at the ceiling, rubbed his face with both hands and searched for the right words.  His thoughts went to the times in his youth when friends jokingly mimicked the motion of pulling an ejection handle and bailing out.  He needed an ejection handle right now, and he couldn't find it.  In a bold move, he decided to face the dilemma point blank, head-on and damn the results.

He continued, "Yes, his name was Stephen, and he took his own life.  And poor Oscar didn't stand a chance with his aging heart, did he?  And one last thing, when were you going to tell me about those pills I see you taking?  What are they for?  If you love me, when am I going to see the real you?  Tell me!"

Melissa stood in shock. "How could you know –
how could you – why didn't you tell me that - "

"I could ask you the same thing. I almost got
myself killed by your ex, and my brother stuck his
neck out so far that I've never, I've just never - seen
him do something like that – and you have the
audacity to ask me, 'how come' about anything?
Who are you, lady?"

"I can't believe you're talking to me this way.

"Yeah, I found out some things about you
because I wanted to know. You grew up here in the
same county where I work. People who know you
see us together, and they tell me things. You mean
something to me, Melissa. But is that a two-way
street? What do you know about me? Tell me, have
I ever been married before?"

She lowered the handkerchief and looked at him
blankly.

"That's right, you don't know. Do you even
care?"

She sniffed loudly and said, "Okay, if you must
know, my previous marriages have been a thorn in
my side for years. I've tried to forget them. And if I
asked you about your past - "

"Then you would have to talk about your own
past, right?"

She simply nodded.

"Did you think I would never ask?  Just enjoying the moments together?  Am I just some kind of fling?  A series of one-night stands?"

"No, Dan.  You're a very special man.  I'm sorry I have not been totally honest with you.  I've never met anyone like you."

Dan could feel his temper beginning to cool down.  He asked softly, "What's the medication I see you taking sometimes?"

"I forget the name.  It's for anxiety."

"Anxiety over what?"

"Just everything!  Put yourself in my shoes."

"No thanks, I like the shoes I have.  Your size pinches my toes."  He smiled and winked.

Melissa forced a smile and said, "As long as we're asking questions, what kind of love life have you had before you met me?  Any old flames still around that I need to know about?"

"No, they all had enough of me and left.  All fifty of them."

"Sounds like you had a hareem."

"Yeah, until they started trying to domesticate me, one by one."

"So, that's your weak spot?"

"No, I think I'm looking at my weak spot.  I need a hug from you, lady."

"Make it quick.  I have to get him to the doctor."  She pointed at her father coming down the stairs wrapped up like he was in Alaska. They both looked at him and stifled a chuckle.

"I can play the game if that's what you're thinking," her father said.

While Dan and Melissa were putting the final touches to their healing of priorities with each other and getting Silas into the car, Aaron sat in his church office waiting for a marriage counseling appointment to show up. The couple was already ten minutes late. He hoped they wouldn't be late for their own wedding, which was six months from now. Talking to young couples about marriage and the joy of sharing a life together was always a pleasure. It was like telling people about adventures that lay ahead, those requiring work and pleasure, challenges and rewards, promises and uncertainty. Aaron always used his own marriage as an example. He and Jane filled each other's gaps. Her strengths buttressed his weaknesses, and the reverse was true as well. A good marriage made two people complete, he would say.

And now, he knew his younger brother was finally getting serious about someone. Dan's choice in women had always puzzled him, but Dan was a mystery all by himself. As he waited, his office phone buzzed. The church secretary had taken the day off to run personal errands. He thought to himself, *How much simpler my life would be without these damn phones.* He looked at the caller ID and saw 'Meadows House' on the screen. He quickly answered in an official tone.

"Osceola Presbyterian Church, this is Pastor Harper."

"Pastor, this is Jonathon Appleton. How are you?"

"Hanging on by my fingertips and busy as usual. What's up?"

"It's your father. Do you have time to come by today?"

"You have caught me short-handed here at the church. Is it urgent?"

"Tomorrow would work, I suppose. Yesterday, your dad took a small tumble. Just fell over his own feet in the hallway. We thought nothing of it until today when he fell out of his bed. He tried to get up, but his legs were very weak. He opened up a gash on his forehead that required stitches. It seems your father has been compensating for a progressive weakness in his legs, and we just hadn't noticed it. We have him in a wheelchair. So, we need to talk about additional medications, a different kind of nursing care, that kind of thing."

"I can be there tomorrow at, say, 10 O'clock. Does that work?"

"Yes, in the meantime, we need to schedule a full neurological workup. The neurologist will be here this week sometime, and I need your permission to schedule a block of time for your father and that doctor."

"Sure, go ahead.  But why do you need my permission?  Something different about this?"

Jonathan hesitated.  "This doctor is not in the network for the coverage your father has.  The insurance requires an extensive write-up to justify our use of this doctor and he won't be back in our facility for another three months.  So -"

"So, it sounds like you're talking around the subject of payment.  How much will it be?"

"Well, his evaluation takes more time than the usual doctor's visit.  He has his own protocol that he uses."

"Jonathan, how much?"

"Eight-hundred dollars."

"You're kidding!  That much?  What kind of snake oil is he selling?"

"No, Pastor, this guy is really good.  The timing is just unfortunate.  If we had known a month or so ahead of time, we could have avoided this out-of-pocket expense, but it just didn't work out that way."

"Do you need the money now?"

"Well, it would be nice, yes."

"Now?  Are you kidding?  You are kidding, right?"

"No, I'm not. Can you pay us when you come by tomorrow?"

"Looks like I have no choice. Let me see what I can do. I'll see you tomorrow."

Aaron hung up the phone just as the young couple knocked on his office door. Time to shift gears. But, the next 45 minutes would be a challenge with other priorities running in the background of his thoughts.

When the couple left, he called Dan's office. Tricia answered promptly, as always.

"Good morning, Mrs. Fulgate. Aaron Harper here. How are you?"

"What's this Fulgate stuff? You've always called me by my first name."

"Sorry, I'm just a bit up tight this morning."

"Have you tried prayer? I hear it works."

Tricia treated both Harper brothers with a dry sense of humor. Aaron had known her for as long as she had worked for Dan, which was several years. She was always solid as a rock.

"Thanks for reminding me. If my beloved brother comes within earshot this morning, could you have him call me?"

"No problem. Speaking of being up tight, your brother's significant other seems to be moving into Harper territory at a steady pace."

"Why is that a matter to be uptight about? Is Dan worried about something?"

"No, I am. I'm the one who's worried. He's seeing that 'Melissa' woman more and more. I know he has a lot of outside calls that take him away from the office, but I see his schedule, and he's away too often for other reasons now. He used to be here at the office when I needed him, but now I have to call him, and half the time, he doesn't answer. I just don't know what to think." For a moment, Aaron reflected on how lucky his brother was to have a loyal employee who was more than just a secretary. She paused, and he could hear her tapping the countertop with her pencil. In the few times Aaron had been in contact with Tricia, he found that to be a habit of hers when she was thinking hard about something, anything. Tap, tap, tap. She suddenly spoke up, "Oh, wait, here he is, hang on! Dr. Dan, your brother's on the phone!"

Dan walked into his office, picked up the phone and yelled through the door, "I got it, Tricia. Thanks." He waited until he heard the click from her phone before he spoke. "Hey, preacher! What's up?"

Aaron explained the situation regarding their father and the need for money up front. His explanation was typical of previous conversations about their father.

"Dan, you mentioned before about stepping up to the plate and helping me with Dad. I know you're busy, and I'm not asking for your time."

"I get it. You just need some money."

"Hey, I've been the nickel and dime bank for Dad for quite a while, and it adds up. I would appreciate some help."

"Okay, just cool your jets. No problem. Can you write a check for now? I'll put one in the mail to reimburse you."

"That works."

"So, what's this neurologist looking for?"

"I'm not sure, but he took a fall yesterday and again today. That has them worried. I don't know how long this neurologist takes to write his report, but I'll see to it that you get a copy."

"Me? A copy? Okay, I guess."

"See, Dan? That's what I'm talking about. Do you really care? Aren't you the least bit curious?"

"Aaron, what our father has is an extended goodbye. That's not going to change. All the high-powered testing in the world won't make a bit of difference. This guy, this doctor, is probably writing a paper for some medical journal, and we're paying for his time to gather data. Yeah, I care. But we don't want our father to become a lab rat. Am I making sense?"

"Dan, I know it looks that way. But what if this work gives them a better idea about caring for him? Does that make sense?"

"They can decide all that without all the testing. But like I said, we'll pay for it just to stay in good graces with Meadows House. I'll have Tricia write the check today. Hey, I gotta' go. Stay cool."

The next morning, after Aaron took care of a few loose ends, he drove to Meadows House. It was an overcast day with a forecast of rain, and he knew everyone would be inside. He signed in at the reception desk and then proceeded down the hallway into the wards on the first floor. Because of Henry's increasing fall risk, he was no longer in his apartment. It had been assigned to another resident. As Aaron approached the corridor that branched off toward Henry's room, he heard a collection of muffled yells and shrieks.

"What's he doing? Did someone call for help? Hey, we need some help here!"

Aaron found himself walking faster past several rooms as he got closer and realized the hub of the activity was centered on Henry's room. He discovered his father pulling himself into the bed while still strapped to the wheelchair. The chair was half-way in the bed along with Henry when two attendants appeared at the door.

"Grab that wheel!" one of them shouted. "Unbuckle him!"

Aaron could only stand back and watch as the two men wrestled with Henry and the chair. Once they freed him from the device, Henry sat up and took a swing at the two men. One of the men shoved him back down with such force that he hit his head on the adjacent wall. They apparently had not noticed that Aaron was standing there.

"Stay down, you old bastard!"

As the man turned to face his coworker, Aaron's fist caught him squarely on the chin, and he went down like a big tree. The other man stood there with his eyes bulging in disbelief.

"You will never treat my father that way! Never again!"

Both men quickly left the room. Aaron looked at the other patient on the adjacent bed and heard him yell, "I saw it! I saw it! I saw what they did to him! I'm going to tell!" The man then shrunk back under his bed covers.

In what seemed like less than a minute, the two male attendants reappeared with three more right behind them. They grabbed Aaron by the arms and shoved him out into the hallway. Jonathan Appleton came running and arrived out of breath.

"What happened?" he asked.

The first attendant said, "We were taking care of a little issue here, and this man," he pointed to Aaron, "This guy comes in like some kind of hurricane, and the next thing I know, Jones is on the ground."

Appleton turned to Aaron and said, "Pastor, what happened?"

The two men looked at each other with blank stares, and one of them muttered, "Pastor?"

Aaron wasn't sure of his liability in this, so the truth was the best answer. "I heard a noise in the hallway and came in to find my dad trying to get into his bed with the wheelchair still strapped to him. They unstrapped him, and he was still resisting, so he got shoved against the wall. You mind if I go back in there and check on my dad?"

The entire entourage moved back into the room with Aaron in the lead. Henry was curled up in a fetal position, holding his head.

The patient in the next bed screamed, "I saw it! I saw it. See! There's blood on the wall!"

Appleton's face turned red. "Go get the ward nurse! Now!" He turned to Aaron with a look of foreboding and apprehension. "Pastor, I'm sorry about this. It should have never happened. I can't begin to tell you..."

Aaron waved him off. "It is what it is, Mr. Appleton. Those men should not be in contact with patients. At least not until they get better training."

"Better training?  Hell!"  He looked at the two attendants in question and spoke for all to hear. "This is their last day.  We're already short-handed, but this is over the top.  Don't worry, it'll never happen again."

The ward nurse appeared, evaluated the situation and directed her attention to Henry's head wound. "We should sedate him," she said.  "And we need to put him in restraints."

"Restraints?  You mean, tie him in the bed?"

"I'm afraid so.  It's for his own good."

The nurse finished dressing the wound and gave Henry an injection of Thorazine.  As he dozed off, Aaron said to the nurse, "Could I have a moment with my dad?"  She nodded and left.

Aaron pulled up a chair beside the bed and leaned his head on his father's tethered arm.  The steel side rail seemed so cold, and the room smelled like antiseptic, death, and human flatulence.  Quietly, Aaron prayed, "Dear God, please watch over this man.  He is a victim of a cruel disease, stripping him of who he is and all the dignity he once had.  Guide the people in this place as they care for him.  Forgive me where I have failed."

He stood and walked out into the hallway. "Amen," he mumbled.

# CHAPTER TEN

The Pastor of Osceola Presbyterian Church went home, went into the bathroom off the master bedroom, sat on the edge of the tub, and wept. Over the last several weeks and months, his pastoral duties, his brother, his father, and now his guilt had taken a heavy toll on his inner capacity. Van Gogh once said that our small emotions are the captains of our lives, and we follow them without knowing it. Aaron's cup of small emotions was overflowing. He sat there, his thoughts flashing through his head like thunderbolts, the world disjointed and coming apart.

Aaron suddenly sensed he was not alone and saw the bathroom door cracked open. Joshua's little face peered through. He and his younger brother had heard their father come home and quietly followed him into the bedroom. They were standing outside the bathroom door when they heard their father sobbing. Slowly, the boys entered the room and stood by him with their little hands on his shoulders. Joshua leaned down to his dad's ear and began to sing softly.

"Jingle bells, jingle bells - "

Aaron raised his head and saw tears on their faces. His own tears of grief now became tears of joy as he wrapped his arms around his children, kissed their cheeks, and stroked their hair. Jane came through the door, looking for the boys, and stopped short at what she saw.

"I guess this is my week for doing stupid things," he said while blinking back the tears.

Jane sized up the situation quickly. "You boys go play in your room. Pick up the Legos you left out. Let's go! Hurry up!" She turned to Aaron and asked, "What's happening, preacher?"

Aaron described the situation as it had happened in Henry's room. He detailed the sequence of events involving the two male attendants and the manager's reaction.

"I lashed out without thinking. I've never done that before. It was just a – just - I don't know."

"A tipping point," Jane offered. "They pushed you over your limit."

"I don't think I can take much more. Dad looked so pitiful, curled up in that bed with his head bleeding." He stopped and blew his nose.

"You need to listen to your own sermons. Just last Sunday, you preached about laying your troubles on God's doorstep."

"Yeah, I remember. Philippians, fourth chapter. By prayer and petition, with thanksgiving, present your requests to God."

"Go ahead, what else?"

"And the peace of God - "

"Yes, that's what you need. Some peace in your life. What you need is something else to think about," Jane said.

He had a perplexed look on his face. "Like what?"

"I don't know. Go fishing? Call your secretary, clear your schedule, go to the marina, and rent a boat. I know you like to fish."

Aaron nodded and mumbled, "When Jesus wanted to get away from the chaos, he got in a boat. Yeah, I guess you're right. Can't hurt." Jane was always an icon of solid thinking.

The bait shop at the lakefront was empty. Along the walls were all sorts of fishing tackle for sale. Rods, reels, and lures of all types created a collage of colors and shapes. Behind the counter, Aaron could hear the bubbling of an aerator in the live bait wells.

"Hello? Anybody around?"

He leaned his rod against the counter and placed his bait bucket on the floor beside him. In the background, he heard a toilet flush, and a bearded man with shoulder-length hair wearing coveralls and a tattered straw cowboy hat appeared from somewhere in the back of the shop.

Trying to be cheerful, Aaron said, "Anyone having any luck today?"

"You see anyone fishing out there? Did you look?" The man speaking was about fifty years old with a ruddy, sun-spotted complexion and a large waistline.

"Sorry, I wasn't really paying attention. Do you have any boats to rent?"

"Did you see the sign out front? It says, 'boats to rent.' That answers your question?"

If Jane had wanted something to take his mind off things, this fellow was the right ticket. He reached for his wallet and said, "How much?"

To which the shopkeeper replied, "For how long?"

"Two hours."

"May as well be six hours. Ain't nobody catching nothing this time a day. Bass, stop biting by nine in the morning."

Aaron just smiled and said, "That's okay. I'm just looking for some time to myself. I need some live bait."

The man shrugged. "It's your money. A dozen shiners will run you twenty-five dollars."

"How about just six of them?"

"That'll be fifteen dollars."

*Creative math*, Aaron thought. He put his bait bucket on the counter. The man took it and walked back to the bubbling live wells.

"That's twenty dollars for the boat, fifteen for the bait, and another twenty for the deposit."

Aaron reacted with arched eyebrows. "Deposit? That's a new one on me. I guess I haven't rented a boat lately."

"You want to fish or not? You'll get your deposit back when you bring the boat back."

Aaron couldn't help but smile just a bit as he pulled his debit card out. The man pointed outside to a row of small aluminum boats, each powered by a five-horsepower outboard. "Take whatever one suits you."

He thanked the man and found his favored vessel. He was thinking that for a deposit of only twenty dollars, it must be a pile of junk he was renting. To his surprise, the engine sputtered to life with the first pull of the rope starter. His father had taught him how to handle a boat, but it had been years since the last time he went fishing. The shoreline of the lake had changed over time, but certain landmarks never changed. On the far side, a point of land jutted out into the lake like a guardian sentinel overlooking the entrance to Shingle Creek. There had not been much rain in the past week, so the water current at the mouth of the creek was slow. Aaron knew that bass could be active in slow-moving water, especially where a deep drop-off had been carved out by heavy rainfall in months gone by.

He anchored his boat in shallow water near the drop-off, baited his hook, and waited. He wondered how many other places one could go fishing like this at this time of year. Actually, the fishing was always better in the cooler seasons in Florida. The water temperature in summer seemed to slow down the fish activity. What seemed like an hour went by, and his plastic bobber moved only when the bait wiggled. He watched a bald eagle soaring at a low level over the main body of the lake. Suddenly, it dove into the water, made a grab with its talons, and rose again with a sizable fish in its clutches. It reminded him of the time his mother caught an osprey on her line. The live bait she was using swam to the surface, and the bird snatched it from the water, sinking the hook into its toe. The unfortunate bird floated down like a lame kite and landed in the water. She reeled it in, and his father managed to remove the hook. It was the brunt of family jokes for a long time. He missed his mother. A white Egret waded near the edge of the water. It suddenly froze like a statue and, in a blink, had a small fish in its dagger-like beak. He felt fortunate to live in a place where one could see such sights in late January while the rest of the country was trying to stay warm.

Try as he may, he could not keep his mind from drifting back to his dad, his brother, his wife, and all the events that had captured his time and emotional energy in the last few days. How does it all end? How does God deal with all this? Staring at the water with the sun reflecting in shimmering ripples, he realized his bobber had disappeared. Reacting, he jerked back and felt nothing. He knew the technique. Watch the bobber go under, count to three, and haul back on the rod to set the hook. He had reacted too soon. As he regrouped his thoughts, the same thing happened. This time, he was ready, and the fight was on. Experience told him he had a trophy on the line. His rod tip quivered, bent down, and almost touched the water. The crank on the reel wouldn't budge, but the drag was screaming as the line went out. He saw the line go away from the boat and then dart back toward him and under the boat. Aaron leaned over the side, trying to keep control and not lose his rod. At most, he didn't want to fall out of the boat. Finally, the fish turned again, and the fight was over. A minute later, Aaron leaned over the side, grabbed his catch by the lower jaw, and grunted aloud as he lifted it into the boat. It was an enormous largemouth bass, at least ten pounds.

When he plopped his catch on the flooring of the boat, it flopped and wiggled for several seconds. Carefully, he grabbed it across the top of the head, avoiding the prickly dorsal fin, and held it up to look closer. It shimmered in the sunlight. The fish's mouth was so cavernous Aaron could put his fist in it. Never before had he caught one that size. The details of the fins and the subtle pattern of black spots on the side were a wonder of nature. A dark stripe ran from the gills to the tail. The back was sleek and muscular, a deep olive-green tone. He watched the mouth and gills gape open and close, struggling. The eyes were enormous. He wondered how this one had managed to stay alive long enough to reach this size. But what does a fish do all day long except just eat and survive? How many close calls did this one have? What hazards had it avoided or overcome? How many alligators had it outrun? Can a fish learn? Can it remember? Did it comprehend anything? What worries did this fish have other than staying alive? When he went after Aaron's bait, he was just doing what all fish do.

The gulping mouth and gills began to slow down, and the eyes were losing their pleading appearance as surrender approached. He held the fish up for one last close look, and through the enormous mouth, he saw something deep down in the fish's gullet. There, embedded in the tissue, was a hook attached to a plastic worm, evidence of a previous battle and apparent escape. The plastic material was mottled and pitted, suggesting it had been there quite a while. But the fish was robust and healthy despite the burden it carried.

He smiled and said, "Looks like you didn't let that slow you down."

Aaron felt a sense of calm and knew exactly what was right at that moment. He looked toward the blue Florida sky and said, "Thank you." Gently, he lowered the fish into the water and watched it slowly swim away, free again. Dark clouds were developing to the west of town.

As before, the engine started immediately, and he headed for the dock. There was no breeze, and the water on the lake was like a mirror, reflecting the cypress tree line in one direction and the city of Kissimmee in the other. Twenty yards away, he saw the outline of two eyes and a nose at the surface. He chopped the engine and drifted until it slowly sank out of sight. Another month or so and the bull gators would be claiming their territory and rounding up a harem of females. Water lilies floated nearby, caught in the slow-moving current.

He walked into the bait shop to recover his deposit and immediately heard a familiar voice. The shopkeeper was half-speaking, half-yelling at someone in the back, someone with a much younger voice. A loud slapping sound followed by a weak whimper came to Aaron's ears. The man stomped through the back door with a blustered look on his face, saw Aaron, and walked to the cash drawer. Behind him was a young, barefoot teenage boy with uncombed red hair and a peach fuzz mustache. He wore a grubby, unwashed grey sweatshirt and jeans that were not much better. His eyes were red, and his nose runny. He was rubbing his face and blinking his eyes. The man gave Aaron his twenty without so much as a word, then turned to the boy again.

"I told you to hose off that decking out back! What have you been doing?"

The boy started to answer, but the man interrupted. "Don't give me any excuses! What have you been doing?"

Again, the boy opened his mouth slowly, and the man yelled, 'Huh? Speak up!" He raised his hand, and the boy lowered his head with a grimace already on his face.

Aaron could not restrain himself. "I think he'll answer you if you give him a chance."

With his hand still raised, the man turned and glared at Aaron with an amazed look. He took a step forward and yelled, "You still here? What do you want?"

"Just give the boy a chance to answer you."

"Mind your own damn business. You got your deposit. Now go home!"

Aaron shifted his eyes toward the boy who was still by the back door. "Where do you go to school, son?"

The boy hesitated, then answered with a weak voice, "Uh, Fairview High School. I'm in the ninth grade." Aaron looked closer at him and thought he looked older than a ninth-grader.

"Oh, yes, Fairview. Then you know Mr. Andersen, the Principal."

The boy nodded, looked down, and shifted his feet. His toes made a scraping, gritty sound on the floor.

The man stepped toward Aaron and growled, "Is there something else you wanted?"

"No, just to talk to this young man, that's all." He looked at the boy again and asked, "Who is your gym teacher? Mr. Lyles? He's a friend of mine. Goes to my church. What's your name?"

The boy spoke softly, "Paul - Paul Mitchell." He looked at Aaron with pleading eyes.

The man stepped even closer and finally hissed, "You're jumpin' in the middle of family business here. Now git your ass gone!"

Aaron locked his feet where he stood and looked at the man squarely without blinking. "Did you say family? Family?"

The shopkeeper had an incredulous look on his face. "Who are you? You don't just walk in here and start asking questions that are none of your business!"

"My name's Aaron Harper. Yours?"

"Never mind." He waved a finger at Aaron. "You got to the count of three, and then I'm calling the cops."

Aaron remained unmoved. He replied firmly, "Good idea. Have you ever heard of the Florida Department of Children and Families? I know two people who have dealt with them on a regular basis – that boy's principal and his gym teacher. Maybe you should call them."

The man suddenly stopped and peered at Aaron. "Harper? Harper? I know that name. Your daddy was-"

"Henry Harper. And I am the pastor of that little Presbyterian church a few blocks from here." He looked again at the boy and said, "Paul, we have a great youth group at my church. Mr. Andersen and Mr. Lyles are both involved in it. They would be glad to see you there." He returned his gaze at the man. "Florida Department of Children and Families. Look it up. That's my next call. With that, he turned and left.

Back at home, he came in the door, and both boys told him he smelled like fish. Laughing, he headed for the bathroom to clean up and bumped into Jane.

"How was it? You weren't gone long."

"Long enough. Couple of hours, maybe a little more. Caught a big one."

"So, where is it?"

"I let it go. Beautiful fish." He held up two hands and said, "About this big."

"Yeah, right."

"No! Really! It was a really big one!"

"Okay, I believe you. When you get cleaned up, come join me in the kitchen."

When he returned, Jane was standing over the sink, washing some vegetables from the Farmers' Market. She spoke without looking up. "Melissa called. Her dad is in the hospital with pneumonia. And you had a call from Meadows House. You need to go pick up your dad's personal stuff."

"What personal stuff?"

"Apparently, when they moved him out of his apartment, they found boxes of junk, papers, books, and other stuff tucked away in a closet. Who knows what all is in them? They have been in storage since he was transferred to the ward."

"I had no idea there were other things of his."

"Well, they want you to come get them. The woman on the phone seemed rather abrupt. You know, Aaron, there might be something important in there. I can go with you tomorrow. Joshua will be back in school and Mildred, next door, will watch Adam for us."

Aaron scratched his head. "Okay, tomorrow works for me. I think it's going to rain today. I saw storm clouds over the lake."

"How was the lake?"

"Beautiful as ever.  I should do that more often. Next time, I'll take my camera."

"Yeah, next time.  Like, a year from now?"

"Jane, you know how busy I am.  The church keeps me busy, and most of it - "

"Most of it is busy work you created and then heaped on yourself.  You're doing what you love to do, so stop your complaining."

"Yeah, I know.  Seems like everywhere I go, there's something else that needs tending to."

Jane turned off the water in the sink and looked at him cautiously. "You went to the lake to relax. Now, what have you started?"

Two minutes later, Jane was shaking her head. "This is incredible.  Aaron Harper, you can't fix every problem in the world!"

"No, just the ones I come across.  What would you suggest?"

"Call the school, alert them to what you suspect, and let them handle it.  C'mere, I need a kiss."

The next day, the 'personal' stuff left behind by Henry Harper filled the trunk of Aaron's car as well as the back seat.  It took both of them three trips in and out of the building to get it all in the car.  When they were fully loaded, they went back inside to visit with Henry.

The hallway was cluttered with medical equipment, computer screens, and wheelchairs. Several residents recognized Aaron and said hello. Jane was deep in her thoughts but kept them to herself. She finally broke the silence when they entered Henry's room. Aaron let her go in first.

"Hey, Henry! You've got your favorite visitors!" Henry's bed was nearest the door and he made not a sound.

The roommate sat in a stuffed chair and said loudly, "He just lays there all day. Never talks. Just lays there. I'm going to tell! I'm going to tell!"

Aaron stepped around his wife and put his hand on Henry's shoulder. The eyes moved slowly in the direction of Aaron's hand and then back up to his face. His mouth tried to form words, but nothing audible came out. Jane and Aaron looked at each other, then back at Henry. An attendant came into the room and greeted them.

"Good morning, folks. It's good to see you." He turned to Henry and spoke firmly, "Henry, you have visitors. Henry, look who's here!"

"How long has he been like this?" Aaron asked. "Is he still sedated?"

"No," came the reply. "Not since that incident yesterday. That was unfortunate. The fellow who did it is no longer with us."

Jane asked, "Do you think it was the bump on his head that's causing this change?"

"No, he's had days like this before yesterday. Tomorrow, he may be as spry as a kid at Christmas."

"Okay then," Aaron replied. I'll be back tomorrow, and we'll see what's different. Thanks for all that you do. We'll stay a few minutes today and then go."

Back home, Aaron cleared a corner spot in the garage and stacked Henry's boxes there. Some of the boxes were on the verge of collapse and required strapping tape to keep them intact. When the unloading and stacking were finished, he wondered when he would get around to the task of sorting out what was there. Maybe Dan would be interested in helping. Maybe.

Three days later, Sally poked her head into his office and said, "Call for you. Someone at the high school."

He picked up the phone, wondering why the high school would be calling, and he got his answer quickly.

"Good morning, this is Pastor Aaron."

"Hey Aaron, this is Cleve Andersen from the high school. You called me a few days ago about a kid named Paul Mitchell. I thought I'd give you an update."

"That was fast. What's the latest?"

"Well, I've never seen the State of Florida move this quick. It's probably due to the gym teacher, Mr. Lyles. I think you know him. So, I passed your information on to him, and he watched closely the next day when the boys were in the showers. That kid has bruises all over him. Department of Children and Families will be looking for a foster home to put him in. His mother is in a rehab facility because of her drug habit. The guy at the bait shop is his uncle. He just works there. No one is sure who put the bruises on him."

"How do they find the right home?"

"Often, the state will use outside agencies like Christian Charities or something like that."

"Christian Charities, I never heard of them."

"Yeah, that's been around for a while. I'm surprised you never heard of it."

"Cleve, did my name come up at all in the process of doing all of this? I try to stay out of the details if I can."

"Your name? I don't know. They probably would want to know how we came to find out about the problem, but it's a minor point."

"Well, thanks for the update. I'm sure someone will find a better arrangement for that kid."

A week went by, and February was just around the corner. A phone call to Meadows House told him that Henry's catatonic state had not changed. He would not eat, and they were considering a feeding tube for him. Aaron wasn't sure what that entailed, so he called Dan.

"They want to install a feeding tube?" Dan asked with amazement. "You know what that means, don't you?"

"It's a surgical procedure, right?"

"Yeah, it is. But it means force-feeding him, watching close that he doesn't pull it out, and it just prolongs the inevitable."

"Inevitable what?"

"Aaron, our dad is going to die. This is just prolonging it. It doesn't really do anything for his quality of life."

"I hear what you're saying."

"Do you? I mean, I know you're into all this faith stuff, but one thing is certain: we're all going to die."

"Death is not the end, Dan. Don't talk like it is. Dad taught us both to believe something different."

"I must have missed that lesson. While we're at it, did the neurologist see him?"

"Oh, yes. I got the neurologist's report. It came quicker than I thought it would. You want me to read it to you?"

"How long is it?"

"Hmm, seven pages. Maybe I'll make a copy of it and mail it to you." He flipped through the pages. "But wait, the last page has some bloodwork results."

"What does it say?"

"Dan, what's BUN? And something called Creatinine?"

"The first one is blood urea nitrogen. That and the other one have to do with kidney function."

"Well, this says they're both off the chart, way above normal."

"Crap! His kidneys are failing. What else?"

"Liver enzymes are up above the normal range."

Aaron could hear his brother breathing hard. Finally, he said, "Has the attending doctor seen this report?"

"I don't know. What does all this mean? Oh, wait, here's a comment about dialysis. They're recommending dialysis."

"No, no, no, we're not going to do any of that. Why put Dad through that just to prolong life a few more days? Dialysis and a feeding tube?"

"Just a few days? How do you know it'll be just a few days?"

"Aaron, I don't know. But I do know it won't be prolonging him for months or years. Dialysis is not a comfortable ride in the park, even for a younger person. It's not going to change his dementia. If it would give him significantly more time and make him more conversant, hell, I'd be all for it!" Dan's voice was beginning to crackle.

"You're saying it's a gamble."

"Yeah, it's a real crapshoot with the odds stacked against us."

"When are you free again?  We can go talk to the staff together."

"Melissa and I were going to take a day off tomorrow.  Let me talk to her.  Can you do this tomorrow?"

"Sure.  I'll call and set up an appointment."

An hour later, he called Dan back.  "Hey, I got an appointment for tomorrow morning.  Does 8:30 work for you?"

"Wow!  That may not be early for you, but it means I have to get up real early and drive an hour, at least, just to be there on time."

"Yeah, I thought that might be the case.  Jane suggested that you come and stay with us tonight. We have an extra bedroom."  He could hear Dan chuckling in the background.

"Can I bring Melissa?  She's housebroken."

# CHAPTER ELEVEN

The sun had been down two hours, and the stars were out brightly when Dan and Melissa pulled into Aaron and Jane's driveway. The night air had a heaviness to it. They had stopped along the way and grabbed burgers for supper. It was that evening that both brothers realized that the two women had not really gotten to know each other. From Jane's standpoint, how often does one invite one's brother-in-law to spend the night and bring his girlfriend along? Especially when married to a Minister of the Word and Sacraments? After the first five minutes, both men could see they had nothing to worry about. There was not a judgmental bone in Jane's body. The two women retired to the living room, and their chatter and laughter could be heard throughout the house. In fact, Aaron had to remind his wife that the children were sleeping. The two men were relaxing in Aaron's home office.

"So, this horse was a direct descendent from Man O' War, and you had your hands on it?" Aaron rarely had the chance to sit and listen to his brother describe a typical day in the life of an equine veterinarian.

"Yeah, that's about all I had a chance to do. He was solid as a rock. Beautiful horse. Tried to kick me, but I saw it coming. You learn to react fast in my business."

"We never had horses when we were growing up. How did you learn enough to know that's what you wanted to do?"

"Remember that summer camp I used to go to every year? They had horses there, and I never left the stables the whole time, except when they had some group activity that involved all the kids. Other kids would be out playing baseball or something else, and I would be grooming horses, cleaning hooves, riding, and learning all I could. Three years in a row, I did that."

Aaron stopped and pondered, "Yeah, I vaguely remember. Mom was always afraid you'd get hurt."

"Yeah, and she really hovered over me when I played football. Remember that?"

"Speaking of which, I brought home all of Dad's stuff from his apartment at Meadows House. There might be some pictures of your football games in there."

"I'd love to see that."

"I really don't know what's in the boxes, but we can look tomorrow after we talk to the nursing home staff. Say, would you like to have a beer? We have some in the outside refrigerator. It's in the garage. Go help yourself."

Dan rose from his chair. "Sure, you want one?" Aaron shook his head.

After ten minutes, however, Dan had not come back from the garage, so Aaron went looking for him. He found Dan, an unopened beer in his hand, and a stack of old photos on the workbench in front of him.

"There's a real treasure here, Aaron. I found them in the topmost box. Have you looked through these yet?"

"Haven't had time. I see you found the beer."

"Yeah, thanks. There are a lot of pictures in here of people I have never met. I guess we'll never know." He opened his beer, took a long swallow, and said, "Oh well, we can dive into this tomorrow."

The next morning, Dan and Aaron left the house while Jane got the boys ready for their day. Joshua was in first grade and Adam was enjoying his preschool time. Melissa decided to go for a quick shopping trip.

The staff members were waiting for the brothers to arrive. Several employees of Meadows House were in the conference room, including the attending doctor and the nurse who had given her attention to Henry's multiple head wounds. The doctor spoke first.

"Gentlemen, my name is Dr. Hartwig. I've known Henry Harper for a number of years, even before he came to our facility. Wonderful fellow. Great guy! I'm glad we are all here to discuss his future."

Dan was the first to speak up. "Looks to me like he doesn't have much of a future."

Dr. Hartwig shifted in his chair. "Based on the lab findings, we feel there is potential here to extend life, with the proper support, of course."

Dan leaned forward and spoke forcefully, "You mean with IV hydration, dialysis, and forced feeding?"

"It would keep him alive." A staff member rose from her seat and whispered in the doctor's ear. He looked up suddenly at Dan, and his facial expression changed immediately. "You didn't tell me your name was Dr. Harper, sir."

Dan leaned back and said, "I didn't think it mattered. Looks like maybe it does."

"Where do you practice?"

"In Ocala. Harper Equine Clinic. Maybe you've heard of it?"

"What a quaint name. What gave you that idea?"

The same woman who enlightened Dr. Hartwig slipped a note to him. He read it, raised his eyebrows, and said, "Oh, I see that you are a veterinarian. With all due respect, sir, that does not qualify you to question the medical judgement of this facility. We are the pinnacle of technology and compassion here." He finished with a forced smile.

Aaron could not keep silent. "Dr. Hartwig, my brother has an abundance of medical understanding and more compassion than ten men. And from what I hear, there's quite a bit of overlap between animal medicine and human medicine. So, let's get back to the subject at hand. We know our father is living on borrowed time. Any fool can see that. We've seen the neurologist's report, and we've done our own reading. Perhaps you could enlighten us more about Lewy Body Dementia. It's mentioned in the report as a - differential. I don't know what he means by that. I thought a differential was on the rear axle of a car."

Dan leaned toward Aaron and whispered, "It means it's one of the possibilities."

Dr. Hartwig cleared his throat loudly, several times. "Well, I don't know about LBD as a possibility." He leafed through the pages until a staff member told him what page to look on. "Ah, yes, here it is. Let's see - "

Dan noticed the gap in the doctor's pontifications, and he was furious. "Doctor, you haven't even read the goddamn report, have you? Have you? You stand in judgement of me because of my profession, but at least I read the damn thing!" He pushed back his chair and stood. At the same moment, a nurse came into the room with a worried look. She quickly walked to the far side of the table and spoke privately to Dr. Hartwig, who then excused himself and asked everyone to stay in their seats for a few minutes.

As he was leaving, the social worker said, "May I interest any of you in a cup of coffee?"

Neither Aaron nor Dan bothered to answer.

Within ten minutes, Dr. Hartwig returned with a grave look on his face. "Gentlemen, ah, this whole discussion is now a moot point." He rubbed his chin before continuing. "This is both awkward and difficult. Ah, Henry Harper just died in his bed. You have my sincere condolences." Without hesitation or further comment, he left the room.

Dan and Aaron looked at each other like they had both stepped into the same bad dream together. The fact that Henry Harper no longer walked the face of this earth was something they had been working up to but had no idea it would happen today, in the middle of a meeting to decide what direction to point his care, like poetic justice proclaimed by a cruel judge. The room was so silent that it felt like stepping into a painting of people gathered around a table, like the Last Supper, but only DaVinci hadn't painted it. Suddenly, a quiet cacophony of muffled voices pierced their ears, expressing condolences, sympathy, and tearful sounds of disbelief. The brothers heard none of it as they continued to stare at each other. Finally, Dan reached out to Aaron, took his hand, and they both leaned into the shoulders of the other and silently wept together. For each of them, an uncontrolled motion picture of memories and images surged through their minds until, finally, Aaron spoke in a whisper.

Still leaning into each other, he uttered words of petition and supplication, thanking God for the time Henry had as their father and requesting God, in His grace and wisdom, to look after those remaining on this earth. Dan listened to his brother and felt an unexplained, profound sense of reality. They both whispered, 'Amen.'

When they glanced around the table, the social worker was the only one left in the room besides them. She patiently waited for the brothers to collect their thoughts, and then she spoke.

She spoke softly. "Gentlemen, uh, I know this is not the way we had envisioned it would end. There are details to attend to, but we will do so at your convenience. The first thing to decide is which funeral home you have in mind, and we will call them. Could you tell us by the end of the day?"

A few minutes later, as they walked out of the building into the parking lot, Dan rubbed the back of his neck and said, "Well, this day is going to shit, that's for sure."

"Yes, it certainly is a low point."

"A low point?  Is that what you call it?"

"Dan, I'm at a loss for words right now.  Maybe we need to go back to my house and decompress for a while.  Perhaps we'll see something in those boxes that tells us what funeral home Dad wants."

"Dad wants?  Dad?  Aaron, he's dead!  He doesn't want anything!  It's a matter of what we want!  Let's decide right now."

Patiently, Aaron thought for several seconds and finally said, "Well, there's Atwell and Reid.  It's a block from the church.  Would that work?"

"Atwell and Reid.  Have you ever dealt with them before?  I mean, you preach funerals.  You tell me."

Aaron gazed at the pavement and mumbled, "Sure, it's okay.  I mean - yeah, it's okay."

Dan turned back toward the building.  "I'm going in there and tell them.  Atwell and Reid, right?  You coming with me?"

"You go ahead.  I'll wait for you here.  I'm not ready to go back in there."

The drive back to Aaron's house was fifteen minutes.  Neither man said anything, but both wondered what to say when they walked into the house.

Jane and Melissa were busy chatting, eating potato chips, and drinking soda when the men walked in. They both saw the look on the brothers' faces. Jane finally asked, "How did it go?"

Dan didn't stop walking until he disappeared into the kitchen. Melissa followed him. Aaron sat on the living room couch and buried his face in his hands. Jane moved from her chair and sat beside him. Just as he started to speak, they heard Melissa's voice shrieking from the kitchen.

"What? Oh, my God!"

Hearing this, Jane looked at her husband, who had tears, fresh tears, welling up in his eyes. "It happened while we were in the conference room. A nurse came in and told the doctor he had died lying in his bed. He died while we were trying to decide what to do next. We were going to go visit him after we finished, and we never got the chance to."

Dan came out of the kitchen with Melissa's arms around him. The four of them stood, looking at each other through a flood of tears, not knowing what to say. Melissa finally found her voice.

"You know, I met Henry Harper - once. But I'm so sorry that I didn't take the time to get to know him better. I can only guess what it would have been like."

"He was an authentic, genuine guy," said Jane tearfully. "You would have loved him."

Dan looked closely at Jane and murmured, "Well, there were times, though, that I didn't feel connected to him."

Aaron glanced up at his brother. "Is this the time to talk about that? His body isn't even cold, and you're bringing up crumbs of bitterness."

"Yeah, see? You know what I'm talking about. I was the second son. The hand-me-down kid. I was always told, 'Be like your brother.' You know what that feels like?"

"Dan, Dad wanted you to follow your own path. He wanted you to create your own dream and follow it. Your path was different than mine. Your path is technical and hard for other folks to comprehend. He tried, but you were always a step ahead of him. When he talked about you, he always referred to you as 'My son, Dr. Harper.' He was so proud of you, Daniel. Don't ever doubt that."

Dan sniffed loudly. "I'll bet he couldn't tell you what color the outside of my clinic is or what street it's on. He never came to see what I had done with myself. But he sure as hell knew where your church was."

Jane stepped in and wrapped her hands around Dan's arm. "Dan, why did your dad have his business here in Kissimmee?"

Dan stopped and looked at her curiously, "I guess because that's where the most customers were."

"No, it's because this was the location when he bought it. It was years before you two brothers came along. Now answer me this – why didn't you open your practice in Kissimmee?"

Dan thought for a few seconds and saw that Jane was backing him into a corner. "I went to Ocala because that's where the horses were."

"There's no horses in Osceola County?"

"Not the kind I work on, no."

Melissa chimed in, "Sounds like your dad loved you enough to let you go where your dream was."

Dan took a step back from Jane's tender grasp and shook his head. "What's this? Everyone here ganging up on me?"

"Only if you see it that way, brother," Aaron said. "We're all on the same side."

Dan was still unconvinced. "So, let's all sit around the campfire and sing songs before we go to bed. I'm just telling you I didn't have the connection to Dad that Aaron had. Now, I never will."

Jane stepped closer to him and said quietly, "Dan, you are so full of shit. But we love you anyway."

"What's this? You know something I don't know?"

"While you fellows were gone, Melissa and I started looking through some old pictures from Henry's apartment that were in those boxes. You need to look at them.  Maybe it'll jog your memory and then tell us if you feel the same way."

Two hours later, they had dozens of photos laid out on the dining room table, hopefully arranged by dates.  Someone had turned the hourglass over, and time was restarted as they saw their childhood, teenage years and young adulthood unfold, come alive, and speak to them.  Pictures of picnics, birthday parties, bonfires, Christmas mornings.  Dan saw countless pictures of himself in his football uniform with Henry standing beside him.  Several others were taken at the summer camp where Dan developed his love for horses.  Henry was there.

Amazed, Dan said, "This one is of me and Mom at the horse barn.  It looks like I was about ten years old.  That horse's name was Spud.  The name fit him. He was about as fast as a baked potato."  He paused a moment, then continued, "But who took the picture?"

"Must have been Dad," Aaron remarked.

"Okay, it's coming back to me.  Yeah, I had a load of fun there.  That was a good time."

Melissa had a question.  "Was that a free camp? Did it cost anything?"

Jane answered, "I doubt it was free.  Nothing's free.  Summer camp nowadays costs a pretty penny."

Aaron pulled another picture out. Here's a picture of Mom. She looks older in this one. You know, I think this was right before she died."

With a question on her face, Melissa looked at Aaron, then at Dan, who spoke first, "She had a stroke. Died about ten years ago. Right about the time Dad started having memory problems. Funny how that timeframe sticks in my memory."

Jane reached into the stack and pulled out a small, framed picture of a little boy sitting on a Shetland pony. He had loads of blond curls and a smile bigger than Texas. He was wearing a sunsuit and sandals. "Who is this little boy?" she asked.

Aaron looked at the photograph and his face suddenly brightened up. "That's Dan! Hey, bro, look at this one. It was your fifth birthday. I was in the second grade. You remember?" Dan shook his head. "This guy, some guy, with a camera and a pony, came through our neighborhood taking pictures of kids sitting on that animal. Mom and Dad were in the front yard when he came through and they had the picture made. They asked me if I wanted a picture, and I said I didn't."

"What a cute picture!" Melissa was all smiles.

"The real story was that Dan thought it was his birthday present. He thought Mom and Dad bought him a pony! He was so disappointed when he found out otherwise."

"Oh, geez! I remember now! Yeah, my feet didn't even fit into the stirrups."

Jane continued to look at the picture and said, "Who would have thought that you would end up doing what you're doing today?"

"There's so much in here. Why did they keep all this stuff in boxes?" The picture went on the pile with the others.

Jane was peering closely at another photo. "You know, this one is a group picture outside your dad's main office at the greenhouses. See? There's a sign in the background that says *Harper's Gardens.* Do you know who these people are?" She handed the photo to Aaron.

"Looks like some of his workers. Some of them are holding garden tools. That's Pepi Diaz, and this one is Mario Ramirez. And that woman on the end, I don't know who she is." Aaron was turning the photo around as though different angles would reveal new answers. "Look at that field behind them! All the colors!" He handed it to Dan.

"The woman on the end, that's Alison," Dan proclaimed proudly. Why do I remember her? She worked for Dad in the office. I remember we would ride our bikes to the place, and she would take us both outside and show us what was growing. She knew the names of all the flowers and shrubs. I remember she told me that Disney was Dad's biggest customer. Yeah, I remember her." Dan's mood seemed to be improving.

Melissa suddenly left the room while pulling her cell phone out of her pocket. She returned in less than a minute. "Dan, we have to go," she said with a tremble in her voice.

All eyes were on her, and she could read their thoughts. "The hospital in Ocala just called me and said they have transferred my dad to intensive care. His oxygen saturation level is falling."

Within ten minutes, Dan and Melissa were on their way back to Ocala. Aaron wasn't sure what to do next. Go to the church office? Call Meadows House? For what purpose? His father probably left a few other things to be picked up and brought home. The more he thought, the more cluttered his mind became. *There's nothing to do that can't wait until tomorrow,* he thought. His mind then drifted to the boxes in the garage. He went into his home office, cleared off a space on his desk, and brought a large trash can in from outside. The first box found a home beside his chair, and it occurred to him that he shouldn't throw anything away without Dan being here. So, he traded the trash can for another empty box and opened the first manilla envelope on the top of the pile.

During his time travel through newspaper clippings, train tickets, horticulture articles, and assorted letters, he lost track of the current time.  It was a welcome diversion but a nostalgic one, at any rate.  A thought that kept running through his head was that he knew it would come to this someday.  He knew his father's days were numbered, but it didn't fit into the reality of the day at hand.  He called his secretary, and she told him all was quiet at the church.  The Sunday worship bulletins were almost ready for the print shop, and Clara Bench called just to say hello and to say she was looking forward to next Sunday's service.  Aaron decided to tell his secretary about his father, and she promised to get a prayer chain started.  It reminded him that he needed to call around to find another pastor to officiate at his father's funeral.  Looking for another pastor was a bit foreign to him.  Bob Weathers was pastor of the local Baptist church, and the two of them frequently had lunch together.   He called, and Bob agreed immediately.  He reminded Aaron that many of his own church members knew Henry Harper and that there would probably be  standing room only at the ceremony.

When he hung up, he fumbled through the box of artefacts and noticed that the next item was another large envelope of photos.  Judging by the faded condition of most of them, these were most likely much older than the ones they had been looking at earlier.  Most of them were of groups of people unknown to him. He found one of his mother's at a very young age with another woman about the same age. Something told him to turn it over and, in some unknown handwriting, were the names of 'Evelyn' and 'Alison.' Alison – Dan had mentioned her. Was she a friend of his mother? Another picture that looked like it came off the same roll of film was that of his father and Alison. His dad must have taken the first picture and his mother, the second photo. Who knows? "Who cares?" he said aloud. At a loss for something else to do, he rose from his desk chair and walked outside into the backyard. Adirondack chairs rested in the shade of a large willow tree, and he sat in one with a magazine. He lingered there until Jane joined him to remind him that he had skipped lunch and supper would be ready in about an hour.

"You doing okay?" she asked.

"Yeah, just trying to keep a rein on my inner thoughts. I had a pretty good rhythm going until today. Things always seem to fall into place, but right now, nothing is where it should be."

"Are you ready for next Sunday? Is your sermon ready?"

"Yeah, for what it's worth. I always end up ad libbing beyond my own notes, anyway. You know how I am."

"So, go back into your office and go over it again. Maybe it'll get your rhythm back. And don't think about anything else, okay?"

"I'm okay right here for a while. Don't worry about me, honey. I love you."

Jane kissed the top of his head and went back into the kitchen.

A week went by, and plans for the funeral were in place. The response to the prayer chain told Aaron and Pastor Bob that the Presbyterian church would not be big enough. The Baptist church had a larger sanctuary and could easily hold the size of the crowd they were predicting. The visitation would be at the funeral home, and then the formalities would move to the Baptist church. At 1 PM on Thursday, the chapel at Atwell and Reid Memorial Home was open for friends and family to mix and mingle. The brothers had crawled through the box of pictures for several hours and had the best of them posted on an easel near the open casket. The reception line extended into the parking lot. After two hours of standing, both men were feeling a bit weary. There had been a plethora of faces that neither Dan nor Aaron knew. The line was about to clear out when a blonde woman in her early twenties approached to shake hands. Her voice was soft and melodic. She was dressed in a solid purple one-piece dress with matching lace trim at the hem and sleeves. The neckline was high and her makeup was tastefully applied and complemented her dress.

"Hi, I'm Cynthia from Tampa. My mother wanted to be here, but she's in poor health. I'm so sorry for your loss."

Dan answered first. "You came a bit of a distance. How did you know our dad?"

"It's not that far, really. I see some other people here from Tampa." The rest of her response was lost in a sudden crescendo of voices nearby. As is the case in many such gatherings, it turns into a semi-social event after the first thirty minutes. Others were pressing forward to speak to the brothers, and the young woman politely stepped aside and proceeded to view the casket at the opposite end of the room. She stopped and looked at the pictures on the easel, and Dan saw her glance back at them. More faces came through the line, and Cynthia was gone.

The brothers had lost count of the number of people coming through the line who said they had done business with Henry. The line seemed to grow longer as the day progressed.

Pastor Bob did a great job with the memorial service. His church was home to a rather large pipe organ that filled the building with holy vibrations. Dan and Aaron both gave a eulogy, and there were hymns galore. The graveside ceremony at

Kissimmee Memorial Gardens was simple, and the earth covered Henry Harper next to Evelyn.

The crowd slowly dispersed and moved toward their cars to leave. The mood was anticlimactic, to say the least. It was ending on a quiet note, with gentle breezes whispering through the nearby trees with the message that life goes on in spite of today's events.

Aaron and Dan waited until only a handful of cars were left. That's when Dan noticed the same young woman he had met at the funeral home, now standing next to her own car, lingering with car keys in her hand.

"Hey, Aaron – do you know that young gal over there? We saw her go through the receiving line."

Aaron looked closely, then realized his gaze was obvious and perhaps embarrassing. He turned back to Dan and said, "No, I guess I missed speaking to her. There were just so many people."

Before they left the cemetery, John Pleasance approached both men. "Gentlemen, there is no appropriate time for this, but now is as good as any. We need to discuss your father's financial estate. It's not much. The business was going downhill about the time your mother died, and when he sold it, he took the first offer that came forward. Then he just lived off the proceeds and his assisted living arrangements costs have eaten into it considerably.

He left instructions with his attorney and with us at the bank that the estate should be divided equally between you two, thinking it would be a gold mine for you both. It isn't. But it still must go through probate. Give me a call when you have time, and we'll set up an appointment to go over it."

There was a coldness about the subject of money at a time like this, but both brothers knew it was an unfinished piece of business. There was a moment of silence, then Aaron spoke up.

"I'm aware of Dad's mismanagement of his money. I have control of his checking account, and I know it's running low. His memory problems started about the time Mom died, and I'm sure his judgement ability was declining as well."

"So, why didn't you do something about it, Aaron?" Dan asked.

"That was before I was given control of his finances. We've been squeezing the pennies ever since then."

The answer seemed to satisfy Dan for the moment.

The four of them drove back to Aaron's house to unwind. Aaron asked Dan what he thought about John's comment regarding the estate and the need for an appointment. Dan gave Aaron a shrugging gesture, which implied he didn't have time and that he wanted Aaron to take care of it. Aaron had assumed that Dan and Melissa would be anxious to get on the road back to Ocala, but they appeared to be in no hurry. It became obvious that they had something more to talk about as they stood in the living room. They showed no indication of leaving at that moment.

Melissa began, "Aaron, Dan, and I have a favor to ask of you."

"Yeah, sure. What's up?"

"I know this is an odd time to bring this up, but we need to talk about a wedding." She looked at them for a reaction. "Our wedding."

Jane and Aaron were both shocked and ecstatic. Jane spoke first. "Oh my God! When did you decide this?" Hugs and kisses flowed through the room. The brothers even hugged each other.

Jane took the lead and spoke at a rapid pace. "So, what are the plans? You have a time frame? Be sure and give yourself plenty of time to plan. This is so wonderful!"

Dan's face blanched. Melissa waited for him to speak, and when he remained muted, she dropped the bomb.

"Jane, time is one thing we don't have a lot of. It's a bit urgent, in fact."

Aaron and Jane looked at each other with wide eyes. Jane blinked and said, "Whenever you're ready! Aaron will be there. You need a maid of honor?"

"This is one of the few times I've seen my brother at a loss for words!" Aaron practically shouted. "I'm finally going to be someone's uncle."

Dan finally found his voice. "As our default minister, can you skip over the need for premarital counseling? I think we're beyond that."

"I have a good substitute. We have an unopened bottle of champagne from New Year's Eve. Melissa, you get Club Soda."

As they raised their glasses to new life, Jane said, "Henry Harper would be so happy if he were here."

Aaron mused, "He is here. He is."

A short while later, Aaron was bending over the kitchen sink, washing out glasses, while Melissa and Jane were busy chatting in the living room. Dan came into the kitchen and leaned against the cabinet next to the sink. He watched his brother silently for a few moments, then said, "So what's it like to be a father? You know, this is all kind of new to me."

Aaron stopped and replied, "I can see that." He thought for a few seconds and said, "I'm happy for you, without a doubt, but I thought you knew how to avoid this kind of thing."

"Yeah, I know. But stuff happens. I'm not going to go into the details. I just have to get used to it."

"When did it happen?"

"I think it was New Year's Eve."

"You think? Did you lose count?" Aaron gave his brother a light poke in the ribs.

Dan returned the poke. "Yeah, come to think of it, that was a memorable holiday. We had Jimmy Buffet playing on the speaker all night."

Aaron continued, "A few minutes ago, you made a light comment about counseling. Let me give you a ten-second version - do you love her?"

"I think so. She kinda' grows on you."

"I'm a pretty good judge of people. From everything I've seen and heard, and for what it's worth, it's obvious that Melissa worships the ground you walk on. I'm sure a guy with all your charm, you've left a trail of broken hearts behind you. Let me tell you, this one is special. She's a keeper."

"What would Dad say?"

"I know he'd agree."

A few days went by, and both Melissa and Jane kept reminding the brothers that they needed to write out thank-you cards for the flowers that had been sent to the funeral home. Both men balked, but they agreed to share the task when each one could find time. Jane gathered all the tags from the flower arrangements and randomly divided the stack into two piles on the dining table. One pile she mailed to Dan, and the other stayed in Kissimmee. It became obvious that finding the addresses for each would be a drudgery, but Aaron, in a spark of imagination, suspected that most of them would be in the boxes of Henry's collection of junk. After an hour of searching, he found an address book and felt a strong sense of accomplishment. Jane joined in and was making good progress until she came across one that defied any lists she had so far.

"Aaron, this is a strange one. It's signed 'Cynthia and Alison,' and that's all. No last names. Do you know these folks?"

"I met a woman named Cynthia at the funeral, and she hung around the cemetery afterwards for a while. Dan and I tried to talk to her, but we never got the chance to do so before she left. But I don't know if that's the same woman who gave the flowers."

Jane looked at him sternly. "And what if it's not?"

"It's a harmless thank-you card."

"Yeah, but it's two names. If this is the Cynthia you're thinking about, who's Alison?"

"I don't know. The only Alison I can remember was Alison Burbidge. And she moved to-"

"Tampa! It's in the diary, I think."

"Yeah. That's right." She paused a second and almost shouted, "Wait a minute! Where's Dad's diary? Where is it?"

Jane reached into one of the boxes and immediately came up with it. She started to hand it to Aaron, and a red envelope fell out.

"See? That's what happened to me. I picked up the book, and this fell out. That was a few days ago, and I had no idea what it meant."

"Aaron, I know what you're thinking, but there are dozens of women named Alison in the Tampa area. This is probably one of your dad's old customers."

"What's the date on that envelope?"

"It's August, 2004. Why?"

"Can you look up the census report for the year 2000?"

Jane whipped out her laptop and, within minutes, had the Tampa report for that year. No Alison Burbidge to be found.

Aaron was having difficulty controlling his imagination as well as his sense of excitement. "Yeah, but what if she got married and her name changed? That young woman, Cynthia, never mentioned her mother's name, but the facts are all starting to add up. I gotta' call Dan!"

Jane convinced him to wait until the evening to call in hopes that he would start to see how outlandish his conclusions were. Besides, Dan probably wouldn't have time to discuss this in the middle of doing surgery. That evening, he called,

and Dan listened to the first half of what Aaron had
to say. The rest was, well, what Dan usually calls
stuff he doesn't believe.

# CHAPTER TWELVE

Time passes as it always does, seemingly at a rapid rate when busy days rush by with so little time to spare. The citrus harvest was finished, and one could still see spilled fruit at the intersections of county roads, where overfilled trucks took their turns too sharp, spilling small increments of their contents into side ditches and across the pavement. It was no more than a couple dozen per truck, but when the passing truck traffic was measured in terms of hundreds, the spilled harvest would accumulate in noticeable amounts, leaving the shoulders of the roads covered in ripe fruit. If needed, one could open a fruit stand with just the spilled cargo. The March breezes arrived, and new blossoms on the trees filled the air of the groves with a fragrance beyond description. Silas Hemphill was finally home from an extended hospital stay after refusing to go to an advanced nursing care unit for rehabilitation.

Melissa and Dan's wedding was as unorthodox as a baptism at a rodeo. The burned-out barn had been rebuilt with tile stalls and cable TV. The floors were of non-slip material, and the sidewalls of the stalls were lined by mosaic tile. Near the entrance was an entertainment room with a small bar, complete with a beer tap, stuffed chairs, and couches.

A small apartment near the entrance gave room for the night watch staff to catch some winks while assuring that Silas's four-legged treasures suffered no untoward visitors, not that any would attempt it, but Silas's paranoia after the fire seemed to set the agenda. The entrance to the barn had been transformed for the wedding with a flower-covered archway with trellises on four posts. It looked like a floral gazebo inside a barn. Everywhere, there were strong hints of Melissa's interior decorating skills mixed with an equine venue.

Melissa wore a form-fitting gown covered with swirling saddle-like stitching. Her baby bump was barely visible and really not noticeable unless someone pointed it out. The hem of the dress was embroidered with subtle images of horse heads. Dan wore riding pants and knee-high boots with a red fox hunter's jacket. Three of Melissa's friends wore various combinations of Western attire that would have made Dale Evans blush. The male members of the wedding party were employees of the Hemphill family, all former jockeys, all wearing their silks and boots as though preparing to mount up and race at any moment.

Dan found out firsthand that wedding plans began and ended in the hands of the bride. The groom was there just to balance out the picture. Their vows included phrases like "crossing the line together" and "running the home stretch." When they kissed at the end, someone rang a starter's bell borrowed from Silas's training track.

Officiating the event, Aaron was the model of tolerance and understanding. He knew better than to insert his opinion into the ceremony itself, except that he insisted that it have a tone of Christian fidelity. He told Dan and Melissa that it would be a deal breaker if they wanted him to preside over the ceremony. There was no debate, no argument, and they agreed. He ended the ceremony with his favorite scripture about love.

"From 1st Corinthians, chapter 13, we hear Paul's words about love, and they are still appropriate today, *'Love is patient; love is kind; love is not envious or boastful or arrogant or rude. It does not insist on its own way; it is not irritable or resentful; it does not rejoice in wrongdoing but rejoices in the truth. It bears all things, believes all things, hopes all things, endures all things.'"* He looked at the two of them and said, "Melissa and Daniel, carry these words with you for the rest of your lives."

The reception was in the enormous living room of Silas Hemphill's home, fully catered, with an open bar and a ten-piece band. Silas seemed to be doing better since he was discharged from the hospital. They played until midnight, with Silas dropping C-notes in the band leader's shirt pocket each time they seemed ready to quit. It was as if the entire population of Marion County showed up, including a few female persons who appeared to know Dan better than Melissa would have preferred. One in particular, wearing a short, flowered cocktail dress with a pound of eye makeup, slipped up beside Melissa and whispered, "Good luck. He likes it kinky once in a while. But who doesn't like a change of pace occasionally?" She ended with a giggle and a wink of the eye.

"Who was that?" she asked Dan a few seconds later.

"Oh, her name's Barbara. Don't believe a thing she tells you. She's the jealous type and always tries to push all the right buttons."

Melissa looked at Dan carefully. "Yes," she said. "I'll remember that." She couldn't help but wonder how someone like that was on the guest list. Then she remembered her own father had had some input.

Tricia Fulgate showed that she could hold her liquor as long as she stayed seated. The band leader called her to the microphone to give well wishes to Melissa and Dan, and Aaron had to hold her arm and guide her to a chair on the dais where her monolog was slightly slurred but happy.

Fortunately, Dan's part-time associate, Dr. MacArthur, the previous owner of the practice and a man with plenty of experience, would watch the clinic while the newlyweds took a five-day honeymoon to Jamaica.

The next morning, Aaron had planned to go to his church office a couple of hours late, but a frantic call from his secretary, Sally Butterfield, changed all that. Aaron had just finished shaving and was wiping his face off when Jane came into the bathroom with the house phone in her hand.

"It's Sally. She sounds upset about something."

Aaron took the phone and spoke calmly. "Good morning, Sally. Everything okay?"

In the background, he heard Sally fumbling with the phone, and suddenly, there was the cry of a baby. Not the wail of a toddler but of a newborn.

"Pastor, I don't know what to do!"

"Sally, slow down. Start from the beginning. What happened? Whose baby is that?"

"That's the problem, Pastor. I don't know!"

"Wait, what? You are holding a baby and - "

"I need you here, right now!"

"I'm on my way."

Aaron turned to Jane with alarm written all over his face. "Jane, I have to get going. Do me a favor. Call the Kissimmee police and tell them we need them at the church, and – and  bring an ambulance team."

"What's wrong? Who's hurt?"

"I'm not sure. Sally's holding a baby, sounds like a newborn, and she doesn't know who it belongs to. She's in a real panic."

Jane was astonished at what he was telling her. All she could say was, "Go! Go!"

Aaron arrived within seconds after the police and ambulance did. The EMT crew was at the threshold of the office entrance as Aaron trotted up the walkway to join them. They found Sally in tears, pacing the floor and holding a baby whose umbilical cord was still fresh and moist. The child was wrapped in a cheap, tattered blanket and covered in meconium; apparently a difficult birth and a stressed infant. Between cries, Aaron could hear the baby's raspy breathing.

The eldest of the technicians said with a definite tone of concern, "This one needs to go to Orlando Medical Center. They have a neonatal intensive care unit there." The ambulance crew swiftly took the child as two Community Service Officers, both women, questioned Sally, who was still in an emotional freefall after finding the baby on the front steps of the church.

As one officer continued to question Sally, Aaron asked the second officer who would be responsible for the baby while it was hospitalized.

She said, "Maybe Christian Charities. They have an office a block from the Orlando hospital. They'll probably be waiting with open arms by the time the baby gets there."

"How will you find the mother?" Aaron asked.

"She's bound to need medical help. We'll canvass all the walk-in clinics and emergency rooms here in town. She'll turn up."

"Christian Charities," Aaron repeated. "I've heard of them but never dealt with them."

"Big organization," the officer replied. "Lots of kids go through there."

"You mean, like an orphanage?"

"No, better than that. Foster care. A foster family will look after the baby while they find suitable adoptive parents. Christian Charities has been around for a long time."

"Any way I can keep track of the baby's progress?"

"I don't know. You're clergy, and that might carry some weight. When you get time, drive up there and see what they can tell you. You'll have to go in person. They won't trust a phone call."

Sally finally regained her composure after the police left and decided to busy herself with menial chores around the building, anything to feel normal again. Three times, she poked her head into Aaron's office and repeatedly expressed her astonishment over the idea of someone just abandoning a newborn. Aaron could hear her talking to herself as she shuffled around the front office amid the copy machine, her desk, various inboxes, and the telephone. The police and ambulance crew had been gone two hours when she decided to empty the office trash cans. Aaron saw her go out the back door toward the dumpster. A few seconds later, he heard a blood-curdling scream from the back parking lot. He raced to the back door and almost ran over Sally, who was trying to get back inside the building. She was speechless and pointing frantically in the direction of the dumpster.

Aaron ran to the parking lot, turned around, and looked back at Sally with his arms raised in a perplexed gesture. Sally finally found her voice.

"Behind the dumpster!"

Aaron cautiously stepped toward the waste container and looked behind it. A woman's body curled in a fetal position, lay on the edge of the asphalt. He looked closer and saw she was still breathing. His fingers could not find 911 fast enough on his cell phone.

A different ambulance crew arrived minutes later, followed close behind by three Kissimmee police cruisers. Two men carefully lifted her body onto a stretcher. Her clothes were blood-stained from the waist to the hem of her skirt. Her arms and neck were limp.

"She's gone," one of the EMT technicians pronounced. "Her gums are already blue."

"I'm telling you," Aaron half-shouted, "She was breathing when I found her!"

"Pastor, she's gone." He lifted the hem of the blood-soaked dress and said, "Looks like she bled out."

Another EMT, an older woman with a tone of authority, motioned one of the police officers to come closer. She said, "Take a look and learn something." She lifted the hem of the dress again and declared, "She just gave birth. See that? See that? This is why we don't waste time when dealing with these cases. Time is of the essence." She kept pointing until, finally, the officers all said they had seen enough.

As the body was enclosed in a zippered body bag, the police questioned Sally and Aaron, who went through the entire episode again, starting with the baby left on the steps of the church, now on its way to Orlando, and later finding the woman's body behind the dumpster. A small crowd had gathered on the sidewalk, a safe distance away from the scene. Three of them were homeless women whom Aaron recognized from a local shelter, and they recognized him. The first responders all left, leaving a strand of yellow tape around the area. Aaron was about to go back into the church when one of the three women called out to him.

"Hey, preacher! Was she really dead?"

Aaron was astonished at the question but answered anyway. "Yes, very much so."

"She weren't dead a couple hours ago."

He turned and took a step toward them. They began to back away. "Please, don't go just yet. Did you see she was having trouble? Did you know her?"

"Her name be Bonnie. That's who."

"Do you know her last name?"

"Ain't nobody got a last name where we go. She just Bonnie."

"Did you know she was having trouble giving birth?"

They just shook their heads. Aaron found it hard to believe.

"Why was she behind a dumpster?"

"I guess she went as far as she could. She sleeps there some nights."

"She wasn't dead when I found her. Why on earth didn't someone call an ambulance?"

They had no response to his question. "That baby gonna' make it?"

"I certainly hope so. Did any of you talk to the police?" He saw the crowd begin to disperse upon hearing his last question.

It took Aaron and Sally a couple of hours to resume a normal daily agenda. Sally tried to perform routine tasks but kept wiping her eyes every time Aaron looked at her.

"Sally, you need to go home. I can handle the office for the rest of the day."

"No, Pastor. I'm okay. It's just all too much excitement to process in one day. That poor baby. I guess we'll never know if it recovers from this, whatever you call this."

Aaron thought for a moment. "Are you willing to take a ride with me? We could go to Orlando and check on it."

She stopped her pacing and exclaimed, "Could we? Oh, that would be so nice! Ah, wait a minute. What car did you come in?"

"My car, of course."

"That little thing?"

"Why? What's wrong?"

"I know where we're going. We'll go in my car, and we'll find it. And I'm driving!"

Thirty minutes later, they were in the middle of Orlando, driving past the hospital, and quickly found Christian Charities nearby. The parking lot was empty. Within minutes, they were standing in front of the reception desk, speaking with a young woman who, by her choice of words and body language, suggested that she was new on the job. Aaron had taken a moment at the church to put a clerical collar around his neck, something he rarely did. He remembered the policeman had said that being clergy would help him get his foot in the door.

"Yes, Pastor, we just got word of a baby who was brought in from Kissimmee. A little girl." She finished her words with a big smile and clasped her hands to one side in a prayer-like gesture.

"How can we know of her condition? Is there any way to keep track of that?"

"We can keep you abreast of things, yessir, especially since you're the ones who found her. What was your name again?"

"Harper. Pastor Aaron Harper."

"Wonderful, let me get your contact information. Oh wait, I typed into the wrong page. I don't know how to work this thing." She stopped and stared at the screen. "Oh look, there's already a Harper on this page. Isn't that strange? Hang on, let me get someone to help me. I'll be right back."

The woman left her desk, and Aaron could hear her talking to someone in an adjacent office. After a few seconds, it became apparent that she wasn't finding the help she needed. She made a brief reappearance and said, "I'll be right back, Pastor. Sorry about this."

It was just then that Aaron had completely processed what she had said before she left her desk. He looked at Sally with puzzlement on his face.

"Did I hear her say something about the name *Harper* on this page? Are there Harpers in Orlando? That's not a common name. I mean, it's not rare, but I don't hear it every day."

Sally peered down the hall in the direction Alice had gone. The rest of the office complex was very quiet.

Just then, a thought occurred to him. "Sally, I know of a kid, a teenager, who was put in foster care, and I think they used this agency to find a home for him."

"What's that got to do with you?"

"I made the first phone call, one of many, that started the investigation, and then the State stepped in. My name was probably recorded somewhere in some confidential record. That could be what she's seeing."

Sally was not convinced. "Pastor, I'll keep a lookout. Go around behind her desk and see what it says on the screen."

Aaron took a step back. "Sally, I can't do that. That's probably confidential information on the screen."

She studied his face for a brief moment and said, "Okay, you come stand here where I am. C'mon, right here. Keep your eyes peeled."

Aaron reluctantly switched places with her, and she quickly stepped behind the counter. Moments later, he heard Alice coming back. In a heartbeat, Sally was back in her original spot, looking innocent as an angel, when the receptionist came back with another woman behind her.

"Silly me," she said. The instructions are right here. Okay, let's get your contact information."

They finished their tasks, thanked her, and started back toward the elevator. Aaron was eager to ask Sally what she saw on the computer screen but was wrestling with the thought of being complicit in violating confidential information. Sally saved him the trouble of asking.

"You want to know what it said? Huh? It was a page with the heading 'Harper, Henry… Kissimmee, Florida. It wasn't your name. It was your dad's."

Aaron stared in disbelief.

"There was a date. I couldn't see it all, but the year on it was 1990."

Aaron went through the rest of the day in a semi-daze. He tried to work on the church budget that was due next month, but his thoughts kept drifting back to what Sally had reported to him. The distraction was so overwhelming that he decided he should not be working on anything critical like a financial spreadsheet. He turned his attention to the church newsletter and looked for errors and updates. He found none.

Having lost track of time, he hadn't realized that Sally had left the building and returned with two hamburgers, fries, and sodas.

"I knew you hadn't eaten, and I didn't want to disturb your concentration. I hope this is to your liking."

"Sally, you're an angel. I didn't realize how hungry I was. Come and sit with me while we eat."

Sally pulled up a second chair to the corner of Aaron's desk and made herself at home. She began to speak with a mouthful.

"So, what do you think about all this?"

"The baby? I hope she's alright. They have such good luck nowadays with those high-frequency ventilators. If the stress isn't too bad - "

"That wasn't what I was talking about. Christian Charities? Henry Harper? Coincidence?"

"It's probably nothing. You were probably looking at an invoice for flowers or something crazy like that. I haven't given it a second thought."

"Yeah, right! Don't give me that line. I know you too well. Almost seven years, I've worked for you. I can tell when something is on your mind."

"Well. I admit. It seems odd. But there's no other explanation. Just a coincidence of some sort. Besides, I have no way of finding out. What am I going to say? 'Hey, I was just looking at your computer screen, and the funniest thing popped up!' Is that how you see it happening?"

"Maybe I can make some phone calls for you," Sally spoke with a bit of a swagger.

"No, Sally, don't. You'll just muddy up the waters. Really, just let it go."

Sally finished her burger and exclaimed, 'Oh, my gosh! Where did the time go?! It's almost 3 O'clock. Time for this old gal to clock out. You coming in tomorrow?"

"Ah, yeah. I hope tomorrow is less eventful than today has been."

"Okay. Bright and early tomorrow. Drive carefully, preacher. Oh, the phone's ringing. Let me get that for you."

Aaron listened to Sally's muffled conversation with someone on the phone. She kept her back to him the whole time and didn't turn around immediately when she hung up. He walked around to face her and saw tears and trembling lips.

"That was the hospital," she said. "The baby, she didn't make it."

An hour later, Aaron was on his way home. There was no way he could keep this from Jane. In fact, he had not called her to let her know the whole story.  That would be a rich dinner conversation.  When he walked into the house, he heard the usual sounds of a happy household.  The TV was playing, his boys were running around the coffee table, and Jane was sitting at her computer.

He walked in and kissed his wife on top of her head.  He sat down on the couch with a faraway look and both boys ran to him and jumped in his lap.  Jane continued her gaze at the computer screen for a few more seconds, then looked at her husband, who had said nothing.

"Looks like you had a busy day.  Is the baby okay?  Too bad about the mother."

He looked at Jane and asked, "How did you know about the mother?"

"The police blotter.  It's right here on the internet.  C'mon, preacher, you got to get with all the technology around you.  The mother died, and the baby was transported to Orlando.  Right?"

"Yeah.  The baby died as well."

She crossed the room and sat beside him on the couch.  She knew that changing the subject had little chance of helping, but after a few minutes of silence, she decided to give it a try.  "We got a text message from Jamaica.  Sounds like Dan and his new bride are having a good time.  Did you know your brother knew how to water ski?"

"Huh? Oh, I think he tried once in high school. Almost drowned," he said with a detached tone.

"I've seen travel brochures of Jamaica; it looks beautiful there. Maybe we should go someday."

"Maybe when my dad's puny estate comes out of probate, we'll do that."

"I'm not holding my breath on that one. What was the rest of your day like?"

Aaron was speaking more responsively. "It has been a very interesting day. We found out about an agency called Christian Charities. Had this baby survived, she would have probably gone to a foster home to await adoption."

"Christian Charities? How are they involved?"

"Oh, you know, foster homes, adoption, kid stuff. Makes sense that they would have an office right next to the hospital."

"How did you know it was near the hospital?"

"Well, we went there."

"Who? You and who else? Aaron, do I have to drag it out of you? Let's start over. How was your day?"

"Terrible. And yours?"

"I guess you'll tell me when you're ready."

"No secret about it. Just Sally and me. Interesting place."

"Okay. Tell me about it. Interesting in what way?

Aaron hesitated before continuing. "Is there some way you can look up people on your computer?"

"You don't know how to do that?"

He shrugged.

"Who are you looking for?"

"Henry Harper. I want to know if there's more than one Henry Harper in this neck of the woods."

Jane moved closer to him and asked, "Living or dead?"

"Both."

"I don't work cheap. My fees are pretty high."

"Name your price."

"A million dollars."

"Check's in the mail."

"But, I also have to know what you're up to. Under threat of torture and eternal damnation, you must tell me why you're doing this!" She ended by burying her face in his shoulder and jabbing his ribs. The two of them wrestled playfully on the couch until they saw two small faces watching. Jane could usually bring Aaron out of a slump. She also knew he was good at keeping his emotions buried.

"Okay, that's enough," she said.

After supper, Jane did as she promised. She immersed herself in a people search that covered the last fifty years and found only one Henry Harper in all of Osceola County. Drilling down a little deeper showed he had been married to Evelyn Harper, and with that, she knew she had the right man.

"Okay, there's your result. Now, you promised to tell me why you're looking for this name."

"Sally and I had a rather unusual opportunity today. When we went to the agency's office, we came across some information in an unorthodox manner. The clerk left her computer screen on and went to a back office for help. Sally peeked around the desk and saw Henry Harper's name and a date of 1990. We're not sure what the document was, but there is no doubt about it. Why would my dad's name be on a document in an adoption agency?"

"Maybe it was some kind of business invoice."

"That's what I told Sally."

"Let's see, 1990, I wonder if they had everything computerized back then."

"It was on the bloody computer. What are you thinking?"

"It could have been a hard copy that was later scanned."

"This is all too crazy. I can't think of a single reason for any of this."

There was nothing of any interest on TV that night, so they played cards and entertained the boys. Just as bedtime approached for the boys, Adam came running into the living room carrying an unusual-looking rag doll made of macramé material. It looked like a knotted rope shaped into a humanoid form with red hair and blue feet.

"Where did you get that?" Aaron asked him.

Adam pointed to the garage.

"Come show me. Let's go in the garage and you show me where you got this." He turned to Jane and said, "I've never seen that before, have you?"

Adam led his father to the boxes that came from Henry's apartment. With a look of guilt, he pointed to a box in the middle of the stack. The corner was protruding, making the interior contents accessible to a small hand. He was relieved when he saw his father look down at him and smile. Aaron saw nothing else of interest and looked no further.

"I named him Knobby," Adam said proudly as they walked back into the kitchen. "He's got knobs all over him. But he doesn't care."

"Come here, boy!" He grabbed Adam and lifted him high in the air, evoking squeals and giggles. Joshua appeared around the corner and Aaron picked him up with the same tactic. He had one on each arm as he came back into the house. "Bedtime for both of you! Pick out a book, and I'll read it to you. Get going now!" Both kids hit the floor running. Jane stood by watching with a rich feeling in her insides.

# CHAPTER THIRTEEN

Dan and Melissa's honeymoon was an apparent success. The only thing flawed was the variety of rum drinks missing from Melissa's daily intake. They landed in Orlando around mid-afternoon, rescued their car from the long-term lot, and made it home by suppertime. Planning a household schedule had not been a top priority before they married and left for their trip, so frozen dinners in the microwave would have to suffice that night.

"Call your brother and tell him we're back." Dan could tell Melissa was getting into the family stuff in a big way.

"Yeah, I'll call him. Let's unpack first."

"Did you remember to put those T-shirts in the suitcase? You know, the ones for the boys?"

"Boys?"

"Aaron's two kids. Remember them?"

"Oh, yeah, I'm sure I did. See, here they are. You think these are the right sizes? They look kinda' big to me."

"They're growing. No worry."

The phone interrupted their homecoming conversation. Out of habit, Dan reached for it, answered, listened for a moment, answered briefly, then hung up. Melissa noticed a look of gloom on his face.

"What is it?"

"That was one of the house workers at Hemphill Farms. Your dad is back in the hospital."

Silas Hemphill had chronic congestive heart failure. Many have called it 'old man's heart.' He had stopped taking his medication while Dan and Melissa were on their honeymoon. His lungs were heavy and fluid-filled. His oxygen saturation was 85%. Melissa and Dan stood helplessly by his ICU bed, watching him struggle with each breath. The room was filled with machines that beeped, whistled, and flashed numbers. Silas's breathing was labored and raspy as a cappuccino machine. Doctors and nurses came and went at all hours of the night. His condition reached a low plateau and leveled off. Nothing better, nothing worse. His urine output varied with the medication given to draw the fluid from his lungs, but without dehydrating him. Melissa reached out to touch his hand; it felt cold and lifeless. When they first arrived, his grip on her hands had been discernible, at least, but now offered no response to her touch.

At midnight, Silas Hemphill breathed his last. In the hallway, a dozen Hispanic employees of Hemphill Farms stood vigil and waited for the couple to emerge with the news. When they did, there were muffled sobs from the women and grown men wiping their eyes. One by one, they approached Melissa reverently, kissed her hands, and called her 'La jefe.' She was in charge of Hemphill Farms now. They all knew it.

The following morning, Dan called his brother and broke the news to them. Aaron offered to officiate at the funeral, but Dan told him Silas had wanted only a graveside committal. Aaron offered that as well, and, with Melissa's consent, he said the last words over her father. Silas Hemphill was buried in Ocala.

Afterwards, the entire entourage gathered at the Hemphill house for memories and refreshments. Aaron and Jane were there and brought both Joshua and Adam. Joshua brought his stuffed horse, Buddy, and Adam brought Knobby. Hammers and crowbars couldn't separate those boys from their fuzzy friends.

Dan noticed Buddy at first. "Hey, what's wrong with Buddy's eye? You want me to fix it? Go ask your Aunt Melissa for some needle and thread and a big button, and I'll have Buddy see out of both sides in just a few minutes."

A short time later, Buddy sported two eyes again, although they didn't match. Joshua didn't care. Uncle Dan also sewed up the rip that was leaking the inner stuffings from Buddy's soul. He was a new horse.

Adam couldn't let the opportunity go by, so he presented Knobby to his uncle for an equal blessing. Dan looked at the ropey figure, then looked again.

He called to his brother from across the room, "Aaron, where did he get this from?"

Aaron was in deep conversation with someone and didn't hear Dan's question.

"Hey, Bro!  Where did he get this?"

Aaron broke away from his private audience and looked at his brother with a confused appearance.

"Oh, that?  He found it in one of the boxes we brought home from Dad's apartment.  Why?"

"I remember this thing.  I had it when I was just about Adam's age.  I haven't seen it for, well, longer than I can remember."  He paused while deep in thought.  "I'm trying to recall who gave it to me. Don't you think it's a little odd that Dad kept it all these years?"

Aaron motioned to Dan, and they both found a private corner to chat.

Aaron spoke first.  "Dan, there are more odd things than you can imagine about our father, and I'm just now finding out about them."

"Like what?"

"It's not just this rag doll thing; it's what I found in Orlando."  He went on to describe the events leading up to visiting Christian Charities and Sally's stealthy way of harvesting information.

"So, there's a document somewhere in their computer files with our dad's name on it. That's all you know?"

"That's it. And I can't just go back and ask to see their files. First of all, it would be illegal, and second, they would want to know why. Third, they'd ask what led me to believe there was something in their files that I should not have seen."

Dan was still fondling Adam's Knobby doll. He turned to Aaron and said, "Well, I guess we'll never know." With that, he handed Knobby back to Adam.

"Aren't you the least bit curious about what's in those boxes?"

"No more and no less than you. I mean, they're at your house, and you still don't know what's in them. Bro, you're really letting your abstract mind get the best of you."

"You haven't been listening," Aaron almost shouted. "I told you about the photos we found. We have looked, but there hasn't been time to do much more than just peek. Besides, I'm sure you'll find stuff in there that interests you. He was your dad, too."

Dan threw his hands up and said, "Hell! Let's do it now! C'mon, let's go down the road to Kissmywhatever and go through Dad's blessed boxes! Sure, I've got nothing else to do, so why not?"

Aaron kept his cool and tried to rephrase his concern. "Dan, I would not ask you to come home with me on a day like today. There are family things here to take care of first. Talk to Melissa and pick a day. I didn't mean to pressure you. I'm sorry."

The next day, Dan called to say he would be there in the early evening and leave the next morning. That should be time enough to do what had to be done. It was all the time he could spare.

Jane had put the children to bed about the time he arrived, and the two men brought all the boxes from the garage into the dining room. The dining table became a staging area for photos, letters, postcards, and all manner of trinkets and assorted junk.

"Did he ever throw anything away?" Dan asked. "Look, here's a picture of Mom in her bathing suit. Looks like they're on a beach somewhere."

"Is there a date on the back?" Dan asked.

Aaron turned the photo over and said, "Yeah, June 26, 1986. Mom looks tired. And all these other pictures in frames. Wait, I saw this one on his dresser. Who is this?" He held up a picture of a young woman. It was obviously a posed studio picture. She had blond curls that left her neck and shoulders exposed. Jane and Dan looked and shook their heads.

Jane picked up a small notebook and began reading on the first page. Ten minutes later, she was still reading and spoke without looking up, "You fellows better take a look at this."

"What is it?" Aaron asked.

"Looks like a journal or diary of some sort."

"He had more than one?"

She handed the book to Aaron. "Look at page 10."

"The date here is March 24, 1990. Dad's handwriting is not so cool, but I think I see what it says," *'Christian Charities is moving to Orlando from their Kissimmee office. They have been an asset to the community. Flowers delivered to their location to enhance their going away party.'*

He looked at Jane and said, "I never heard of them until recently."

"That may explain seeing Henry's name in their files," she said.

"Why would he take the time to make note of something so trivial? What's on the first 10 pages?" Dan asked.

Aaron turned to the first page and squinted his eyes. "Something about Dr. Wilson. It's about Mom and this doctor."

"That's the start of his journal? Does the doctor have a first name?" Jane asked. "What's the date?"

"No first name. The address is on Church Street. *'Appointment for Evelyn on February 18, 1985.'* That's all it says." Aaron turned the page. "Oh, wait.

There's more. *'Medication prescribed for depression.'* Depression? Mom?"

Dan and Aaron launched into a deep discussion about their mother while Jane pecked away on her iPad. She interrupted their debate and read from the screen perched on her knees, "It says 'Dr. Adrian Wilson, 27 Church Street, Gynecologist.' I know that office. He's not there anymore."

"Gynecology and meds for depression?" Dan shook his head. "How would those two things connect in any way? Makes no sense."

Jane interjected, "How long had your parents been married at that point?"

Both men looked at each other, and Aaron finally said, "I think they got married in 1965." Dan nodded in agreement. "The year 1985 would make it twenty years. Why?"

"Twenty years and no children? She was going to a gynecologist out of frustration, I'll bet, and he gave her a script for depression. Makes perfect sense to me."

Jane interrupted and said, "Here it says that Evelyn went to visit her parents in Atlanta sometime in May of 1989. Doesn't give an exact date. That's strange. Henry was usually so detail-oriented."

Dan asked, "When did she come back?"

"It doesn't say on this page."

"So, Dad was alone for an undetermined period. Did they have an argument? This is starting to sound creepy."

All three of them were beginning to feel a growing need for sleep. Jane looked at her watch and said, "You know, it's almost midnight. Why don't we table this until tomorrow?"

The brothers agreed and soon all three were in bed, asleep.

True to his nature, Dan was up at the crack of dawn and sitting in the dining room, looking at the journal Jane had found. When Aaron and Jane appeared in their bathrobes, he looked at them with a note of satisfaction.

"I know where Adam's Knobby doll came from." His smile had a bit of swagger. "Remember Alison Burbidge? Didn't she used to work for Dad?"

Aaron was still in the process of waking up, but Alison Burbidge's name grabbed his attention.

Aaron was puzzled. "Wait a minute. What does this have to do with Adam's Knobby doll?"

"Alison Burbidge made it for me out of macramé. I remember it now like it was yesterday! He was my imaginary friend."

"There's lots of pictures of Alison Burbidge here," Jane exclaimed. "She must have been good friends of your parents."

"Okay," Dan said. "I think we've accomplished something here."

"Like what?" Aaron was puzzled.

"Now, don't get all wound up. Brother, for someone who knows how to handle people and their issues, you surprise me. I'm just saying that certain pieces are starting to fall into place."

Aaron was not impressed. "Okay, so you figured out the history of a rag doll. Why is that a big deal?"

Dan shook his head, folded his arms, and looked at the floor. "You know, I should really get back to my new bride. The funeral party may have drained her energy level."

Jane put her hand on Dan's shoulder. "There's a lot more in these boxes. We'll keep you updated. But you must have something to eat first. At least a piece of toast and coffee."

Fifteen minutes later, Dan wiped his mouth and said goodbye. Jane and Aaron stood at the door and waved. Aaron dressed and prepared for another day at the church, but his mind kept wandering back to those boxes of Henry's.

He had been gone almost an hour when Jane saw Melissa's number appear on the caller ID. She hadn't heard the phone ring and realized the ringer was turned off.

"Hey, Melissa! Dan's on his way. He's - "

"Jane, listen to me! Where's Dan? He's not picking up when I call."

"Dan left here around eight. He should be pulling in very soon. Melissa, what's wrong?"

Her voice was becoming more frantic. "It's my ex! I think he's coming back!" Her voice crackled.

"No! He's in jail! Isn't he?"

"Jane, apparently, he found some judge that would grant him an appeal process, and his lawyer talked the court into letting Jack out, and now they can't find him!"

"Melissa, wait a minute. How do you know all this?"

"My divorce lawyer, the one up in New York, has been keeping a close eye on things, and he called me this morning. Oh, God! I'm by myself! Where is Dan?"

"Are you by yourself? Have you called the police?"

"And what do I tell them?"

"Melissa, they will recall Jack being arrested on the side of the highway, remember? I'm sure they'll send someone over to, to ah, well, to do whatever they do. It doesn't matter. Just call them!"

Both women hung up, and Melissa called 911. The dispatcher couldn't understand Melissa's frantic explanation and decided it was just an over-excited female with a vivid imagination. In the meantime,

Jane called Aaron, who, in turn, called his friend, the Chief of Police in Ocala. He was promised a cruiser would be sent to Hemphill Farms immediately.

Melissa stood by the window, anxiously waiting for either Dan or the police. After ten minutes, she began to panic and withdrew to her father's bedroom, the one room that was the furthest from the front door. Then, she changed her mind and came back out to sit at the bottom of the stairs behind a large potted plant.

Footsteps on the porch made her skin tingle and crawl. The front doorknob rattled, but she had locked it. The deadbolt made a strange clicking sound, and the door burst open. Jack Gibson was all alone with a screwdriver in one hand and his gun in the other. Melissa stood up, but still behind the plant and Jack saw her.

"Hah! There you are! I heard your old man croaked! And I heard you got married! Poor guy. You happy now?"

"Jack, I've already called the cops. You need to leave. Now!"

"You bitch! Not until I'm through with what I came for! You called the cops on me the last time I was here, and I spent those weeks in that lousy jail because of you. That's the last time you'll ever do something like that to me."

He looked at the ceiling, raised his .38 in his right hand, and pointed it in her general direction, then nonchalantly reached up and scratched his nose with the other hand. She saw his thumb go to the pistol hammer. From behind the potted plant, she brought out her dad's old Colt .45 automatic, the one he always kept in his bedroom. There was a live round already in the chamber, and the safety was off. Jack's eyes dilated, and his mouth flew open a split second before the Colt roared, and Jack dropped his gun and clutched his right ear. He looked at her in amazement as blood trickled down between his fingers.

"Are you crazy? You shot me!"

Melissa was breathing heavy. She screamed at him, "Jack, I wasn't aiming for your damn ear! I forgot this gun pulls to the left!"

He stumbled backwards through the open door just as Ocala police cruisers pulled up in front of the house. She sat down on the stairs and laid the gun beside her. Two policemen peered around the doorframe.

Her voice was weak and trembling as she held her hands up in plain view. "Officers, come on in. You can see he's right there, and I don't have any gun in my hands. His revolver is right there beside him on the floor. Be careful, it's still cocked."

Cautiously, the two policemen grabbed Jack's arms and put handcuffs on him. Blood was dripping down to his fingertips and onto the floor.

"Could you please take him out to the porch so we don't get blood on my carpet? Thanks."

There was the sound of tires sliding on the gravel driveway out front, and she saw Dan running up the front steps. He stopped when he saw Jack Gibson with two policemen trying to stop the bleeding. He reached inside his truck and came up with a large wad of gauze. They immediately took it and applied pressure to Jack's ear. One of them said, "We need an ambulance. Which one of us should ride with him?"

Melissa stood at the foot of the stairs with a drained, empty look on her face. Dan made his way into the house and rushed to where she stood. She looked at him and couldn't summon up the courage to speak. With little imagination, he could see what probably took place before he arrived.

He spoke softly, "I was doing fine until I saw two police cars in front of the house."

She reached for a pack of cigarettes, but her hands were shaking like a tuning fork. Dan tapped one out for her and held her lighter.

"Just this once," he said. "Remember, you're smoking for two of you."

She glared at him and spoke through clenched teeth, "Next time, answer your damn phone!" He took her in his arms, and her whole body trembled.

It took about an hour for the police to take Melissa's statement and examine all details of the scene. Then, a quick phone call to New York and all were satisfied that Melissa had acted in a 'stand your ground' situation. The ambulance had already arrived, and Jack was whisked away. Two housekeepers arrived, stood in stark terror at what they saw, then rushed to Melissa to reassure her they would clean up the large spot of blood on the hardwood floor. When the last of the official visitors had left, Dan and Melissa sat on the couch, and she spilled enough tears to streak her mascara.

When she had regained a portion of her composure, she said, "I've never shot anyone before. It feels so empty, so unbelievable. If Daddy had been here, Jack would never have gotten beyond the porch steps." She wiped her eyes and took a deep breath. "So, what was so pressing at Aaron's house?"

# CHAPTER FOURTEEN

The airways between Kissimmee and Ocala were flooded with calls from the two brothers until everyone had the latest information about the shooting. Jane and Aaron were almost frantic to hear what Melissa had gone through but relieved that they were hearing of it after the fact. Aaron mentioned that Melissa might benefit from a few counseling sessions and Dan said he would pass it on to her.

When Aaron came home that afternoon, Jane was stirring something on the stove and reading from Henry's journal they had rescued the night before. She barely paused to look up when he came through the door.

"Did you know your father had twenty-five acres in nothing but pansies? I can't picture that."

"Yeah, I remember walking down the rows of stuff like that. He knew how to make things grow."

"And five hundred potted mums! And that was just one order!"

"You know, with that kind of operation, they probably took very little time off. Probably no more than one day at a time."

"Maybe that's what your mother needed more than anything."

Aaron decided to ignore her comment. "What else did you find?"

"Lots of trivial details that mean nothing to me. But there's still one box to go through."

"Another one?"

"Yes, you didn't bring all of them in. Let's re-pack all of that stuff and go through the last one after supper."

Aaron agreed and relaxed on the couch while the boys got busy with new coloring books. Supper was simple, and he helped clean up the kitchen. The last box was heavy and filled with an assortment of paperwork.

Copies of property deeds, house titles, insurance bills, and an eclectic collection of unrelated documents made up the bulk of the box's contents. Jane pulled out a large, thumb-worn mailing envelope with nothing written on the surface, and the clasp was secured with several layers of tape.

"Aaron, look at this. Have you ever seen this envelope?" She handed it to him.

Aaron looked at it, then looked closer because it was not like Henry to leave something like this unlabeled. He glanced up at Jane and started to fumble with the clasp that held it shut. Shut, apparently, for many years.

What he pulled out was a thick stack of folded documents. The first thing that caught his eye as he unfolded it was the letterhead of each one, indicating it came from *Christian Charities*.

The cover page showed the names of both Evelyn and Henry Harper. The adoption was that of a baby boy born in Orlando. The rest of the page was blotted out with redacted lines that covered the birth mother's name and the date. The child's birth name was also covered, but it had been redacted with a different colored pen.

"I can't believe this! Mom and Dad? Look at all the other pages. They're all covered with redactions. What is all this about?"

Jane looked at what Aaron was holding and noticed his hands were trembling. The look of disbelief on his face was almost alarming. He flipped through the papers, page by page, with his mouth open and his eyes ablaze.

"You need to call your brother. I'm going to see if there is a website for adoption records in Florida." She looked at Aaron, who was still standing in the middle of the room with a look of bewilderment, disbelief, and betrayal. "Okay, take your time," she said. "Call him when you're ready."

Aaron rifled through the entire contents of the envelope and found nothing to reveal more information. There was a listing of pediatricians, counselors, lawyers, and an assortment of other individuals. One page was entitled, 'Child Custody

Rights.' Another page was from the *Florida Department of Children and Families.* There, the names of Henry and Evelyn Harper were listed along with general information, but nothing to identify a child or birth parents.

Aaron had regained his senses and said, "There are documents in here that tell me this was no ordinary adoption. Maybe an unwilling birth mother? How many adoptions do you know of that involve 'child custody'?"

Jane replied, "It's all foreign to me. You said there was a lawyer involved. Is his name listed?"

Aaron flipped through the pages and stopped on one near the end of the pile. "I know this guy. George Denzil. He died last year. Don't ask me why I remember it. I think they closed his office."

"Okay, are you ready to call Dan?"

Aaron rolled his eyes, called his brother's number, and Dan answered promptly. "Hey, dude, what's up?"

"Dan, are you sitting down?"

"I can be. Why?"

"Jane and I went through the last box of Dad's. Remember, there was one more in the garage? Remember?"

"Yeah, yeah. One more box. What's in it?"

"We found some startling papers in it. You're not going to believe this."

"Aaron, is there a point to this phone call? Maybe sometime this evening?"

Aaron took a deep breath. "Dan, it would appear that maybe one of us is adopted."

Aaron could hear his brother breathing on the other end. Finally, Dan said very slowly, "Preacher boy, what kind of bullshit are you pedaling now? Maybe one of us is adopted?"

"I figured you would react this way. I'm trying to break this to you gently. There's paperwork here you should see."

Dan exhaled loudly. "Geez! If it isn't one thing, it's another. C'mon, man! What – what are you talking about?"

"Just what I said! There're adoption papers here with Mom and Dad's names, and a whole bunch of stuff blacked out. You know, like some kind of secrets and -"

Dan cleared his throat. "Then bring it to me. I can't come to you. I've been out of town on my honeymoon, then taking care of family business, cleaning up the house after someone got shot and almost killed - I could go on, but I'm not. I simply don't have time for some ridiculous story about one of us being adopted. You must be eating the kids' breakfast cereal again. The one with the cartoons on the box."

"Dan, I'm serious."

Dan exhaled loudly into the phone. "Bring it to me, and I'll look at it. Good God!"

The following morning, Aaron called Dan's office and spoke to Tricia. He found out there was an open block of time right after lunch for them to speak in private, and Tricia assured Aaron that she would keep the time open. The drive to Ocala seemed to fly by as Aaron was lost in a blur of his own thoughts. He was patiently waiting in the outer reception area of the clinic for thirty minutes when he heard Dan coming in through the back door. He was kicking his boots off and yelled from the hallway.

"Tricia, what else do I have on my schedule? I need to call my brother."

"Come to the front, Dr. Dan. Your next appointment's already here."

"Tricia, I said get my brother on the damn phone!"

Dan was immediately confronted by an angry secretary, storming into his office. "Young man, I don't care how many things you have hanging on the wall of your office. You will not talk to me that way! Understand?"

"Yes, ma'am." He paused and continued, "Now, could you please get my bro…"

Aaron stuck his head around the door, and Dan stopped cold. "You didn't tell me you were coming."

Aaron held up the old envelope he and Jane had been looking at. "You said bring it to you, so I did. You want to look at this here or somewhere else?"

A half-hour later, Dan stood and stretched. "It's like I said on the phone, this is pure unadulterated bullshit. Someone was adopting a child or trying to, and there's no indication that it was either of us. Your imagination is getting the best of you. Just put it to bed."

"Daniel! First, I can't believe this paperwork, and now I can't believe how you're sticking your head in the sand! Not in so many words. The whole intent of this paperwork is obvious, and Mom and Dad's names are in here. I just don't know what it means to us."

"Exactly! I'm glad we agree on that part. We have no idea what it's about. Maybe they tried to adopt and were turned down."

"So, you have no interest in pursuing this?"

"You haven't given me a reason to. It sounds strange, I'll admit. But it's a dead end. Maybe they sponsored someone, I don't know."

"Sponsored someone? What's that about?"

"I don't know! Maybe someone needed a character witness." He stopped and looked closely at Aaron. "Okay, the thought just occurred to me; I don't know." Dan was half-stomping around his office, looking at the ceiling. "Okay, get this -

remember, Mom and Dad had trouble getting pregnant. Mom went into a state of depression. Maybe they wanted to break the spell or something like that. And it must have worked! I mean, here we both stand, alive and well, with the same parents. Anyone will tell you - no one could deny that Henry and Evelyn Harper are our parents! There's plenty of folks who have seen us grow up together. You know, I've heard lots of stories of people who couldn't have kids, and as soon as they adopted one, then bingo! They make the next one from scratch, the old-fashioned way."

"But, you're saying they probably didn't adopt anyone."

"Maybe just the thought process is all that's needed."

Tricia's voice spoke softly but firmly from the office door. "If you're going to discuss confidential family business, you should shut the door."

Both men looked at her blankly. Finally, Aaron asked, "What did you hear?"

"I heard enough." She folded her arms and leaned against the door frame. "You're both educated men. You should know what to do in this case."

Dan and Aaron looked at each other, then back at her.

"Buy one of those DNA kits, each of you. In fact, buy one from two different companies and see if you get the same results. List your names on the forms. They'll tell you if you're related or not." She started to turn but added one more remark, "Frankly though, I agree with Dr. Dan. I think it's a bunch of bullshit."

Dan looked at Aaron as if to say, 'I told you so.' Then he finally spoke. "Okay, I'll make this easy for you. My office will order four kits from two different sources, two for you and two for me. I'll have yours mailed to your address. Happy now?"

Trying fitfully to maintain a calm demeanor despite his brother's patronizing manner, Aaron said he was satisfied with the plans.

That evening, Dan went home to his new bride and filled her in on the happenings of his day. Everything except the phone call and visit from Aaron. She had stopped taking her anxiety medication because of her pregnancy, and at that moment, Dan didn't wish to stir the pot over what might be a non-issue.

While he was thinking about it, he asked, "Did you ever figure out what was causing your anxiety? You were taking that stuff when I first met you."

"I always thought it was from being around Jack. But that's over now. I should be feeling better. I wish I knew what to do."

Dan sat next to her on the couch and put his arm around her. "Mrs. Harper, you shot and almost killed a man. He would have done something awful to you, for sure, and that justifies what you did, but it still has had an effect on you. Give it time, give it time."

"I love you, Dan Harper. Nothing's going to happen to us now." She wrapped her arms around his neck and kissed him. "Have you thought about any names yet?"

"Yeah, in my sleep. Problem is, I can't remember what I dreamed when I wake up. Do you have any ideas?"

"I was thinking I liked the name, 'Henry,' like your dad. He needs a namesake. Would your brother approve?"

Dan sat up straight and almost shouted, "Aaron has no say in this matter. None at all!"

"Whoa, calm down! What brought that on?"

Dan was shocked at his own visceral response. There was now no way to hide what was weighing on his mind. He rubbed his eyes and said, "I had a long day. Aaron showed up with some papers and a crazy idea. He seems to think that one of us is adopted. I told him he was crazy."

Melissa looked at him carefully. "He seems to think, you say. Does he, or doesn't he? So, are you going to elaborate? What did he say that was so crazy?"

Dan went into detail about what Aaron and Jane had found among Henry's papers and personal items. Melissa listened carefully.

"Daniel Harper, your brother is no fool. Yes, I'm shocked. But if he has a reason to suspect this, you should at least listen to him."

"I did today for almost a solid hour. He's convinced. So, we decided to do DNA testing. I had Tricia order some kits for us to spit in."

"Spit?"

"That's what the sample consists of. Cells from the inside of the mouth will be in the sample and -"

"I get the picture. Spit? Really? Is that like 'Spittin' Image?" She almost laughed at her own words. Whose idea was it?"

"Tricia. She heard what we were talking about. I have to hand it to her; she comes up with good ideas."

"So, you both are going to do it?"

"Yeah, that would make sense, wouldn't it? To see if there's a match?"

"Will that tell you who the parents are?"

"Only if the parents submit a sample."

"Just think," she said with a grin. "Our baby could say, 'I don't know who my granddaddy is, but I'll bet I'm a spittin' image of him.'"

Dan grinned and felt the muscles in his neck loosen up. He kissed Melissa again and held it for a long time. She made him feel so complete.

Earlier, Aaron had arrived back in Kissimmee around mid-afternoon. Sally showed him the hymns the music director had picked out for Sunday. Andrew Frazier was his name, and the church knew him as 'Andy.' He had been the pianist at Osceola Presbyterian for longer than Aaron had been there. During the week, he wore a straw hat and played a smoking hot piano at Walt Disney World. Foreign travelers came from the four corners of the world for entertainment, and they were usually advised to seek out Andrew and get his autograph. Collectors in France and Japan were paying nice sums of money for anything with his autograph on it. He never considered his music to be a task. Yet, he remained humble and devoted to this small, humble church. Aaron often told him the worship services couldn't be what they were without him. Andy was someone Aaron could confide in.

They were sitting together with hymn books on their laps and came to a pause in the conversation. Aaron closed his book and looked at Andy.

"Andy, I have a question – no, never mind." The music director looked at him inquisitively. The trust that flowed between them prompted Aaron to continue. "Okay, let me ask you this. If you found out that one of your parents was really not your parent, how would you feel?"

Andrew looked closely at Aaron. "Strange question, but I guess some people have to face that once in a while." He scratched his chin. "I guess it would depend on the person. If it was me, it would be a whole new world opening up, and I would wonder why I had not been told earlier."

"But would you resent either of them for not telling you at a younger age?"

"I guess I would wonder why, but, no, I wouldn't resent them. I'd have a lot of questions, but I guess that eventually, my life would settle back down to an even pace like before."

"Really? That's all?"

"I guess so. You are who you are on your own merits, right? Our reality is what we have waiting for us each day when we get up and come home. That's what counts, I guess. As long as I have my family and a piano to plink on from day to day, I'm fine. Why? Is something going on?"

"No, I just needed to bounce that off someone else."

As Aaron walked back to his office, Andy watched him and told himself that even pastors have a personal life with family dynamics that no one knows about.

Aaron arrived home around dark with Andy's words still bouncing around in his head. He noticed the kitchen light, which usually shines all the way through the living room, was not on. Something about the sounds of his house was not the usual greeting. The kids were playing quietly, but Jane was not in the kitchen. She sat in the living room with several items spread out before her.

"Hey, honey, what's all this? What have you been doing today?"

She rubbed her eyes and looked up at him. "Digging in that last box and reading the journal. You and Dan have some work to do. Come see what I found."

He sat beside her and looked at the parts of the journal she had earmarked with sticky notes.

*March 14, 1989 – Alison has asked for time off to go to Europe.*

Two pages later:

*June 10, 1989 – Alison back at work.*

And three pages later:

*August 12, 1989 – Alison asks for more time off*

*August 19, 1989 – Alison wants a year away to be with her mother in Tampa.*

Aaron said quietly, "There's a lot of stuff in here about Alison."

Jane remarked, "I didn't see anything about her mother living in Tampa. In fact, there's no other mention of Alison's mother at all. Aaron, that note you saw about delivering flowers to *Christian Charities* was dated as 1990. Although we don't know the exact date, right?"

"Right, we don't. Was there any notation about Alison coming back from Tampa?"

"No, in fact, that's the last mention of her at all. I wonder if she really went to Tampa."

"Why would you question that?"

"It's the only mention of Tampa so far. It would make sense that she would have said something about her mother at an earlier time. But then, as I think about it, this isn't her journal, it's Henry's."

He nodded. "I guess I'm getting skeptical like my brother. What we have is a bunch of notes and dates, with a lot of partial information that leads to nothing."

Jane paused, moved closer to him, and looked at him with that look he had seen before when she had something profound to tell him. She posed her next question carefully. "Okay, have you ever heard of shadow printing from a copy machine that needs cleaning?"

"Shadow printing? Never heard of it."

"Sometimes the glass on a copy machine, particularly the old ones, if they are not cleaned regularly, will retain an image of what was just copied for a few seconds. You copy one side of a page, turn it over, and copy the second side, and you see a faint image of the first side, but as an overlay on the second side."

He sat back on the couch and pulled his shoes off. Her question sounded bizarre and out of context. "Can't say that I have. Sounds like something out of *Twilight Zone*."

She handed him a page from the adoption folder. "Look closely at this. Do you agree this is a photocopy?"

He nodded.

"And the redaction marks were made after it was copied?"

"I guess."

"You guess? They wouldn't go marking up an original document. They'd make a copy first and then mark up the copy, right?"

He nodded again.

"So, look again. Look between the lines that were copied. It's faint, I know, but it's there."

Aaron squinted and finally said, "I see something - yeah! I see it! But I can't read what it says. Looks like two words, and the first letter of each word is capitalized." He turned the page over a bit as he couldn't see it from the other side.

"Go in the bedroom," Jane said. Hold it up to the mirror. The image is backwards. Go ahead! Go look!"

Aaron hurried in his socks to get to the mirror. He held it up and leaned as close as he could. On the mirror, the faint image of a name - *Alison Burbidge* – appeared.

"Jane! Come look at this!" He turned and almost bumped into his wife, who was standing in the doorway.

"I know," she said. I saw it this afternoon and decided to wait for you to get home."

"Why is her name on any of these documents? What does she have to do with any of this?"

"I can think of only one reason. She took a long time off back in 1989. I found her expired passport in that last box. It was definitely hers. Aaron, she went to Switzerland, not Tampa. Henry took the time to mention it. I'll bet you she's the mother of whoever was being considered for adoption."

"But why Switzerland?"

"Hey, fella! Why does an unmarried pregnant woman go to Switzerland?"

Aaron's eyebrows began to rise. "To either have the baby and keep it a secret," he paused, "Or to terminate the pregnancy."

"She must have changed her mind on both counts."

"Jane, where is the registry book from Dad's funeral? I need to find a name, and I need your help locating someone. I don't remember the name, but I do remember she said she lived in Tampa. We've got to find that book."

# CHAPTER FIFTEEN

The week went by fast, and the DNA kits arrived. Aaron called Tricia, and she confirmed that Dan's had also arrived. He had decided against telling his brother about the shadow printing image, which would only give him another reason to argue against what only seemed to be strong intuition. Aaron filled both sample bottles that night and stuck them in the refrigerator. The next morning, he dropped them off at the post office, then called Tricia to confirm that Dan had done his as well.

"You may as well talk to him yourself, Pastor. You don't need me for a messenger every time you call."

"You're right. I just don't want to start any more arguments. I really thank you for your help, however."

"Okay, just don't make me come pull you two apart. I don't make a good fight referee. I'll send you both to your rooms with no supper." She laughed as only she could. "Let us know when you hear something."

At the end of the day, Aaron came home to find Jane, yet again, immersed in the contents of the last box. She glanced up at him with a look of slight guilt, like a child caught stealing a cookie.

"I haven't made any plans for supper," she said. "Sorry, I just got involved in this, and time got away from me. You okay with pizza tonight?"

Although he knew better than to emphasize it, Aaron saw Jane's occasional childish habits totally endearing. "That's fine with me. What did you find? Anything?"

"Not much. Just some old bank statements. Same bank your church uses. In one of his last years, your father was the king of internet orders. He bought all kinds of stuff. Bought it and then sent it all back."

"Like what?"

"Here's a bird feeder. That's twenty-nine dollars. How about a kitchen spatula? Seven dollars."

"I could see how he would want a spatula. He tried to cook."

"How about dining room place settings? Enough for twelve."

"Geez! But on the bank statements, does it say what the items were?"

"No, but the transaction number is there, and it doesn't take a genius to look it up on Amazon."

"Depends on how you define 'genius.' Let me look at those statements."

286

She handed the bank statements to him, and the first page showed an automatic withdrawal by the bank for a security portal.

"Security portal. What's that?"

Jane looked at the sheet. "Yes, I saw that, too. I was going to ask you about it."

"I never heard of such a thing. Security portal in a bank. Sounds like something out of a science fiction novel."

Jane was already ahead of Aaron. She had the bank's webpage on her screen and was looking at additional features the bank offered. "Here it is," she said. "The page says, 'Protect your valuables and documents with our *Security Portal* safe boxes for a reasonable annual fee.' Aaron, your father had a safety deposit box. *Security Portal* is just a fancy name the bank put on it. Sounds like a marketing gimmick."

"When was the annual fee last paid?"

She looked closer at the page and said, "Eight months ago. So, it's still an active rent. I wonder - "

"Yeah, what's in it?"

The following morning, Jane and Aaron were both at the bank's entrance when it opened. They carried the package of bank statements with them in a folder along with Henry's death certificate. The teller listened and directed them to an empty office where they could make their case to an assistant manager.

"Pastor Aaron, good to meet you." Through the door came a young man in his mid-twenties with a pencil-line mustache. The nameplate on the desk read 'Derek Middleton.' "We haven't met, but I know of your church and your father's untimely death."

"Thanks, but it was hardly untimely."

"Sorry, just a memorized phrase. I didn't mean to be insensitive." He sat behind the desk and asked, "So, what can we do for you on this wonderful morning?" His face was frozen in a plastic smile.

They both started to speak at once and Derek looked back and forth rapidly between the two of them.

"Sorry," said Jane. "Go ahead, Aaron."

"What we have here are bank statements belonging to my father, and it seems to indicate that he has a safety deposit box here."

"And you want to open it. I see."

The look of skepticism on his face caused Jane and Aaron to wonder what the rest of this day would be like.

"What else do you have? I mean, everyone knows he died, but do you have something more official, something that allows you access to the contents?  Are you the only offspring?  We can't be too careful in these matters."

"The bank statements aren't enough?" Aaron asked.  "I had control of his account."

"Accounts are one thing.  This is something entirely different.  Furthermore, bank statements don't give us the cause or mechanism of death.  I remember once, we had a case - "

"I have the death certificate if you care to make a copy of it," Aaron said firmly.

Aaron handed the document to the assistant manager and felt a glare coming over his face.

"This says the cause of death was failure to thrive.  That could mean anything."

Even Jane noticed her husband, usually a quiet, patient man, beginning to steam.  He opened his mouth to speak, and another man popped into the office.  To Aaron's relief, it was John Pleasance, a familiar face on Sundays at church.

"Hey, Pastor!  What brings you here?  Jane! Didn't see you there.  How's everyone?"

Derek Middleton was visibly irritated at the interruption.  "We were just going over a request with the Harpers.  Be done in a minute."

John quickly evaluated the scene in front of him and said, "Aaron Harper has power of attorney over his dad's assets.  I think that includes the safety deposit box. In fact, I'm sure it's mentioned in the document."

"Well, I need to see it first. If the board finds out…"

"Derek, why don't you go get a cup of coffee? I'll take care of these folks." He turned to look at Jane and Aaron. "So, what kind of day are you having?"

The younger man stood silently, then left. He made sure the door was closed, but he did so with a bit more firmness than was needed.

John sat down behind the desk and silently looked at them both with a sly smile. "I know why you're here. I was expecting you to come in at some point, and I wanted to be the one to help you. I just didn't know when. I guess I could have told you about the box ahead of time, but you had a lot on your mind. You've already closed your dad's checking account. There's only one thing left that connects him to this bank, and that's why you're here. Hang on, I'll be right back."

Five minutes later, John was back with a large metal box. He placed it on the table along with an empty plastic bag bearing the bank's logo. "Don't worry about Derek. We gave him the job because his dad is on the board of directors." He looked at them both and said, "So, I think you might need a bag or something to carry home all that's in here."

"You talk like you know what's in there," Jane asked.

"Pastor, your wife is very perceptive. Henry and I go way back in time. A time before, he married Evelyn. A time before, well, you'll see. At any rate, he and I were best buddies, and we made a pact about the contents of this box. I suggest you take it all and go home. Don't sort through it here."

Everything in the box was either in envelopes of various sizes or in plastic bags. It took a few minutes to fit all the contents into the bank bag John gave them. It was so tempting to look at the items as they were transferred out of the box, and twice, Aaron gave in to that temptation to stop and look at something intriguing to the point that Jane reminded him what they were trying to do. A bit bewildered, Aaron and Jane walked to their car with an undisclosed amount of mysterious treasure. Neither said a word until they returned home and were safely inside.

In the dining room, Aaron pushed the remaining worn-out box from Henry's apartment over to a corner. They sat across from each other at the table. Each reached into the bag and started pulling out papers and notes, one at a time. Jane spoke first.

"What's a DD Form 214? I've never seen something like this."

"Let me see. Oh, I know, this is a discharge form from the military. Military? Dad never mentioned the military. U.S. Army?"

"Okay, set it aside, and we'll come back to it. Wait, here's some more military stuff. It says, 'Permanent Change of Station' and then a number. The date is November 15, 1958. Oh, geez! On the back, it's stamped 'Top Secret.' Aaron, what do we have here?"

"This is too much. Is his name on it?"

"No. Just a personal serial number. Do you know if this was your dad's military serial number?"

"How could I? I didn't know he was in the military."

"Go back and look at that form, that DD 214, or whatever it is."

"Yeah, here it is! It matches! Same number on both forms. But there's no location listed on either one."

Aaron pulled out a small silver object the size of a matchbox. "And what's this? A cigarette lighter? Dad didn't smoke, did he? There's something inscribed on it. It's faded, but looks like it says, '6913th RSM, Bremerhaven.' Germany? Was Dad in Germany?"

"I don't know. Maybe some old buddy had been there."

"Jane, if we had known this, we could have had a military funeral for him. I think he would have liked that." He threw his hands up and said, "Too late now."

Jane barely heard what he said. "Wait, here's some letters. The stamps are German. It's addressed to your dad at a residence in St. Cloud, just a few miles from here. The return address is smeared. Looks like it got wet or something."

"Yeah, he lived in St. Cloud during his younger years. What's the date on the postmark?"

"I can't read the whole date, but the year is 1963. Aaron, these things are really old!"

Aaron carefully opened the unsealed envelope and pulled out the letter. The whole text of the letter was handwritten in German. But he noticed the greeting contained the name 'Henry.' He looked at the closing, and all it said was 'Helga.' *Who is Helga?* he thought.

"Look, there's more letters! German, all in German! Did my dad speak German? What the hell is this crap? Who is Helga?"

"Careful, preacher. You're starting to sound a little like your brother. Let's keep digging."

"Wait a second. Here's one with a postmark from Switzerland. The date is 1989. It's addressed to Harper's Gardens. But look! The letter inside is written in German, just like the others."

"Who's it from?"

"I don't know.  But the handwriting resembles that of the earlier letters, the ones written in German.  And it looks like the last page is missing."

As they gazed at each other in amazement, the phone rang.  Jane picked it up, and Aaron heard her say, "Yes, John.  He's right here."

Aaron looked at Jane quizzically as he took the phone and was surprised to hear John Pleasance's voice.  Twice in one day.  "Pastor, have you looked in the bag?  Do you want some help?  I told you I knew what was in it."

"Ah, yes, we are at a loss here.  Can you help?"

All he heard was a slow chuckle and a voice that said, "I'll be right over.  Put the coffee pot on."

John arrived thirty minutes later while Aaron paced the floor, waiting.  He greeted the man at the front door like John was a house-call doctor coming to look at a sick child.  Jane was a bit calmer.

"John, how do you like your coffee?"

"Just black, please."  He turned to Aaron and said, "Now, what have you looked at so far?"

Aaron could barely control his eagerness.  "First of all, why does my dad have a discharge form from the military?"

"Because he was in the military, wouldn't you say?"

"I thought you knew."

"Just pulling your leg, young man. Yes, he did a tour in the military before he met and married Evelyn. We both were stationed together. What else you got?"

"Lots of references to Germany. Even a cigarette lighter."

"Your dad never smoked that I knew of. Let's see it."

Aaron fished out the lighter and handed it to John. He turned it over and around, pulled the insert out, and smelled it. "The inside's dry. Never had fluid put in it. And here's the inscription." He looked closer and mumbled, "Well, I'll be damned."

"What? What's so important about that inscription?"

"Your dad and I were both in the Army back in the late '50s and early '60s. But this inscription is that of an Air Force unit we were assigned to in Bremerhaven. That's right on the North Sea, where the winters are cold as well digger's butt in Idaho. Bremerhaven was a tri-service base. Army, Navy, Air Force. We were both in Army intelligence, but they attached us to this Air Force unit because they had all the communications equipment we needed. You see the initials, 'RSM'? That's Radio Squadron Mobile. They had more electronic stuff than you can imagine, and it was all on wheels. They could do air traffic control at remote outposts, they could do forward air control, and they let us play with their toys when we needed to."

"Like how?"

"Oh, like sitting at a teletype and watching messages about Gary Powers and his U2 getting shot out of the sky."

"Geeze! My dad was that close to that stuff?"

"Yeah, we had access to it, and that's the reason we rarely ever wore uniforms. We spent most of our time in German ratskellers and on street corners. We learned to nurse the same beer mug for hours while listening to the locals loosen their tongues and drop crumbs of information that we could piece together."

Aaron interrupted the direction of the conversation. "John, I have the sense that you have known more than you've admitted to for a long time. I must say, you've done a great job staying hidden in plain sight all along."

John made an exaggerated motion with his arms in the air. "Yeah, real cloak and dagger stuff. Ha! In your dreams, Pastor! In your dreams. Let's get back to the subject at hand."

Aaron was still not satisfied with John's answer, but he pressed on. "Okay, you've explained why he was over there. But these letters, who are they from?"

"You have letters from someone?" John glanced through several of them. "Oh, these are probably from Helga." He stopped and smiled. "Yes, that's who this is. She was our contact for a lot of what we learned and reported. I lost track of her after we shipped back home and got out. By the way, all this stuff I'm telling you is obsolete information, so don't worry about the Secret Service knocking on your door."

"Helga? How old was she? Young woman, older woman?"

"Young, bright, pretty. Your dad thought the world of her."

"And you don't know where she is now?"

"It's a big world, my friend, a big world with lots of possibilities. What else you got there?"

While the two men talked, Jane went through some of the remaining content. She pulled out something with letterhead from the State Department. It wasn't clear at first, but it appeared to be a visa application. She handed it to Aaron. He scanned it quickly, looked at her, and shrugged. She pointed to a name in the lower corner and his eyes fixed on the clearly typed name, 'Helga.' He looked at John and asked, "Was 'Helga Röder' her full name?"

At this point, John Pleasance had been enjoying the nostalgic trip back in time, thinking of younger days and high adventure. When Aaron mentioned the name 'Helga Röder,' he stopped daydreaming and sat up like someone had just shaken him awake from a make-believe fantasy world and thrust him back into reality.

"Let me see that." He studied it for almost a full minute and finally said slowly, "Yes, I knew she had plans to come here. She said she was going to try. Henry didn't believe she would. The State Department probably helped for her own safety. She was very resourceful. She came looking for your dad and found him – married to Evelyn. I wonder where she is now?"

Aaron was confused. "Wait a minute! You say she found him?"

"Umm..."

"Safety?" Jane was now more intrigued than Aaron.

John continued, "Well, she got a lot of information for us out of East Germany. She helped a group of people escape, including herself, and worked for us as we intercepted messages from the bad guys. She helped us decipher what was the truth and what was intentionally misleading. And the East German government had embedded contacts on the Western side. Contacts that just blended in without anyone knowing who they were. Helga's work was like skating on thin ice most of the time, but she never quit. Amazing young woman.

"Before we met her, there was a time when her friend, Anna Richter, came up with a plan to get Helga and her two cousins across the border. It was December of 1960, the Berlin Wall wasn't up yet, and Anna was very instrumental in creating a diversion. She worked for the utility company and found out what relay station supplied the lighting for the section of the wall that was undergoing repairs. She had Helga and her cousins hiding in the shadows while she went into the relay station and disabled one of the transformers, putting the whole neighborhood in the dark. In the process of doing that, she came in contact with a high-voltage line and had severe burns on her hand. Anyway, they took advantage of the darkness, made their way through the barricades, and Henry and I were waiting for them. From there, we took them to Bremerhaven. I took a liking to Anna, but your dad couldn't get enough of seeing Helga."

"So, once they were in the American zone, why were they in any danger?"

John had a distant look on his face, then a frown, recalling crucial events. "In the process of escaping, she encountered an East German guard who was about to draw a bead on her fleeing cousins with an AK-47. She clobbered him with a brick, took his gun, and pumped a single round between his eyes. Your dad and I were the only people she told that to. But the bad guys figured out who had escaped, and they drew their own conclusions. Furthermore, Helga's job was intercepting messages, translating them, and sending her report to Henry. She had a code name, and it changed every week. One day, she inadvertently signed a report with her real name and transmitted it. Two days later, East German agents tried to come onto the base. After we interrogated them, we knew they were looking for Helga, and they had multiple reasons for wanting her."

Jane and Aaron sat mesmerized by the story John was telling them. "So, what did you do to protect her?"

"We transferred her to a post in the British zone for three months where she would be harder to find. Henry found all kinds of excuses to go see her."

Aaron interrupted John, "This is all so incredible. This kind of stuff only happens in spy movies. So why didn't he bring her back to the States?"

"She was a loyal German. She wanted to come here, but she also wanted to help remodel her country into something to be proud of. Henry hated to go home and leave her there, but he did. Remember, he hadn't met Evelyn yet."

The remaining contents in Henry's safety deposit box simply amplified the information John had already given them. Why had his father never mentioned any of this? The Iron Curtain was a real issue back in the years his dad had served, but who knows why some people bury the past like a bad dream?

John was in the process of saying goodbye, and Jane disappeared back into the dining room.  When she came out, John was gone, and she had the visitors' registry book from the funeral home in her hands.  "You were looking for this?"

Aaron was still trying to connect all of this information if there was any connection at all.  He tried to think back to the time of day when various people had come in for the final viewing of Henry's casket.  With a rough idea in his head, he started flipping pages and then stopped.  There was only one 'Cynthia' listed in the entire book.

"Jane, you said you could find people on the computer.  Can you look for this woman who lives in Tampa?"  His finger pointed to the hand-written signature of 'Cynthia Kramer.'  From outside, they both heard the familiar noise of the mail delivery truck stopping at each residence.  Jane walked out to the curb to meet it.

"Shouldn't you be at work?" she asked Aaron when she came back in.  "Oh look, the DNA results came in."

"Okay, I'll look at them later.  I have a meeting at the church in – my gosh! Fifteen minutes!  I have to hit the road.  Bye!"

He grabbed his jacket and car keys and was out the door. By the time he arrived at the church, he noticed there were several cars in the lot, many of which he recognized as belonging to the church elders. It was a Session meeting of elders, and he had completely forgotten about it. He noticed John Pleasance was there, and he acted like he was seeing Aaron for the first time that day. The group assembled in the conference room and made short orders of the business at hand. Aaron decided to stay a while longer to confer with Andrew Frazier, the pianist, who, in Aaron's absence, had made his own musical choices next for Sunday. At that moment, Aaron was beginning to feel overwhelmed between balancing church duties with new discoveries in family life.

He was about to walk into the library to look for a reference book when Sally Butterfield said there was a call for him.

He half shouted from the hallway, "Who is it, Sally?"

She yelled back, "It's from your brother's office in Ocala. He sounds excited about something."

Aaron hurried around the corner and took the phone that Sally was holding out to him.

"Hey, what's up?"

"Aaron, did you get your DNA results? Man, I can't believe this! You gotta' see this!"

"Dan, slow down.  What are you talking about?"

"Aaron Harper, I take back everything I said about you and your silly DNA tests.  This is some weird shit!"

"Okay, okay.  Start from the beginning.  What does it say?"

Dan was almost shouting into the phone.  "It says that you and I are half-siblings!  Can you believe that?"

Aaron took a moment to digest what his brother had just said.  "What?  Dan, how can that be?  We have the same parents.  Everybody knows that."

"Do we?  What was all that adoption crap you were talking about?  Remember?  That's why we did these stupid tests to begin with.  And listen to this – I got results back from both test labs, and they both say the same thing!  Half-siblings!  Can you believe this shit?"

"What else does it say?  Does it mention any other relatives?"

"Just cousins and so forth.  Only people who have used the testing service.  And I didn't see any unfamiliar names."  He stopped and caught his breath.  "But can you believe it?  Half-siblings!  You need to go home and read yours.  Maybe it's a big mistake.  Labs make mistakes, you know."

"I don't know about that, Dan.  Two independent labs?  Same results?  I have some church business to finish up here, and I'll go back home. I'll call you this evening."

He slowly hung up the phone and felt like he was in someone else's dream world. This can't be true! It was just too much information for one day. Try as he may, he couldn't concentrate on church business. He stood at the office window and looked at the Spanish moss hanging from the oak trees, swaying in the breeze. Was he in the same world as everything he saw outside that window? Was anything he saw or touched real? A mood of otherworldliness slowly crept over him. What else did he not know about who he was, who Dan was, who anybody was? What information could he trust? Why had his father or mother kept such a secret? He noticed that Sally passed by his open door several times and quickly peeked in to check on him. Finally, he got up and shut the door.

An hour passed, and he decided to take a break. Where was Sunday's worship plan he had been working on? Did he print it out? He couldn't remember. Maybe it was still in a folder. A budget sheet caught his attention. What was that item someone had asked him about? His mind was a jumble.

He rose from his desk and left without saying goodbye to Sally. As he approached his car, Sally looked out the window at him, picked up the phone and entered a number.

"Jane, he's on his way home.  He seems to have a lot on his mind.  God bless him."

# CHAPTER SIXTEEN

Jane met him at the door, lab results in her hands. She started to speak but could only look at her husband's face and realize how much she loved him. The look of near-emotional exhaustion was clearly evident. His eyes were red and darting, and his breathing came in short huffs and puffs. She cupped his face in her hands and let the language of her own eyes speak to him. He was home. He was loved; he was not lied to or abandoned.

All he could think about was what his brother had told him. And yet, it opened a whole new batch of questions that may never be answered.

"Aaron, you need to sit down, gather your wits about you, and let's go over this. Who have you been talking to?"

"My brother. He got his results in." Aaron caught himself staring off into space, then looked at Jane and continued, "He says we are half-siblings. I don't know what to say now. This is just too much for one day. We have one parent in common. We have the same father or the same mother. What in God's name is this all about?"

Jane held up a small, folded group of pages. "These are your DNA results. We got them in two separate envelopes from both labs. It's just - "

"I know. Dan got his results today, too. It's unbelievable, and it creates so many new questions, especially having seen those adoption papers we found. What do they mean?"

Jane measured her next words carefully. Looking straight at him, she said, "Hey - you're repeating yourself. You need to stop talking and listen to me. Look at your results. There is a similarity to Dan's but with one big difference. Here, look at what it says."

His eyes darted all over the pages until Jane directed his attention to the paragraph about siblings.

"Yes, I see here. It says I have half-siblings. It says – what? More than one? I have two half-siblings? How can that be?"

Jane gently pointed out what Aaron could not see through the emotional fog. "You both have the same father. Dan has one half-sibling, that's you. You have two half-siblings. It says here that Dan is one, and the other one is not listed. But someone out there has turned in a sample and withheld the name. Whoever that is now has your name."

Shock would not describe Aaron's state of mind. It was totally foreign to him. It was as strange as looking in a mirror and seeing a different face.

Aaron's voice could be heard a block away. "Stop! I can't think about this anymore! I don't want to think about it! Damn you, Henry!"

Aaron looked up in time to see his own two children peeking around the corner, then retreating to the safety of their own domicile where everything was safe, understandable, believable, dependable. He started to follow them to their room, and Jane stopped him.

"Hey, just let them go. Tomorrow, they'll barely remember what they just heard. Kids are funny that way. They know how to filter out the bad stuff. Maybe that's what you need to do."

"Bad stuff? Bad stuff? I can't change the past. What's done is done. Now, I just need to re-calibrate my thinking. It's a whole new paradigm for me."

"Tell me, Pastor. Is who you are today based on who your parents were or were not? What would you tell a parishioner who came to you with the same story?"

"Jane, not now. Don't throw this back in my lap. It almost makes me think this whole thing is my fault. It's not!"

"That's right, it's not, and you are not a victim. And you won't see that until it's right there in front of you. I know you too well. That's why I'm throwing it back at you. You need to look at it through a different lens. I've heard you say that in your sermons. Homiletics, you called it. A lens through which you see the truth in love. Those are your words, my dear."

Aaron went through the rest of the week in a fog. He told Sally to double-check everything he wrote and certainly everything he signed. Appointments came and went, and all seemed to run together. In the evenings, he gave his children just token attention, and his wife could not find anything to divert his thoughts away from what had imprisoned him. As Sunday approached, he retrieved an old sermon that seemed to work the last time he preached it. For the first time in his career, he approached the pulpit unsure of what he was going to say.

Andy played a magnificent prelude, and Aaron welcomed everyone to the service. All the steps of the liturgy were falling into place, and he was about to start his sermon when he looked up and saw a few stragglers coming in, including a young woman who entered quietly and found a seat in the rear. He had his reading glasses on and could not focus well on any of the faces, especially those in the very rear of the sanctuary. But the sermon took on a life of its own, and he fell into his usual speaking rhythm. Feeling more comfortable, he switched glasses, and the faces came to him in sharp focus. Sitting in the back row was a woman named Cynthia Kramer. Jane had found her name on the computer, but the address and phone number were unlisted. He realized he had paused, and people were beginning to shuffle their feet and look distracted.

The service was finally finished, and he walked in front of the podium to give the benediction and a parting prayer. When he opened his eyes and raised his head, she was gone. His first impulse was to run down the aisle, but he restrained himself. As he walked toward the door, the ushers stood by, and he asked, "Where did she go?"

One man said, "Who? That young lady? She left in a bit of a hurry. I didn't see which way she went."

Aaron almost felt like crying. Who was she really? Why had she come here? The usual line of parishioners formed to exit the building and to bestow Pastor Aaron with their best wishes and private commentaries. Try as he could, he could not invoke his gift of listening as he usually did. The notion of Cynthia Kramer, with all the possible answers she may have, lay just outside of his reach. But then, he realized he must remain objective and fully accept the possibility that her presence could mean absolutely nothing, and his dilemma may continue on with her fading into the background.

Clara Bench approached him, and Aaron was expecting the usual story about her daughter in New York. She shook his hand, looked at him intently, and said, "I've been on this earth long enough to notice when someone is troubled. Pastor, whatever is on your mind, I pray God will take you by the hand and give you peace."

Her words caught him by surprise. After a moment, he gently reached down and gave her a soft hug. She wiped her eyes, smiled, and she left.

The last of the well-wishers and gossip merchants came and went, and Aaron re-entered the building to go to his office. The hallway was crowded with people, and he remembered there was a potluck lunch planned for that day. That meant he was obligated to remain there at least until the meal was blessed and afterwards for as long as it seemed necessary. He was trying to read the mood of the crowd as they migrated into the dining room. There was a low hum of voices and clinking of plates and utensils. What he needed was a moment, just a moment, to collect his thoughts and redirect his presence toward being a pastor despite all the background thoughts and images running through his head. If his distress was obvious enough for Clara to notice, then others would also. Hypocrisy or not, he had to show a stoic image to his parishioners. Right now, he needed the haven of his office where he could breathe deeply and put on a happy face. He found himself on the far side of the room from the hallway, which meant he had to wade through the crowd to get back to the office. As he looked in that direction, he saw Cynthia Kramer walking down the hall and leaving by way of the side door. She must have come back into the building through the kitchen entrance while he was still greeting people on the front sidewalk. Over the incoming tide of voices, he knew he could not get her attention, nor could he make his way through the crowd fast enough to intercept her.

A minute later, he was standing outside his office door, still trying to process all that had happened. He stepped through the door and sat behind his desk. There on the keyboard of his computer was a note written in beautiful, flowing penmanship. It said:

"As I told you at the funeral, my mother is not doing well. Time is running short." The note finished with an address and a phone number. There was no signature.

Looking for an escape route, he noticed only a handful of people on the front sidewalk. He gathered up his briefcase and laptop, walked out the side entrance and around the building to the parking lot. The Miata brought him home quickly. Jane saw him pull in and came into the living room with a dishtowel in her hands.

"How was the potluck? Did you eat?" Aaron's face told her that his mind was somewhere else. Patiently, she walked to the couch and sat next to him. He pulled the note from his shirt pocket and handed it to her.

"This is all that I know. It's like she's reading our minds and handing out clues in small bits. I don't get it. This is one big innuendo, but nothing concrete."

"Maybe she's as unsure as you are. Did you think of that?"

"Jane, there have been times in the past few days that I feel like I'm dreaming. I need a pinch or something to tell me this is real."

She left Aaron sitting on the couch with his own thoughts. With her children, she gives tender care to skinned knees and hurt feelings. It comes natural to her, and she's good at it. How hard for the mother of two kids to realize there are some things in her husband's life that she cannot fix? An hour went by, and Aaron was still sitting on the couch. A thought occurred to her, and she gave herself adequate time to consider it. Quietly, she approached Aaron and sat beside him.

"Hey, preacher, I think you have a job to do, and you're dreading it."

He turned and looked at her with vacant eyes. He said nothing, but the look in his eyes told her he was listening.

"You have a task to do, and you see it as painful. It's not. I think you can recall your scriptures and remember so many people who had really painful tasks ahead of them. And they found the faith and courage to do it. You get my drift? What you need to do is nothing compared to what they did." She put her fingers on his chin and turned his face toward her. "Hey, look at me. Are you listening?"

A moment passed, and he said with a quiver in his voice, "Yeah, I hear you. I have that Tampa address, and I'll go there tomorrow."

"Yes, you will, and I'm coming with you. There's no way you are walking into this alone. Call first."

The rest of the evening went without any discussion of family, of Tampa, of lab results, of responsibility. That night, Jane heard Aaron get out of bed around 2 AM. She peeked through the bedroom door and saw him sitting, alone on the living room couch. Two hours later, he came back to bed.

# CHAPTER SEVENTEEN

The kids were staying with a neighbor. Cynthia Kramer had expected them, and the phone call she received to break the ice was well-timed. The address in Tampa was on Palm Court, just a stone's throw from MacDill Air Force Base. Jane and Aaron had left before the sun peaked over the horizon, and they arrived on Palm Court around 9 O'clock. It was a small frame house with one sickly, small tree in the front yard and an open carport, just like all the others on that street that were built in the late 40's early 50s. The siding was old, faded, and cracked at the corners. Attached to the porch post was a small American flag on a rusty flagpole. The yard had numerous bare spots. Three small children were playing in the front yard next door. Cynthia met them at the door before they could knock. Aaron immediately remembered her from the funeral. She was dressed more casually than the last time he had seen her, but the sparkle in her blue eyes and the carefree curls of blonde hair were the same.

"It is so nice of you to come to check on my mother, Pastor. She had been close to your family, as you know, and she regretted losing touch with them after so long a time."

Aaron felt a twinge of guilt as Cynthia talked. They had used the initial excuse of visiting because Cynthia had said her mother was not doing well and, after all, her mother had, indeed, been a friend of the family for so many years. On the surface, it had all the appearance of a social call. But Cynthia had her own lab results, knew the real reason for the visit and had the fortitude to let Aaron and Jane take the lead in the conversation.

"Was your drive here a pleasant one?" she asked politely. "Traffic on the Tampa highway can be brutal sometimes."

Aaron cleared his throat and started to speak, but Jane interrupted him. "Cynthia, we want to thank you for allowing us to visit. This has been an eventful few weeks for us. Henry Harper left behind a large collection of personal information that needs to be brought out into the open."

"By the looks of the crowd at his funeral, he must have been a very popular man."

Aaron remarked, "Yes, popular and with a history of mysterious facts that my brother and I were unaware of. That is, until recently. He was a packrat apparently who never threw anything away."

"You have a brother?"

"Yes, his name is Daniel. He lives in Ocala. Dan usually takes the high road on things of emotional entanglement, but I think he now has a deep desire to find out where all this family history is leading."

"Perhaps you should start at the beginning."

Aaron glanced at his wife, took a deep breath, and started by asking, "Have you ever heard of an agency called Christian Charities?"

Thirty minutes later, he stopped and watched Cynthia closely to see if she grasped everything he had told her. Apparently, she had.

"And that prompted you to do the DNA testing?"

Aaron hesitated, then answered, "Yes, in a roundabout way, and we are not the type of people who ignore family ties, no matter what the circumstances are." He stopped and let that sink in. "And you need to know, we are not here to intrude or violate your privacy in any way. To the extent that you feel comfortable, I think it would be best if you now tell us what you know."

Cynthia clasped her hands together on her lap and cleared her throat. "My mother is from Germany. She came to this country under mysterious circumstances, which I still do not understand. I am twenty-seven years old, still single, taking care of her, and she has never told me her full story. It's always been a vague, cloudy thing that hung between us. There was a time when I asked her if she had a birth certificate, and she showed it to me. It has her maiden name and date of birth, but it was issued by the U.S. State Department. I have friends who were stationed overseas, and they tell me that American babies who are born abroad are issued a birth certificate from the State Department. She was not born to American parents. She's German and a naturalized citizen. Why would she have a State Department certificate of birth?"

Aaron inquired, "Did you ask her?"

"I have been afraid to ask for too many details about that time in her life. I tried once and found only a cold, stone wall."

Jane was thinking clearly. "What was the date of issue on her State Department certificate?"

Cynthia thought for a few seconds and said, "I believe it was around 1991. I can get it if you like."

Aaron replied, "That's okay. Do you happen to remember what her maiden name was?"

"Her name was Burbidge, Alison Burbidge."

Aaron felt like he had stepped off a cliff. When he could gather his thoughts, he looked at Jane, then at Cynthia. "Yes, we know of that name. Now, it makes sense. Well, almost."

Jane chimed in and said, "I'm sure she has reasons to hold her past to herself."

To this, Cynthia replied, "And I have the sense that you know more than I do. I feel so lost in all of this."

Jane spoke softly, "We've been going through a similar frame of mind these last few days. When did you get your DNA results back?"

"Three weeks ago. It was just a fun thing to do, and I was hoping to find some German connections. I did not use the option of letting people know who I was in case any odd connections popped up, and I could deal with them on my terms. I'm so glad you chose to reveal your name." She ended with a nervous laugh.

Aaron asked abruptly, "Does your mother know about the lab work?"

"No. I haven't told her, and I'm not sure I will."

"Why not?"

"I think she will tell me what she wants me to know when she feels like telling me. She might see this as an effort on my part to go places she wants kept private."

"And your father? Or is that a sensitive question?"

"No, not at all. Joseph Kramer passed away five years ago. He didn't leave much for Mom to live on. I moved in with her and took over running the house, which, you can see, isn't much. At least it's paid for."

"How do you manage to do shopping? Just leave her by herself?"

"What choice do I have? I can't depend on the neighbors, not in this neighborhood. Nice folks, but they all have problems of their own."

Aaron rubbed his eyes and asked gently, "So, I guess the last question is, 'Where is she?' Is she here?"

"She was sleeping when you arrived. Let me go see if she's awake. Would you like some coffee to sip while I tend to her? It's already made."

They both agreed to the offer and sat in the living room while Cynthia went into her mother's bedroom. They could hear her softly speaking from down the hallway, but the words were not discernible, perhaps not in the English language. Aaron and Jane both looked around the room, silently reading each other's minds. The living room was small, like the rest of the house. The furniture was modest, similar to what could be bought as used items from a rental agency. Or it could be just old and in need of replacement. On one end table was a picture of a young woman, a copy of the framed picture he had seen in Henry's apartment. Although he had not noticed it at first, he began to see that the entire living room had small hints of macramé. The doilies on the end tables were fringed with macramé, as were the edges of the lampshades. The curtain tie-back strips showed someone's handy work with that form of art. He whispered to Jane, "The person who made Knobby lives in this house and has been here for a long time."

"Knobby?"

"Adam's knobby. Remember the doll?"

Aaron could see into the kitchen and clearly recognized mismatched asbestos tile flooring with signs of wear in the center, the heavily trafficked areas. The kitchen chairs were early 60's vintage with plastic seats and chrome legs. He was about to go into the kitchen to look closer when he heard Cynthia clearing her throat in the hallway.

"She's awake. I took her into the bathroom, and she's back in bed now, all propped up and ready to receive guests." She gently motioned toward the hallway and said, "Come this way, please."

The bedroom walls were covered by pink, muted floral wallpaper with a blue border near the ceiling. Jane saw several corners were loose and starting to peel. The bed's headboard was dark veneer with cracks at the edges. Two small lamps on bedside tables, one on each side, gave soft illumination to the head of the bed, and the foot was in faint shadows. A small dresser and mirror were on the opposite wall, and she noticed the drawers were crooked and cracked. Alison's hair was grey and beginning to thin in the front. She was wearing a dark maroon housecoat with the logo of the Tampa Bay Buccaneers on the left shoulder. The bedspread was thin, pale yellow, and pulled up to within inches of her neck. The blue veins in her hands were prominent and corded like tree roots under a thin vellum of skin.

Cynthia spoke first. "Mama, these folks are here to see how you're doing. Can you see them?" She turned to Jane and Aaron and said, "I don't know which is worse, her sight or her hearing." Then she repeated a little louder, "They're here from Kissimmee. They came to see how you're doing. This is Aaron. Aaron Harper. Do you remember him from the time you lived in Kissimmee?"

Aaron stepped closer and reached out his hand. She clutched it, trembling, and her eyes moistened as she explored every detail of his face. Her voice was weak and raspy. The words came slowly with labored breathing. "Yes, I remember you. You used to play in the pansies. You've grown up so much now. You always looked after your little brother."

Aaron could not stop the tears. He released her hand, backed away, and turned to face the door. Jane walked to the bed and took her other hand. "Alison, my name is Jane. I'm Aaron's wife."

She looked at Cynthia with a puzzled expression. "He's married?"

Jane responded, "Yes, and we have two little boys."

Her response was a muffled mumble. Her eyes drifted away from Jane and toward the door where Aaron was standing. She tried to sit up but struggled.

"Aaron, I think she wants to talk to you," Jane said.

Approaching her bed and wiping his face with bare hands, he saw her looking at him through cloudy eyes and slowly reaching up with both arms. He took her hands in his, then bent down toward her, and she hugged her son for the first time in decades. Then she settled back and said, "Please say hello to Henry for me." It was almost more than Aaron could bear to hear. He lifted her hands again and kissed them both gently, and she smiled.

"I will tell Henry you were asking about him." He looked at Jane, and they both left the room.

After a few minutes, Cynthia joined them in the living room. She was wiping her eyes along with Jane and Aaron. The three of them sat in silence for a full minute.

Cynthia finally broke the stillness and said, "This was a very special day for her."

Jane asked, "Do you think she knew who we were?"

"I think she had a glimmer of the truth. Before I turned the light out, she said, 'Tell Henry it's okay.' And I suppose you know what she's talking about."

Aaron said, "I can only guess." He looked at Cynthia intently. "I was wondering, what does she need? Better yet, what do you need?"

"We're okay. We're living on her Social Security checks, and I work from home for an advertising agency. I have a certification in graphic design. It brings in enough, I guess."

"But the time is coming when she's going to need more than you can provide. Something like skilled nursing care or hospice."

Cynthia shrugged. "In a perfect world, that would be nice. But that's not the case, is it?"

Aaron looked at Jane and she turned her head to an angle like she always does when she's thinking. Cynthia was perceptive and quickly said, "Oh, no. Not what you're thinking. No, we're okay. We don't need help. Perhaps another visit would be nice, however."

Aaron lifted the framed picture from the end table. He asked Cynthia, "Who is this?"

"That's her. Look on the back. The photo studio is in Germany." He looked, and it was a name he couldn't pronounce, but he clearly recognized the word, 'Bremerhaven.'

With a few more polite comments and words of appreciation in both directions, they left and got into their car. Jane fastened her seatbelt and saw Aaron with his forehead resting on the steering wheel. His lips were barely moving, but she heard no words coming forth. After a minute or so, he took a deep breath and looked at Jane like he had just seen the burning bush.

"What's wrong?"

"Did you see what else was on the back of that picture? There was a name – 'Helga.'" He spoke with his eyes closed. "I don't know what I am supposed to think. Should I be happy? Sad? Angry? I don't know. Let's go home. I have a lot to think about. There're still so many unanswered questions."

Two hours later, Jane dropped Aaron off at the church. Sally had a pile of work on his desk that was calling out to him and demanding priority. The Presbytery office needed an annual report, which was due in a week. He normally started on such things about a month ahead of time, but that kind of proactive planning was nowhere to be found this time. He had been giving Sally bits and pieces of the personal issues at hand, and she was careful to respect his privacy, keep it to herself, and not ask too many questions. But when she did ask, her questions came forth like a bank shot into a corner pocket.

"So, you have a bunch of letters written in German. You think that was to prevent anyone from reading them?"

"Could be. But don't you think Mom - Evelyn - would be suspicious if she saw letters in a foreign language?"

"Your dad must have handled it carefully."

Aaron stopped and formed his next question carefully. "Sally, should I be angry with my dad? I'm seeing him in a totally different light now. Why would he cheat on Mom?"

"Pastor, how many times have you had that question put to you by someone with the door shut?"

Aaron rolled his eyes toward the ceiling. "You're just like my wife. I'm asking you. What would you do?"

Sally simply looked at him for almost a minute. Then she hit the nail on the head. "Aaron, you don't have enough information to answer that question. Don't judge your father until you do. Go back to those letters. There's got to be something in there."

The phone rang. Sally retreated to the front office and listened intently, then came back into Aaron's office in a state of concern and excitement.

"Aaron, it's your brother. He's been taken to the Ocala hospital in an ambulance. A horse kicked him, and they think he's bleeding internally."

Aaron stopped in mid-stride as Sally spoke. He probed his pockets and said, "Where are my car keys? Oh geez, Jane dropped me off! She should be coming back soon."

Sally didn't miss a beat. In a flash, she had her keys in hand and said, "C'mon, I'm taking you home to get your own car. You can call your wife while I'm driving!"

Minutes later, he was on the Florida Turnpike, and the old Miata's tachometer was at 6000 RPM. Luckily, the traffic was light. He passed two State Troopers going the other way and counted his blessings. Light poles, rest stops, exit ramps, and billboards whizzed by. The reality of today's troubles, compared to what he had just witnessed in Tampa, stood in stark contrast, but he had no idea what to do with the things he now had to put on the back burner.

The Ocala Hospital was a state-of-the-art facility. Fortunately, he found a parking space near the emergency entrance reserved for clergy. He rushed in, flashed his clergy I.D., and asked where to find Daniel Harper. He was directed to a family waiting room and there, beautiful as a picture with her baby bump, sat Melissa, wringing her hands and blowing her nose. When she saw Aaron, she bolted out of her chair and ran to him. She spoke with her face buried in his shoulder, and her words were muffled.

Aaron let her uncork for about a minute, then loosened his hug and said, "Okay, suppose you tell me what happened. Were you there with him?"

Melissa composed herself and tried to speak without sobbing. "Yes, I was. I saw the whole thing, and it was awful! He – he was examining this mare, and the mare's foal let out a squeal for some reason. I was wa-watching.  And well, mothers being mothers, she turned toward the foal, and Dan - Dan was in the way.  She struck out with her front feet at the handler and somehow, Dan ended up by her left hindquarter, about three feet away." She stopped and sniffed loudly. "Dan always said, if a horse is going to kick you, it's better if you're standing close.  Then all she can do is push, not kick.  But he was in a perfect position.  She caught him right below his ribs, and he went down hard!  Then, she stepped on him, trying to get to that damn baby of hers.  These thoroughbreds are nuts sometimes!"  She stopped to catch her breath.  "Stupid damn horse!"  Two other people in the waiting room squirmed nervously in their chairs.

"What have the doctors said?"

She turned and threw her arms up in frustration. "I don't know!  They've been in there a long time!" A scrub nurse appeared on her way through the room, and Melissa screamed in her direction, "Nobody will tell me anything!"

Aaron quickly caught up with the nurse, showed her his clergy I.D., and asked, "Is there any way you can give us an update on Daniel Harper's condition?"

The nurse looked over his shoulder at Melissa and whispered to him, "Who is she? A relative?"

"That's his wife. Seems no one has updated her. Can you help us?"

She glanced in Melissa's direction and hissed, "That woman has been screaming bloody murder ever since they brought him in. I'll try to find out something. Just keep a tight rein on her."

Minutes later, another nurse came into the room, untying her surgical gown. "Are you folks here for Dr. Harper?"

Aaron was surprised to hear his brother's name in such formal terms. He and Melissa hurried to meet the nurse in the middle of the room. Melissa was breathing heavy and trying to form words. Aaron wrapped one arm around her shoulders, put a finger to her lips, and turned to the nurse. His eyes answered the nurse's question.

"The patient has a ruptured spleen and a small tear in the liver capsule. We've repaired the liver, but we had to remove his spleen. It was beyond repair. He lost a lot of blood. His abdomen was so full it was distended. We spent the first ten minutes just trying to suction it all out. It kept filling back up until we could find the bleeders. There were several bleeding vessels, and the spleen itself was bleeding like a big sponge." She stopped and looked at them both. "I'm sorry, I should have a more sensitive way to describe things. We've transfused three units of blood already, and he's probably going to need more."

"Is the surgery finished?"

"They're closing him up now. It'll be several hours before you can see him, maybe even more."

"Do you need more blood donated?"

"They always need more. What's your blood type?"

"I'm O negative. My brother is A negative.

"Your brother?"

"Dr. Harper is my brother." He felt his voice trailing off at the sound of the word.

The nurse pointed to Melissa. "And her? What's her blood type?"

"She's pregnant. Just stick with me. Where's the blood bank?"

Melissa walked with Aaron to the blood bank after he convinced her she could do nothing to help by staying in the waiting room. While the technicians drained a unit from Aaron, Melissa stood by and watched.

"Where have you been today?" she asked.

"Jane and I went to Tampa to check on some family business."

"Top secret stuff? Or just on a need-to-know basis?"

"What has Dan told you about the DNA results?"

"He said you two are half-siblings and that means one of you is adopted. He's convinced it's him."

Aaron raised his head from the bench he was lying on and asked, "Why is he saying that? He has no earthly reason to think that way."

"So what did you find out?"

He laid his head back down and stared at the ceiling. "Like I said, he has no earthly reason to think that way."

Aaron stayed at the hospital until well past supper time. Dan finally recovered from the anesthesia, went to a room in intensive care, and never lost his sense of humor, although it came with difficulty.

"I heard you donated some blood," he said with a look of fake concern.

"Yeah, I heard you were running a little low on the dipstick. How are you feeling?"

Dan's voice was weak. He half-whispered, "Like a horse kicked me, what'd you expect?" He pointed to Melissa and asked, "I didn't get any of her blood, did I?"

"No, we told them your voice was high-pitched enough as it was. Put her blood in you, and you'd be sounding like Michael Jackson."

"My incision probably looks like some unknown horse doctor put sutures in me. I bet could have done a better job." He tried to sit up, but Melissa stopped him.

"We'll see your battle scar later. Just be still, will you?"

Dan was doing his best to stay distracted from the obvious, but he grimaced when he tried to move, and his discomfort was apparent. He looked at Aaron and asked with his eyes half-shut, "So, what did you find out? You got your DNA results, didn't you?"

Aaron saw it coming and had his answer all prepared. "Yeah, we got something back. They said the sample was contaminated. We'll resubmit it."

Dan coughed painfully and hissed, "My God! You can't do anything right!"

Melissa interjected, "Hey, I'm going to run down to the gift shop for a few minutes. I'll be right back."

After she left, Aaron stood by his brother's bed, waiting patiently to let him talk at his own pace. When Dan suddenly stayed silent, Aaron noticed a far-off look on his face.

"You're quiet all of a sudden. What's cookin'?"

"Just thinking about what could have happened."

Melissa returned, and Aaron said goodbye with the promise of coming back in two days. She walked to the door with him, and he said, "Call me and give me an update tomorrow. Call me tonight if you want." She gave him a quick kiss on the cheek.

Dan spent the next day in the ICU, then was transferred to an intermediate-level post-surgical care room. The doctors were pleased with his recovery rate. Three days after surgery, Aaron and Jane both appeared at his doorway. His bed was propped up into a half-seated position. His eyes looked tired, but his face was smiling when he saw them.

Jane was the first to speak. "I hear you're keeping the staff busy around here." She ended with a smile and kissed him on his forehead.

His voice was still a little weak, but definitely that of Dan Harper. "They changed my dressing this morning, and I saw the sutures. I could have done a better job, and I told them so."

Melissa said, "This place will be a lot quieter when they send him home. Then, I'll have to put up with him!"

They all laughed, and the two ladies excused themselves to go sit in the visitors' lounge area.

Dan started twice to speak, then stopped and looked at his brother. Finally, he said, "Aaron, I wouldn't tell this to anyone except you. Not even Melissa."

Aaron's pastoral radar instinctively turned on. He waited a few seconds, then responded. "Okay, it's just the two of us. Go ahead." He noticed Dan's eyes beginning to glisten.

"Last night, I dreamed that I died." He glanced up at his brother before continuing. "I woke up with such a feeling of, I don't know how to describe it –

Christmas, Easter, 4<sup>th</sup> of July, fireworks, all scrambled together, just welling up inside me. I felt like I had had a hundred shots of Demerol. It was so unreal."

"Okay, so that's how you woke up. What was the dream before you woke up?"

"I was at my own funeral. I was lying there in the casket with the lid shut, and I could see right through it. People were walking by, and everyone was crying. I couldn't understand it. Why were they crying? I felt like a million bucks!"

"Okay, that's it?"

"No, no, man, and this is the weird part. The scene changed, and we were at a cemetery somewhere, I don't know where. The hearse had just stopped, and they were pulling the casket out. But I wasn't in it then. I was floating up somewhere above it all, looking down, and it was the same thing again. Everyone was so sad. Everyone but me! I kept asking why they were all crying, and no one answered me."

Aaron listened intently. He had never heard his brother speak like this, so he knew he was telling the truth about his dream. "So, then you woke up?"

"Yeah, and like I said, euphoria isn't a strong enough word for it."

"How long did it last?"

"Not long, maybe fifteen minutes. I'll tell you this: I'll never forget it. I can't forget it! Aaron, what do you think happened? Was that one of those near-death things?"

"No, nobody said anything about having to revive you or anything close to that. I just think God gave you a small taste of heaven."

"What? Nah! Well, maybe. I don't know."

"Okay, think of it this way: it may not have been heaven, but it gave you an idea of what it could be like dream or not. You follow me?"

"Oh, the other thing about it was that I knew it was Springtime. Everything was in bloom. Azaleas, dogwoods, redbuds, you name it. I was dreaming in real vivid technicolor."

"Lots of blooms, huh? Did you see Dad there? He could make anything bloom. If you see him again, give him my best!" Just as he finished, Melissa and Jane came back from the gift shop with a stack of magazines. They found both men laughing fiercely and Dan clutching his midsection.

Dan stopped and took a breath. Don't make me laugh anymore. It hurts too much."

Aaron reached down and ruffled his brother's hair. "I gotta' go. It's getting dark out there."

As they said their goodbyes in the hallway, they left Dan alone in the room, and he felt the smile on his face gradually fade, leaving him alone in his thoughts. *Why was everyone in the dream crying?*

Aaron and Jane stopped at the Turkey Lake rest area on the Turnpike and grabbed a burger. He let his mind drift at random, but his thoughts kept coming back to Dan's dream. He had never seen his brother so visibly affected by something so ethereal.

Mornings after mornings began to pile up, and Pastor Aaron Harper felt like the hinges of hell itself. The previous few days had been full, to say the least, and today held the promise of meetings, appointments, a conference call, and countless other things. In Seminary, one of his classmates talked about constant interruptions during his internship. The professor, hearing the complaint, told him it was his job to be interrupted. Get over it! This week's events bore witness to the truth of that advice. But he managed to get through it with no mishaps or significant social faux pas.

John Pleasance stopped by the church to see what Aaron and Jane had accomplished with the remaining contents of the safety deposit box. He also brought along two men whom Aaron didn't know. One was a young man, about thirty, with brown, straight hair and dark, piercing eyes. He was wearing a blue blazer and a dark maroon tie. The other gentleman was much older and had a headful of tousled grey hair. His wrinkled face betrayed years of cigarettes, stress, and strain. He was dressed more casually with a plaid sports shirt, grey pants, and loafers. The introductions were formal.

"Pastor Harper, this is Jason Burrows from the law firm of Stamp and Reed up in Orlando." He then pointed to the older man. "And this is Herr Wagner. Noah Wagner, correct? They came by the bank this morning looking for some information and, by luck, they asked the right person. They were looking for you, and here you are. Jason, Noah, meet Pastor Aaron Harper."

Aaron felt more than slightly blindsided by this unscheduled event. John excused himself, said a few words to Sally, and headed for the coffee urn in the next room. Burrows sat in a corner until the three of them were alone, then rose from his chair and shut the door. He cleared his throat several times and tried to speak but could not look Aaron in the eye.

Aaron spoke first but cautiously. "Mr. Burrows, make yourself at home. You seem to be in a stressful state of mind. Just take your time and tell me what the problem is. I'm sure God has an answer for you."

"We're not here about God. Pastor, we know your father died not too long ago. We at our firm had not heard about it until yesterday. I'm so sorry for your loss."

Aaron's radar went on full alert, but he posed his question gently. "Okay, is that what you have come

337

here to tell me?"  He watched and could see the younger man try to regroup his thoughts.

"No, I apologize for sounding insincere.  But our reason for being here does have to do with your father's demise.  Rather, that is the aftermath of it. There is a chain of events that have started a domino effect from years ago, and I, I mean, we – we need your assistance."

Aaron leaned back in his chair and looked hard at the man.  His words came low-key but firm. "Okay, first tell me who is 'we?'  Then, tell me why you went to a bloody bank looking for information and you just HAPPENED to bump into John, who just HAPPENED to know where to find me?"  He leaned forward and continued, "You better start making some sense really quick, or else I'll consider this to be some kind of sales spin that I really don't have time for.  I'll give you five minutes to gain my interest.  And this better not be some ploy to get me to sue my dad's nursing home or something like that."

"Well, I'm sorry if this has offended you, but we really need your cooperation in this matter.  It is a matter of significant proportions."

Aaron nodded, sat back, and frowned.

Burrows shifted again in his chair, rubbed his fingertips across his pursed lips, and was about to speak when the older man interrupted.  His words carried a distinct European accent. "Pastor, we mean no disrespect, but enough is enough. Does the name ''Helga Röder' mean anything to you?"

Aaron sat up straight in his chair and hissed, "Who are you? What do you want?"

Burrows suddenly appeared calm as a farm pond on a windless day. "I think we hit a sensitive nerve."

Noah Wagner spoke up. "Pastor, maybe this will help. I am from Germany, as you probably suspect already, specifically from Bremerhaven. I worked there from time to time for an American communications squadron, the same one this woman, Helga, worked for. I did not know her very well, but I knew enough that now, I have been able to put pieces of a puzzle together. I need to find her."

Aaron felt outside of himself. The seminary had not taught him how to handle this. He opened his office door with the intent to physically assist the men in leaving, and John Pleasance was still standing there, talking to Sally. He leaned toward the open office door and asked, "Get what you need, Mr. Burrows?"

Aaron was totally speechless. Was this something John was privy to? Why was he still here and saying nothing? John looked at the three men and decided to intervene.

"Pastor, I have not been totally honest with you. I knew your father more than you are aware of. And others knew that I knew. Can the four of us talk in your office with the door closed?"

John walked back into Aaron's office and shut the door. He was calm and collected as Burrows was trying to straighten his tie while Aaron was trying to cool off. Wagner waited patiently. Aaron finally spoke.

"Gentlemen, I have had a rough bunch of days, all of it personal. Some family issues from the past have been bearing down on me, and several nights ago, my brother almost lost his life in a tangle with a horse. I have a stack of unfinished business, and I'm operating on a slim dose of sleep. It would help me immensely if someone would just cut to the chase and tell me what you want from me. And you can start with your request about Helga **Röder**." He looked at Wagner with daggers in his eyes.

Burrows finally seemed to have his thoughts together. "My firm has been hired by a German law firm to find this woman for her own benefit. Herr Wagner represents parties who are keenly interested in finding her. You may not know, but she worked for the American government in Germany when it was still under the Marshall Plan. She gathered information for Army intelligence. Then she just disappeared. Our inquiries revealed she came to this country and worked for a wholesale nursery in Kissimmee for a number of years, off and on, and then she disappeared again.  We have been trying to catch up with her for, well, since before I was born."

"Wait a minute!  Helga worked for a nursery? Which one?"

Burrows saw himself being backed into a corner. "Harper," was all he said.

"Why are you looking for her?  We won't proceed one step further until you answer that question.  Understand?  Not one step!"

"Sir, you are implicating yourself as an accessory."

"To what?"

John spoke up and said, "Burrows, stop playing Dick Tracy and answer the man's question."

Burrows considered his options and made a decision.  "Okay, but I must report that I did not tell you this upfront.  I was given explicit instructions - "

"Tell the man!"  John almost shouted.

Burrows recoiled in response to John's visceral expression.  He continued in almost a timid fashion. "Helga **Röder** worked for the U.S. government for several years.  She was a loyal German whose family was ridiculed and persecuted by Hitler's crowd because, along with many others, they supported the Declaration of Barmen and they -"

"Wait!  The what?"  Aaron was almost standing out of his chair.

"The Declaration of Barmen. I hope you've heard of it."

"Of course I have! It's in our Book of Confessions." He stood and grabbed a thumb-worn book off the shelf behind him. "It was written by a group of German clergymen who opposed Hitler. They wanted to dispel any notion that God had given His blessing to the Nazi movement. They didn't want the church to become an agent of the state. But that was in the early 30s, before Helga's time. She wasn't even yet born when that came out."

Wagner's eyes widened. "So, you do know, at least, something about her, yes?"

"Keep going."

"Yes, it does help that you know about the Declaration of Barmen." Burrows continued, "You see, Helga's father helped organize the meeting in Barmen. It was very clandestine and difficult to maintain secrecy. There were spies everywhere. Her father's name became known, along with others who were helping, and she later heard of the way her family had been treated because of his involvement. Among other things, her father was an art collector. One of the punitive things the Nazi government did to them was confiscate all their pieces of art. The Nazi oppression was the cause of the war and, therefore, the ultimate reason Germany became divided after the war. So, she vowed to do anything to help restore Germany to its previous intact state without an oppressive dictatorship. She started at a young age and ended up working for the Americans and the West German government."

"Is there a point to all this somewhere?"

Wagner continued, "And one more thing - I am doing this out of a sense of indebtedness. After she escaped, Helga was instrumental in getting me and my family out of East Germany. I owe her this."

Burrows' mouth dropped open. "Herr Wagner, you did not tell me this. What else have you withheld?"

Wagner ignored him and picked up the conversation. "The art collection is worth a significant amount of money. Through considerable effort, it has been recovered and is now being held in escrow by my government, pending auction, until the rightful owner, or heir to the rightful owner, can be found. They have been looking for decades. We finally have reason to believe that you know the whereabouts of that heir." He stopped and let Aaron cogitate on his words.

"You have reason to believe that I know of her whereabouts. Do you mind elaborating on that?"

"Do you know Henry Harper?"

"That's a rhetorical question. You know the answer, obviously, and you want to see my reaction."

"Is Henry Harper your father?"

"Why don't you ask Henry?"

Herr Wagner paused, slowly smiled, and said, "I'll bet you are a good chess player. You have us in a checkmate. You know we cannot ask questions of a dead man. But we found out just recently that Helga worked closely with Mr. Harper. We felt if we could find Mr. Harper, we might find her. You are the closest thing to finding him."

"She worked closely with him? Yes, in Germany. We all know that now."

Wagner did not take the bait. Instead, he shook his head, "No, we mean here in Florida."

Aaron felt himself getting a second wind. "Does the name Alison Burbidge mean anything to you?"

Wagner was puzzled. "No, why should it?"

John's posture and expression remained unchanged, except that his eyebrows levitated ten feet. Aaron and John made eye contact with each other but said nothing.

Aaron now felt he had the upper hand in the conversation. "Never mind. Okay, I've sparred enough with you. How can I help you?"

Burrows took a deep breath and continued, "Helga **Röder** is the heir to this art collection. The executor of the escrow has put a deadline on delaying the auction. That deadline is three weeks from now."

"The executor?"

Wagner leaned forward. "That would be me, Pastor. My family was also persecuted, and we have recovered much of what was taken from us. I heard about this art collection and started to look into it. I am not a young man; my health is not so good, and I will not look for this woman forever."

It was all clear now. This sounded like a legitimate inquiry. But he wanted to protect his birth mother's privacy.

"At auction, how much are we talking about?"

"Easily six figures, maybe more. And it's tax-free. It's her money."

Aaron was staggered when he heard the amount. There was a moment of silence in the room until he saw clearly what to do.

"Forget about asking where she is because I will not divulge that information. I have met her and her daughter." Burrows and Wagner sat up and looked at each other. "I will tell you, Helga's health is failing, and her days are numbered, for sure. Authorize the auction. I can tell you where to send the money. Will that work?"

Wagner scratched his head. "The purpose in finding her was to inform her of the art recovery and to ask where to deposit the money." He rubbed his eyes and looked at John with a weak smile. "I feel my search is coming to an unexpected conclusion.

Mr. Pleasance, can you vouch for Pastor Harper? Can I trust what he tells me?”

John just nodded and smiled. Aaron reached for the phone.

Cynthia answered in two rings. “Hello?”

“Cynthia, this is Aaron Harper. Please pardon this unannounced phone call. Do you have time to talk? You do? Great! I have some good news for you. Perhaps you should sit down for this. First of all, do you have signature authority over your mother’s checkbook?”

“Hang on a minute. What’s this about? Yes, I do handle her checking account, but why do you ask?”

Aaron went on to explain in detail what he had learned, except for the value of the collection. As he spoke, he could feel a strong sense of purpose. Ten minutes later, when he finished, he asked, “So, what do you think?”

“I’m overwhelmed! I just can’t imagine what all you’re telling me. My mother – our mother! A spy? To look at her now, you would never guess. I didn’t know about her family and the art collection. Oh, Aaron, there is so much that she didn’t tell me. Do you think this money would be enough to help me take care of her so much better than I am doing now?”

Aaron could only smile at her question, so selfless, just like her mother – his mother. "Yes, I'm sure it will help quite a bit. So, here's what I want you to do. Go get your mom's checkbook and bring it to the phone." He waited until she returned. "Now, there's two sets of numbers at the bottom of each check. Read them off to me."

"What are these numbers?"

"They are the account number and the routing number to your bank."

"I don't know. Are you sure about this? There's a lot of scams out there."

He turned to the other men and asked them to give him some privacy. When they left the room, he went back to the phone. "Okay, I have some privacy now. Cynthia, DNA results don't lie. You and I are brother and sister. I think you would agree she recognized me and remembered me. I have a wealth of information at my house that supports everything I told you. This is no scam. This is for you and your mother. You can turn it down if you want, and I will not bother you again. But there is a deadline from the German executor, so time is important. If I were scamming you, I would give them my own checking account number and put your good fortune in my own hands, but I'm not. I'm giving it to you. They do not know we are related."

There was silence on the phone for several seconds. She finally said, "I see. Well, okay. Right now, there's not much in her account to begin with. What do I have to lose?"

"Okay, and I'll be there to see you in a few days. You said she would appreciate another visit. By then, I should know when the auction will take place."

Aaron came out of his office with two numbers in his hands. As the three visitors were about to leave, Aaron shot a focused, inquiring glance at John, who simply smiled. John then invited Burrows and Wagner to his bank, where they sat down at one of the bank's computers and recorded the information Aaron had given them.

The next day, Aaron called Melissa to check on Dan, and she said they would have to tie him to the bed to keep him still. Apparent good news.

Three days later, he called Cynthia. She answered the phone with an ecstatic tone in her voice. "Aaron, I just checked the account on my computer! It's all there! Just like you said! Oh my God! It's one million four-hundred thousand and some change!"

"It's there? Already? I guess the word got back to the Germans quickly, and they did the sale."

"Did you know it would be this much?"

Like Noah Wagner had said, it was of significant proportions.  Aaron drew a deep breath and said, "Cynthia, go to your bank.  Open a new account and move all your money into it.  All of it.  Then, cancel the old account.  Do it now, today."

"Why?"

"No one will know the new account number."

"My God, you are an angel!  Then I'm going to have Hospice in here tomorrow, and I'll tell them I'm paying cash!"

# CHAPTER EIGHTEEN

It seems that life always has surprises hiding around corners, waiting to pop out when we least expect them. So many husbands do not appreciate their wives who do small things behind the scenes, oftentimes responsible for those surprises that give spice to an otherwise lackluster existence where one day runs into another with no discernible separation. Jane Harper was one of those wives.

A week after breaking the good news to Cynthia and seeing the sheer joy it created, Aaron was immersed in a project of feeding the homeless at the Osceola Kitchen shelter. He was taking advantage of that opportunity to preach a short message about love.

"I want you to take from here the bible verses I started with today. Remember, it is from 1ˢᵗ Corinthians, chapter 13. Here it is again for you:

*When I was a child, I spoke like a child, I thought like a child, I reasoned like a child; when I became an adult, I put an end to childish ways. For now we see in a mirror, dimly, but then we will see face to face. Now I know only in part; then I will know fully, even as I have been fully known. And now faith, hope, and love abide these three, and the greatest of these is love.*

Aaron closed his sermon notes and said, "I hope this message today has spoken to you as it did to me while I was writing it."

The shelter was one of his stops just prior to lunch and was a short hop away from his house, so he decided to have lunch at home. Jane was sitting on the living room couch with a thin stack of papers in her hands. She looked up at him with glistening eyes and chewing at her lip. Aaron had seen that look before, and he immediately paused.

"Hey, sugar, what's doing?" Hearing no answer, he sat down beside her. "What is it?"

Jane swallowed hard and handed the pages to him. "This requires some explanation. Remember that letter we found dated 1989? The one from Switzerland?"

"Yeah, it was addressed to Harper's Gardens and written in German. What about it?"

"I have spent all morning trying to make out the handwriting and then translating it on the computer."

"You can do that?"

Her voice sounded flat. "Aaron, there's all kinds of translators on the internet. Yes, you can do it."

He noticed a twinge of fatigue and impatience in Jane's words. "Okay, what do you have here?"

"This letter was sent to your father a few months before you were born. We don't have the last page, but it stands to reason that it was from Alison. It looks like her handwriting. She's telling Henry that she needed to get away because she was pregnant. She expressed her love for him, but she knew it was a forbidden love. She assured Henry that she would never break the promise of confidence they shared, and his marriage to Evelyn would never be in jeopardy."

To Aaron, it sounded like the ending to a steamy romance novel. "That's amazing! Did she know the risk of Evelyn finding this letter?"

"I guess so. But she didn't send it to the house. She sent it to Henry's office, and she wrote it in German. That must have given her some sense of safety and seclusion."

"I never knew my dad spoke German."

"To be in Army Intelligence in Germany? It would make sense. But wait, there's more. She says she cannot afford to keep the baby, but she will come back to the U.S. to have the baby if he agrees to adopt it. She goes on to say she understands his loneliness, and she was glad to be there for him when he needed intimacy and affection."

"What? My God! What is she saying?"

"Aaron, remember the doctor prescribing medication for Evelyn's depression? Evelyn must have really driven a wedge between herself and Henry. And Alison was there for him."

His eyes suddenly widened. "Yes, and I remember the notation in Dad's journal about his wife going to Atlanta to be with her parents. Wasn't that about the same time as this letter from Alison?"

"The letter was a little later, and we don't know exactly how long Evelyn stayed away."

"And so, with no kids, my dad tells his wife that he knows of a baby who will be available for adoption, and he never tells her where it came from."

"Apparently not. In her depression, she would probably agree to anything. Your adoption brought her out of her depression, and she mothered you like you were her own."

"And then Alison showed up, ready to go back to work for Harper's Gardens. No questions asked."

"And two years later, here comes baby Daniel."

Aaron smiled and brought a faraway look on his face. "I was too young to notice or remember Evelyn's pregnancy with my brother."

"There's one other thing. It requires a little imagination, so let me show you. Here's the framed picture you found in Henry's apartment. Take a good look at it. See the eyes, the shape of the nose, the cheekbones. It's a copy of the one you saw in Cynthia's living room." She stopped and watched him gaze at each detail. "Now, look at this." She handed him the passport belonging to Alison Burbidge. The face in the framed photo was a few years younger than the face in the passport photo, but the resemblance between the two was striking.

Jane mused, "So, that completes the story, doesn't it?"

He thought for a moment. "We'll never know. There's so much detail that could go through someone's mind; I guess there's always more to tell, but-"

Jane put her hand in the crook of his elbow and said, "Maybe you should go see her again. Go by yourself this time."

"I will, but I need to see my brother first."

In Ocala, Daniel Harper was acting like a hostage held for ransom, chomping at the bit to get home. The hospital staff knew if he went home too early, he would try to go back to work before it was advisable. On Monday, Aaron showed up with balloons and a pizza. Melissa saw him in the hallway.

"Thank God you're here. He's a handful, that guy. I wish I had half his energy. Go on in. He'll be glad to see you."

Dan's room was like a greenhouse due to the abundance of flower arrangements and potted plants. Aaron's balloon joined countless others, floating near the ceiling. Several stuffed animals occupied the available furniture.

"Have a seat, bro! Wipe your feet first. This is hallowed ground, pal. I didn't know I had so many friends. Cool, huh? So, what's new on the family front?"

"I have a lot to tell you." He let a pregnant pause pass between them. "First of all, I told you a white lie about my DNA sample. It was not contaminated. It was a good sample."

Dan looked at his brother with a scowl on his face. "What the hell? So, why the deception?"

"I wasn't ready to cross that bridge yet."

Dan tried to sit up. "Wait a minute! I should have known. My report said you were my half-sibling. How could it say that if your sample was unreadable? Geez! What a dunce I am! Of course!" He stopped for a few seconds. "Okay, so what else?"

"It turns out I have another half-sibling." He paused and let it sink in. He watched Dan's eyebrows almost touch each other. "Remember the young woman who came to Dad's funeral? The one who gave her name as Cynthia?"

"Yeah, and no last name." Dan's scowl was becoming a dark frown.

"She submitted a DNA sample recently, maybe out of having nothing else to do, but she did. She's my sister, Dan. My half-sister."

"And Alison is -"

"Alison Burbidge is my mother." He stopped and let his brother digest the information before he continued. "Dan - I am the adopted child, not you.

355

Furthermore, Jane and I went to Tampa to see Alison and her living conditions are sparse. Maybe Spartan would be a better word for it. But that's going to improve soon if it hasn't already."

"Looks like you have a lot of explaining to do. Go ahead, I'm listening."

For the next hour, Aaron told Dan the story of Henry Harper, John Pleasence, and a young German woman named Helga, who worked as a team to take one small chink out of the Iron Curtain. He showed him the framed photo and the passport photo.

Daniel Harper was never known to be at a loss for words. "Holy crap! These two pictures are the same woman! That's Alison!"

"Also known as Helga. And I need to go see her again. But I thought I would wait until you felt like taking the trip with me. That is before you start back to work. I think she'll be glad to see us both."

Dan laid back in his bed and stared at the ceiling. "I'll be damned. Here, all this time, I thought I was the chosen child. Still trying to upstage me, huh?"

Another five days went by, and the doctors agreed that Dan could be released. Melissa took him home, made sure he was comfortable and tried to resume the normal life of an expectant mother. They had been home only a few hours, and the phone rang. It was Aaron.

"Hey, sister-in-law, you got the hero home now?"

Melissa couldn't help but smile. She saw so clearly why he was a good pastor, always thinking of others before himself. And Jane made it a matching set, made for each other. Melissa's marriage to Dan had been a quick one, but she never regretted having married into the Harper family.

"Yes, he's home and roaring to get back to work."

"Sounds like he needs a distraction. I can help you for at least one day of that. Put him on the phone."

When Dan hung up, he said, "Aaron's coming by tomorrow, and we're driving to Tampa to see someone."

"Oh, yeah? What are you two up to now?"

An hour later, Dan had told her everything Aaron had told him. Melissa thought to herself, *You couldn't write this stuff and call it nonfiction! No one would believe you!*

The next morning, Aaron had a long drive ahead of him. First, he had to leave Kissimmee, go to Ocala, pick up his brother, and then drive to Tampa. He knew the way and didn't want to guess the miles it would take.

By 10 o'clock, he had Dan secured in the car and headed in a southwesterly direction. After they had cleared the Ocala traffic and were on a major highway, Aaron proceeded to tell his brother what the translated letter said.

"So, Dad had an affair with Alison because Mom was gone, he was lonely, and she got pregnant with you, right?"

"Dan, I am sure there was more to it, but yes, those are the high points. We don't know all the details."

"Details? Like what? What else could there be?"

"Jeepers! Everything has to be so cut-and-dried to you. Black and white. No shades of gray."

"What are you talking about? You told me what was in the letter. I just said it back to you."

"Dan, the letter doesn't really get into the deeper, unspoken, emotional aspect of it. Think about this. Alison was trying to give our dad the freedom he needed by not mentioning what she needed, and can you imagine what that did to her? Sending him back to his wife and giving up her baby for his wife to raise and the wife not knowing where it came from?"

"C'mon, I can't imagine Mom not asking critical questions, Aaron. Can you?"

Aaron briefly looked in the rearview mirror, trying to come up with an answer. Finally, he said, "No, I can't imagine her being that naïve. But I can imagine our dad having a damn good story cooked up that covered all possibilities."

Dan grinned at his brother's choice of language for emphasis. "Okay, let's see what we can find out. Can this thing go any faster?"

And the old Miata began to sing.

Once off the highway, they could see signs to MacDill AFB, and Aaron knew they were getting close. The familiar worn-out neighborhood came into view, and Dan silently took it all in. "This is low-income stuff. Not exactly a nightmare, but not uplifting either," he said.

They pulled into the driveway, and Aaron opened the trunk. He pulled out a small tote bag and Dan saw him carrying it toward the front door but said nothing. Aaron rang the doorbell, and Cynthia answered it quickly.

"I'm so glad you're here." She gave Aaron a quick hug. "I told her we'd be having visitors, and she's been excited all day. Well, as excited as she can be."

"Cynthia Kramer, this is my brother, Dan. We were wondering if your mom would remember him."

"Great. Hang out here in the living room, and let me set her up." She left them waiting and disappeared down the hall.

"Dan, don't expect too much. She doesn't process a lot of information all at once." They both waited casually until Cynthia reappeared.

"Come on in, guys. She's wide awake."

Entering the bedroom, Aaron noticed a small cluster of hospital equipment in one corner and a bedside toilet near the foot of the bed. Hospice had clearly been there. Alison was half-sitting up with pillows behind her shoulders. Her eyes slowly looked at one of them, then the other. Finally, Aaron spoke.

"Good morning, Mom. Remember me from a few days ago? I've come by to see you again." He leaned closer for her to see more clearly. She smiled and put her hand on his face.

"Henry!"

Cynthia was quick to correct her. "Mama, this is Aaron. Remember him?"

She nodded and tried to smile.

"And this is his brother. This is Daniel."

Dan stepped closer, and her expression first looked confused, then beamed. But she said nothing. From the tote bag, Aaron pulled out Knobby and handed it to him. Dan looked at him, puzzled.

"Show it to her. Let her see it."

Dan put the doll in her hands, and she immediately touched the red hair and blue feet. Almost by instinct, she pulled on the loose ends as though the knots needed tightening. She then looked up suddenly and exclaimed with a wheeze, "Danny boy!" Her smile almost split her face.

After several moments, her gaze went back to Aaron, and Dan moved away from the bed. Her mouth moved, but the words were too faint to hear. He leaned closer and heard her voice like it was the murmur of a soft morning breeze. She said, "Das ist gut." Her hands stroked his face and pulled him toward her. She rose up a mere inch to meet his lips and kissed him. Aaron felt her kiss like a message from heaven. Lips, old quivering lips, lips that had loved someone intimately in the far gone past. But the message was clear. She lay back down and said, "Ja, das is gut. Ich liebe dich, mein Kleiner."

Both men stayed by her bed for several minutes, making comments that might spark more memories of times passed. They weren't sure if any of their messages got through, but her recognition of them both was clear. After a half hour, she started to doze off, and they all retreated to the living room.

"What was she saying in German?" Aaron asked.

Cynthia spoke up and replied softly, "She said, 'This is good. I love you, little one.' That's what she said."

Dan asked, "You speak German?"

"Of course, I grew up learning to speak two languages. She and I have conversed in both English and German for years."

Aaron thought before he asked the next question. "Does she know about the art sale?"

"No, I haven't caught her at a clear moment to tell her. You see how it was today. Our conversations have been limited to only a handful of sentences for the last month or so."

Dan had a pressing question. "She left Kissimmee when Aaron and I were in elementary school. Why was that?"

"I wouldn't know," Cynthia answered. "She kept a lot to herself. Maybe she needed a clean break."

"What did she do here in Tampa? Obviously, she must have had a job."

"Apparently, she learned a great deal from your dad about exotic plants and how to cultivate them. She got a job at a nursery here just outside of town. She taught me a lot as well. I went to work with her in the summers when school was out. I also had a part-time job at the nursery where she had worked. That is, up until recently, when I couldn't leave her alone for long periods."

Aaron saw no need to withhold what he had discovered on their previous visit. He picked up the framed picture from exactly where he had left it and pointed to the name, 'Helga.' He asked her, "Do you know who that is?"

"Mother always said it was a friend of hers. Why?"

"Why would it be on the back of a photo of your mother? You said she had a State Department birth certificate. The name on it is Alison Burbidge, right? Is it possible that her original German name was Helga?  **Helga Röder**?"

Cynthia gazed at him with no expression. "I don't know. This is all too much for me to think about right now. Too much, except for the providence that we both had DNA samples submitted close to the same time. At this point, names don't matter to me."

Aaron stood and said, "We need to be getting back. Let me peek back in there one more time. Maybe she's not completely asleep." He stood by her bed for several minutes and watched her breathe. The truth still evaded him – this was his mother. His mother, who defied East Germany and escaped, then worked in a clandestine fashion, under immense pressure, to help the Americans. Her withered body did not fit the story.

When Aaron came out of the bedroom, Dan could see he was ready to leave. He extended his appreciation to Cynthia, and both men gave her a quick hug. "I hope this is the start of regular visits," she said. "I really am starting to feel a connection, like I have a family now."

Traffic was heavy and it took twenty minutes to gain access back onto the highway. Just as they pulled into an open lane to head toward Ocala, Aaron's cell phone rang.

"Get that for me, Dan, will you? I can't talk in this traffic."

Dan answered the call, and Aaron was shocked by the one side of the conversation he could hear.

"Cynthia? - Yeah? - Oh my God! Have you called an ambulance? Okay, we'll try to reverse course at the first opportunity. Traffic is backed up, and we just got on the highway. Okay, we'll turn around as soon as we can."

Aaron gave his brother a panicked look. Dan said, "Bro, we gotta' turn around and go back. It's Alison. Cynthia said she heard her coughing and went in to check. She was making choking sounds and turning blue. She's calling an ambulance right now."

It was another thirty minutes before they could find an exit, reverse their direction, and be close to the house. As they approached, they saw the ambulance parked in front. Three EMT technicians were on their way out, pushing a gurney containing a human figure, completely covered, head to toe. Cynthia stood in the doorway with red eyes and her hands over her mouth.

The two men rushed toward the house, and Aaron wrapped his arms around her. Dan stopped the ambulance crew, pulled back the shroud that covered her face, a heavenly face that showed no sign of distress. He wondered what she was seeing. He whispered to her, *Alison, is everything in bloom?* He waited a moment and replaced the shroud. From there, all he could do for his brother was put his arm around him.

"I'm sorry, man."

Aaron turned and looked at him through tear-filled eyes and mumbled, "How can I – I mean, what should I – I don't know what to say." The two brothers embraced and included Cynthia in their grasp.

Cynthia finally composed herself and said, "I knew this day was coming. I've been dreading it for so long. I'm glad you two were here."

Dan suggested they go back inside. "May as well give each other some more time together." For a moment, Aaron was surprised at his brother's newly found level of sensitivity.

Through her tears, Cynthia smiled weakly and said, "Yes, and give the traffic time to clear out."

As they sat silently in the living room, Cynthia got up from her seat and went into the bedroom. She came out holding Knobby and handed it to Aaron. "I think she meant to give this back to you fellows."

An hour later, after they said their goodbyes, the two brothers sat in the car in silence, still in the driveway. Finally, Aaron spoke.

"I keep thinking about Dad. Why did he do it?"

"Do what, adopt you?"

"No, why did he cheat on Mom?"

Dan put his hand on Aaron's shoulder and said, "Was it really cheating?  Or was it reaching out to someone from the past in a moment of weakness?"

"Weakness?"

Dan continued, "Okay, call it loneliness.  Mom was depressed. She was heavily medicated and away in Atlanta.  He was alone, or at least he felt that way.  Don't you think?"

Aaron was surprised at his brother's apparent depth of thought.  "He could have reached out to Evelyn. She was a phone call away."

"Was she?  Was she there for him?  Bro, we'll never know."

"I feel like I'm not supposed to be here, not supposed to have been born.  I was an accident of nature."

"Hey, preacher, our dad acted out of love and then dealt honorably with the consequences with the same love.  You know that.  And look how you turned out.  Look at the people you have led to God.  If you hadn't been born, well…"

Aaron looked closely at his brother.  "I'm thinking.  You just hit the nail on the head.  Dad never impressed me as a man who would sleep around all over town behind his wife's back.  With all my social contacts, I would have heard something years ago.  But the one time it did happen, he wasn't intimate with just anyone.  John said Helga meant a lot to him.  So, if he was seeking refuge with anyone, it would be someone special. I know who my parents are. That woman we saw today was Helga **Röder**, my mother, now known as Alison Kramer. I have no doubt."

Dan put his hand on Aaron's shoulder and gave it a squeeze.

Aaron gave his brother a weak smile. He handed Knobby to Dan and said, "That's a cute doll. Just remember, my mother made that for you."

Dan held the doll in his hands and wiped his eyes.

Two weeks later, Alison Burbidge Kramer was buried in Kissimmee Memorial Gardens under oak trees and within sight of Henry Harper's grave. John Pleasence was with a tall, slender, older woman with straight, flaxen hair, standing at the back of the crowd. She stood quietly with a walking cane. John said goodbye to her, departed, and she waited for a private moment to approach the grave. Both brothers saw her standing there alone and approached her out of courtesy and hidden curiosity.

"Excuse me," Dan said, "Do we know you?"

She turned and showed no emotion on her face. "No, you don't know me, and it appears I am too late. My name is Anna Richter. Helga and I escaped from East Germany together. I had been working for the U.S. Government for a long time before I retired. I found ways to track various people. Now, I'm just closing the loop, so to speak, before my time is up. It's painstaking, but I'm happy to say I found John

Pleasence. What a remarkable man he is! That man has an awesome memory for details, names, and places. And he led me to this place today. So, you see, Helga was not the only one who made it to America."

Dan asked, "In spite of her American name, you knew her as Helga."

"Like I said, John Pleasence has an awesome memory."

"Can we give you a ride somewhere?" Aaron was intrigued and wanted to talk more to this interesting woman.

"No, thank you. I have my car, and I must go now." She held up her car keys in plain view and then walked away without further comment to a Mercedes parked nearby. Both men saw the terrible, disfiguring scars on her hand and arm.

As they walked in the opposite direction, Dan said, "Did you see her hand? I wonder what did that?"

Aaron thought *Helga would have known. She was there.*

A month later, Alison's gravestone was put into place. The main inscription was:

*Consider the lilies of the field, how they grow.*

At the base of the stone, in small font, were the words, *Helga, we love you.*

# CHAPTER NINETEEN

Three months went by.  Melissa was approaching her third trimester of pregnancy and was beginning to be grouchy as a bear waking up from hibernation.  The Florida summer climate did not sit well with her and the extra weight she carried, and it was only bound to get hotter.  She stayed indoors most of the time.  Jane had been reading more of Henry's journal, and the facts with the corresponding dates confirmed that Alison had taken a leave of absence about seven months before Aaron was born and reappeared eighteen months later to continue working for Henry.  One year after Aaron's adoption, Evelyn became pregnant with Daniel.  The news of a second child on the way corresponded closely with Alison's return.  She stayed six years before moving to Tampa.

It was May 15, 2025, and Aaron was in the pulpit.  The choir put the congregation in the right mood with a spiritual message in music, and Aaron finished delivering the children's sermon.  His voice always went through a quick metamorphosis as he stepped up to the podium and spoke with authority.

"In Hebrews, chapter 11, the first three verses speak of faith.  I know you have all heard that word scattered throughout sermons both here and in other places.  It's something we need to revisit from time to time because it holds the key to all our beliefs. As the scripture says, it is belief in something we cannot see. My math professor in college once explained a statistics problem by saying it does not offer us proof, but it gives us sufficient evidence to behave as though we believe a certain thing to be true. In legal terms, a judge might say the court is looking for a preponderance of evidence. Our scripture today says exactly that, in so many words."

Aaron looked down at his notes and looked up again to see three people coming in late. There was room on the back row, and they were soon seated. He tried to continue, but the distraction of the latecomers kept pulling his attention away from his sermon. He tried to be subtle as he kept glancing toward the rear of the sanctuary. It was all explained when he heard a familiar voice.

"Hey, don't stop for us! We just came in time to hear the good part!" Daniel's voice was unmistakable. The whole congregation laughed and turned to see the owner of the voice. It was then that he noticed the two women with him were Melissa and, to his utter surprise, Cynthia Kramer. He couldn't stop smiling, and the congregation enjoyed the interruption.

After the service, Aaron, Jane, Dan, Melissa, Cynthia, Adam and Joshua all gathered on the front lawn while refreshments were served under the old live oak trees. The voices were gentle, and the sense of harmony and belonging was palpable. It was like a scene from a movie set with Spanish moss swaying in the breeze and mockingbirds singing their hearts out overhead. It reminded Aaron of *Steel Magnolias.*

"So, what brought you to God's House today?" Aaron was always quick to imply that his brother could use some more church exposure.

Cynthia spoke up first. "I wanted to announce something of good news, and I talked your brother into coming with me. Sunday was the only day he could get off, so here we are. We knew where to find you."

Aaron folded his arms and gave a slight nod, ready to listen.

She continued, "Well, I heard that the old nursery, Harper's Gardens, was going bankrupt. John Pleasance from your bank told me about it. I looked into it, and I could easily see it was going downhill because the owner had no idea how to run it. I approached them about a business deal, and, as it turns out, I am now the proud owner of Harper's Gardens."

Jane was as surprised as Aaron. "You're what? Which part?"

"All of it. The land, the greenhouses, the flower shop, the little cottage that went with it, all of it. We closed the deal on Friday. I paid cash. And your sermon about faith is weighing heavy on me right now because my cash reserves have diminished greatly, and there's no cash flow as yet."

Dan interjected like a kid at Christmas time. "Yeah, and here's the best part! I bought into it as well, and we have room for another partner." He looked at Aaron and said, "Interested?"

Aaron and Jane looked at each other like they had stepped into someone else's fantasy. Aaron spoke in stumbling words, "Are you kidding! I'd love to do that – but you are way over my pay grade here. I wish you all the best, but I can barely meet my own expenses on a preacher's salary. Dad's estate was so small. I – I can't, but I really thank you for the offer."

Melissa spoke up and said, "We knew you would say that. How about we loan you the money in the meantime? You can pay us back at, say, $19.99 a month?"

"Wha – what? This is impossible, it's just…"

"No, it's not," said Cynthia. "We want the name to be changed to 'Harper and Sons' Nursery.' Gotta' have you in for a penny, at least."

Dan turned to his sense of dry humor. "Don't worry about the loan. It's interest-free, and you'll be paid up when you turn 95."

Aaron and Jane were speechless.

They all gathered at Aaron's house and Dan brought in a case of beer from his car. It had been chilling in a cooler since they left Ocala that morning.  The Harper house was full of kitchen noises, laughter, and remembrances.

The two men relaxed and listened to the women's conversations, knowing they were outnumbered and outvoiced. Melissa had one bit of news that hit a high note.

"We have been thinking about names, and two days ago, the ultrasound told us we should focus on boy's names."

The cheers went up, and Dan stood to quiet the crowd.  "Not just one boy's name. We need two names!"

They all looked at each other in amazement, then in realization of what Dan had just said.  Twin boys were due in late September.

Dan managed to insert one jab at his wife, "Sorry, my dear.  I know you would love to have one of these brews, but I don't think that would be a good idea. Look at Jane!  I know she likes a beer every now and then, but she's avoiding it just so you won't feel alone.  Isn't that right, Jane?"

Jane spoke slowly in her Texas drawl to her brother-in-law. "Dr. Harper, you are so full of crap. I have my own reasons for not drinking today. Aaron, you haven't told them, have you?"

It took a moment for the news to sink in, and when it did, one could hear the cheers from the Harper house for many furlongs.

Then Cynthia had an announcement. "I can't run a nursery business from a long distance. My house in Tampa is up for sale, and I already have a buyer. I need someone to show me around Kissimmee so I can find where I want to settle."

Jane spoke up. "That could take a while, with all the time to look, then wait to go to closing, moving in, and so forth."

Aaron immediately caught the drift of Jane's thoughts. Carefully, he said, "You could stay with us while you house hunt. We have an extra bedroom."

There was an immediate tone of agreement and excitement among everyone there. The women then gathered in the kitchen to discuss whatever they discuss when they want to get away from the men. Dan and Aaron sat alone in the den, each with a beer in hand, and looked intently at each other.

Dan finally spoke. "I have a question. Knowing what we know now, should we feel less attachment to each other? I mean, should being half-brothers mean less than full siblings?"

Aaron answered quietly, "I think I'll let you answer that one."

Dan swirled his beer and took a sip. "I mean, all those years when we were growing up, you always had my back. You were always covering for me, making excuses for me, keeping me out of trouble. Do you still feel that way?"

"Well, I can say this. When those things happened, I was never thinking in terms of anything genetic. You were just my younger brother, and I never gave it a second thought. You're a grown man now, but I'll always have your back. Some habits are hard to break."

"Yeah, and it almost got your head blown off. I still can't believe how you stood up to that Jack fellow."

Aaron took a long sip of his beer. "Me, either." He looked at Dan and winked.

Then, a serious look came over Dan's face. He said thoughtfully, "You know, you're kinda' responsible for me even being here."

"Huh?"

"Well, you remember how we talked about some couples who can't have kids and then finally do, but only after adopting one? Remember us talking about that?"

"So, my adoption led to your being born?"

"Something like that, yeah. I know, it's a crazy way to connect the dots, but who knows?"

Aaron's face changed into a devilish grin. "So, I'm as much your mother as Evelyn was, right?" He waited for Dan to answer but heard nothing. "So, back to your question about the connection between us. If anything, I feel like it's stronger now than it ever has been."

Dan stared at the floor, then looked at his brother. "Yeah, you've always been there for me. Maybe someday I'll have the chance to return the favor."

Aaron responded, "Fair enough. One thing, though, that I'll never understand, and that's how Henry Harper was able to keep such a secret for so long."

Dan nodded. "That's big shoes for us to fill. He was a flawed man like all of us but had the courage and commitment to - I don't know what to call it - provide and protect?"

Aaron saw his brother suddenly plunge deep in thought with his eyes closed. Dan was breathing hard and staring at the ceiling like his restraint was about to burst. Finally, he half-shouted, "Hey, Dad! You got any more secrets? Any more surprises?" He dropped his head and cupped his face in his hands.

There was silence in the room – and in the kitchen. Jane peeked around the corner, saw both men looking upward, and asked, "What are you two doing?"

Aaron answered quickly, "Talking to Dad."

Jane was joined by Melissa and Cynthia. The three women glanced at each other. Finally, Jane joined the drift of the moment and asked, "So, what did he say?"

Dan looked at her and answered, "He said everything is in technicolor, and the azaleas don't ever have to be trimmed."

Through tears, they both laughed weakly. As though the two men had the same thought at the same time, they joined their free hands with each other, and both raised their glasses. Dan sniffed loudly and spoke first.

"To Henry Harper. God be with him in heaven, where everything is always in bloom."

Aaron answered, "And with enough love to go around and some left over. Amen, brother."

****